Sharon started her career as an entertainment journalist, writing non-fiction books about film and television. She is also the author of multiple children's books. Sharon and her husband live in a small village in northern Cumbria. She can be found on Twitter @sharongosling.

SHARON GOSLING

The House Beneath the Cliffs

**SIMON &
SCHUSTER**

London · New York · Sydney · Toronto · New Delhi

First published in Great Britain by Simon & Schuster UK Ltd, 2021

Copyright © Sharon Gosling, 2021

The right of Sharon Gosling to be identified as author
of this work has been asserted in accordance with the
Copyright, Designs and Patents Act, 1988.

3 5 7 9 10 8 6 4 2

Simon & Schuster UK Ltd
1st Floor
222 Gray's Inn Road
London WC1X 8HB

Simon & Schuster Australia, Sydney
Simon & Schuster India, New Delhi

www.simonandschuster.co.uk
www.simonandschuster.com.au
www.simonandschuster.co.in

A CIP catalogue record for this book
is available from the British Library

Paperback ISBN: 978-1-4711-9867-0
eBook ISBN: 978-1-4711-9868-7

Typeset in Bembo by M Rules
Printed and bound by CPI Group (UK) Ltd, Croydon, CR0 4YY

MIX
Paper from
responsible sources
FSC® C020471

For Ella, who made me write it, for Angela and Polly, who read it first, and for Marie, whose home inspired it in the first place.

The House Beneath the Cliffs

So, my own selkie lass,

Did ye like the flowers? The boy chose them himself. I thought something a bit more special than daffs might be in order but he pointed out that yellow is your favourite colour, and we both know he's right. So no moaning about me being a cheapskate, ye ken?

Love you.

PS: Bought more beetroot. It is Mother's Day, after all. Don't say I never treat you. It's in the cupboard.

One

The spring sky above the ocean was a bright and brilliant blue, streaked with the occasional wisp of white cloud, as if someone careless had released candyfloss into the North Sea wind. Anna drove to the edge of the cliff, where the road vanished over what seemed to be a blunt edge, and then on past the sign declaring the point beyond which only the cars of residents should pass.

Around her grassy farmland tipped towards the water, until the slope became an angle that not even the cattle could abide. The road cut down and over the cliffs, sinking quickly between green-covered clefts splashed with the paint of wildflowers nodding in the breeze. Halfway down, a precipitous footpath divided itself from the tarmac, a wooden sign pointing the way on foot. The road continued on, curling back on itself in a bend so sharp that Anna wasn't sure she'd make it, even in her tiny tin-can excuse for a car. Beyond it the village of Crovie unspooled below her to her right, a string of houses clinging like colourful limpets to the wild lip of the narrow shoreline beneath the cliffs.

The road opened out slightly as it reached level ground,

backed by one or two wooden huts before it turned into a rocky beach that curved away from the village towards a towering promontory of grass-shrouded red rock. Before her the North Sea stretched into the horizon, the edge of the land crashing down to meet it in overlapping folds that reached far into the softening distance. The tide was out, the road squeezed between the cliffs and a sheer drop down onto a jagged field of wet black rocks and smaller tumbled stones. Anna pulled up and switched off her engine, staring out at the dip and swell of the blue-green expanse ahead and trying to gather her thoughts.

She'd been there less than two minutes before a shadow slanted against her face, swiftly followed by a single, sharp rap on the glass. Through it scowled an old man. Anna wound down the window.

'Hel—'

'You canna park here,' he said. 'Tis for residents only.' He turned briefly to shake his cane at the backside of another sign she'd ignored. 'Tourists have to park at the top an' walk.'

'But I am a resident,' Anna told him. 'I—'

'B&B and holiday rentals dinnae count,' he interrupted, still scowling. 'Tourists park at the top.'

Anna decided that she was done being at a disadvantage and so unclipped her seat belt and pushed open the door. Once she was on her feet she stood a head over him, yet he remained imposing. His shoulders, hunched now, were still broad and must have once been powerful. Lines traced around his eyes and mouth, deep creases weathered by a life probably lived largely outdoors.

'I'm not a tourist,' she said. 'I'm a resident. A permanent one. I've bought the Fishergirl's Luck.' Anna tried for a smile and put out a hand. 'It's nice to meet you, Mr . . .'

He recoiled as if she was holding out something offensive, then looked her up and down with clear contempt. 'You?' he hissed. 'You're the one?'

'I . . . yes. My name's Anna. Anna Campbell. I—'

He shocked her by turning away and spitting violently at the ground. 'That bloody place,' he said, 'Auld Robbie should ha' let the ruddy sea tek it.' Then he turned his back and began to hobble away, faster than she would have given him credit for.

'Wait,' she called, after a moment. 'Please, I don't want to get off on the wrong foot. Can't we talk, just for a minute?'

He didn't stop. Anna watched his retreating back with a sense of dread. She leaned against the car, feeling suddenly defeated. She hadn't even been here five minutes and her worst fears had been realized. This wasn't going to be a haven. No one was going to want her here. A wave of nausea coiled up through her gut and she took a deep breath, drawing in a lungful of salt air. Overhead the gulls screeched and wheeled and for a moment it seemed to her that they were laughing.

Of course they are, she thought. *What were you thinking? Why didn't you go abroad, like Cathy suggested? You could have just rented a cottage in Spain, or Italy, somewhere warm. Why here? Why buy the damn place at all? Why?*

After a moment Anna dropped her hand and squared her shoulders, regarding the village. The single row of houses had been built on a narrow curve of sloping ground beneath a rolling bank of green cliffs. Between them and the shore there was no road, just a concrete path that edged the sea wall. On occasion, she had read, a stray wave had dragged the unwary out to sea and in high tide or during storms this route was often impassable. The idea of this had seemed both extraordinary and romantic as she'd read about it, but now, faced with the reality, Anna realized that though the former was true, the latter most definitely wasn't. Most of the houses had been built with their gables pointing towards the sea. Here, survival against the elements was more important than a view.

This little line of homes made up the village of Crovie. Anna had bought the smallest one of all. She could see it from where she stood. It looked – it *was* – little more than a stone shed, standing directly on the sea wall halfway down the village, its back to the North Sea and its face to the other houses and the cliff. The path that had now revealed itself to be terrifying rather than romantic was Anna's only route to the home she had bought, sight unseen, because it was better than staying another month, another week, another *day* in Geoff's pristine Kensington penthouse.

'Idiot,' she muttered to herself. 'Anna, you complete and utter *idiot*.'

Still, there was nothing for it now but to go and collect the keys. Anna locked her car door and took a deep breath before striking out towards her new home.

The last building in the village, the one nearest the road, wasn't a house at all, she realized. The gable end was whitewashed and faded into the grubby paint were large grey letters proclaiming it as the Crovie Inn. There were old menus still taped up in the windows, but it had obviously been shut for some time. Anna wondered where the nearest pub was now and thought it was probably at Gardenstown, another coastal village that was situated across the large natural bay in the Moray Firth on which Crovie had also been built. Anna turned to see it emerging now, across the gently chopping water and beyond the monolith of rock that truncated the far end of the rocky beach. Gardenstown spilled down a wide cleft in the cliffs, zig-zagging in steps until it reached the bay and harbour below, both of which, though not large, dwarfed Crovie's by comparison. In fact, Crovie's harbour was really no more than a little pier with moorings for a few boats, though the single one there now was a battered-looking wooden dinghy sitting precariously atop a forest of rocks as it waited for the tide to turn.

No wonder most of the buildings here were holiday homes, Anna thought. Who in their right mind would live here permanently by choice? Even now, in the brightest sunshine of spring and when the sea was calm, it was a forbidding prospect: fascinating, yes, but a place to visit, surely not to stay. She knew, also from her reading, that it had been established in the wake of the Clearances. The first people to live here full time had done so because they'd had nowhere else to go and this was one of the few places the English had no use for. As a result Crovie had seemed to her from a distance to be a symbol of something beyond how cruel the powerful can be. Of what, she wasn't entirely sure. Ingenuity? Tenacity? Hope? Or was it because she had nowhere to go either?

Idiot, she thought again. *Idiot*.

Then, before her, there it was. *The Fishergirl's Luck*. It was the name that had caught her attention as much as the setting. It was painted on a letterbox to the left of the door, below the single square window. The door itself was painted a cornflower blue that matched the sky above the small building's roof, a cheery colour despite the fact that it was beginning to peel slightly in the strong salt wind.

Anna stared at her new front door. The For Sale posting had featured photographs of the interior, but right now all she could remember of them was a tiny wooden staircase leading to an attic room scarcely big enough for a single bed, and a sense of compact cosiness that could easily be put down to estate agent trickery with a camera. Looking at the dimensions of the place, it couldn't be more than one room downstairs. It really was a shed – it must have been converted from something originally built as storage.

Anna tried not to panic. It had water and electricity. It had a shower, for goodness' sake, it wasn't a hovel. Just because from the outside it looked like a shack didn't mean it would be one inside. The peeling paint of the door meant nothing. She'd grown too accustomed to living in show homes, that was all: apartments with space and taste but no character.

Steeling herself, she rapped on the door, hard. The letter the estate agent had enclosed from the seller had told her he'd meet her here to hand over the key. It wasn't an arrangement that would have happened in London, but then this wasn't London and besides, Anna herself had no previous first-hand experience of house buying. That had always been Geoff's department, in the same way that the places she'd followed him to over the past two decades had always been his choices, steadily growing more opulent as his star had ascended, but never expanding enough to make more room for her than one side of the wardrobe, one side of the bathroom sink.

The wind caught at her hair as Anna waited. She noticed for the first time that on one side of the Fishergirl's Luck there was an empty stretch of concrete, wider than the pathway and enclosed from it by a rickety little fence and gate. A garden, of sorts, though one that would surely be drowned by each high tide and therefore not suitable for plants, or indeed anything much at all.

Two minutes passed; three, and there was no answer. Perhaps Robert MacKenzie was as deaf as a post. What had that old curmudgeon at the harbour called him? 'Auld Robbie'? If they were contemporaries, it could certainly be true.

She knocked again and heard a door creak open, though the sound came from behind her. Anna turned to see a woman in her early sixties with short-cropped silver hair and smile lines around her eyes looking out at her from the house directly opposite.

'Are you looking for someone?' the woman asked, her accent as lacking in the Scots burr as Anna's own.

11

'I'm supposed to be meeting someone here,' Anna told her, raising her voice against another sudden gust of wind. 'Robert MacKenzie?'

The woman looked doubtful. 'He doesn't live in Crovie,' she said, pronouncing it as '*Crivvie*'. 'He definitely said to meet him here?'

'I – yes,' Anna said, the general weariness imparted by the past few weeks catching up with her all at once. 'I – this is my house. I'm supposed to be moving in today, he needs to give me the key . . .'

'Oh!' The woman exclaimed. 'Of course! You're Anna Campbell.'

'Yes,' Anna said, a little taken aback.

'Old Robbie said you'd be coming,' she said, 'but I'd thought it wasn't until next week. It's not like him to be late, perhaps the boat's been called out.'

Anna had no idea what the woman was talking about.

'He's on the lifeboat roster out of Macduff,' her neighbour clarified, with a smile at Anna's blank look. 'If they got a call he may not have had a chance to make alternative arrangements for you. I can call Barbara, she'll know. Why don't you come in and I'll put the kettle on? You look as if you could use a cup of tea.'

For one brief, unbalanced moment Anna thought she might actually burst into tears.

'Oh,' she said. 'Yes. Yes, please. Thank you.'

'I'm Pat, by the way,' the woman said, as she stood back to usher Anna in. 'Pat Thorpe.'

Two

Pat Thorpe's home bore the name of the Weaver's Nook.
It was spread over three levels that reached back against the
cliff, the original builder tapping a well of ingenuity to make
a comfortably spacious home in this unforgiving place. The
front door was up a short flight of stone steps to one side,
where a small patio housed a rattan table and chairs.

'We take guests in through there,' Pat told Anna, 'but you and
I will use what my husband calls the "tradesmen's entrance".'

This was the door that Pat had opened in order to speak to
Anna. Inside it was a narrow passageway, which on one side
housed a door through which Anna could see a tiny WC.
Ahead was another door, which Pat pushed open and walked
through to reveal a large, warm kitchen. The floor was
laid with grey flags, the walls had been taken back to their
original stone and then rendered and painted white. In one
wall a well-sized hearth housed a wood-burning stove. The
rest of the room was taken up with beautiful units painted a
sunny yellow and a big oak table surrounded by sturdy chairs.
Pat filled the kettle and flicked it on, telling Anna to take a
seat before going up a flight of steep wooden stairs to use the

telephone. Anna listened to the murmur of her voice filtering down from above as she looked around. Against one wall was a dresser full of what looked like hand-thrown pottery, each piece glazed with a wash of glorious colour.

Robert MacKenzie had, in fact, been called out with the lifeboat, to aid a struggling pleasure boat that had set out from Lossiemouth and had run into trouble in the busy shipping lanes of the Firth.

'It shouldn't be too hard a call to set right,' Pat said, as she busied herself making tea. The kitchen smelled of the fresh shortbread that was cooling on the rack beside the huge range cooker. 'With any luck he'll be here soon enough. Although I can imagine that the last thing you want is to be watching your P's and Q's with a new neighbour on moving day. You must be tired.'

'A bit,' Anna admitted, with a smile. 'And as it happens, I've already failed on that front.'

'Oh?'

'I met an old man as I came in,' Anna explained. 'Didn't want me to park in the residents' area.'

'Ahh,' Pat said. 'Carried a cane? Looked as if he could have gone ten rounds with Tyson back in the day?'

'That sounds about right.'

'Douglas McKean,' Pat said, with a sigh. 'Oh dear. Don't take it personally. It's not about you, it's about the Fishergirl's Luck. Some dispute over ownership that goes back literally decades. He hated Bren because of it too. Although to be honest, I don't think there's a soul on this earth that man actually likes. Except Old Robbie, perhaps. Douglas is the last of the Crovie born and bred and he's got a chip on his shoulder about us incomers. I should sympathize, I suppose, but I don't, really. He works hard at being unpleasant.'

Anna smiled, obscurely relieved to hear she wasn't the sole focus of the old man's anger. 'How long have you lived here?'

'Frank and I bought the business about fifteen years ago. It was our retirement plan. Perhaps not the best idea we've ever had, but I can't imagine living anywhere else now.'

'Business?'

Pat offered Anna the plate of shortbread. 'We run this place as a B&B in season and we've also got another one of the houses further along as a self-catering rental. That's where Frank is now, doing a bit of fixing up. Both get quieter every year, but then again, we're not as young as we were so that's perhaps for the best. We love it here, though. But you, Anna – what brings you to Crovie?'

'Oh,' Anna said, looking down into her mug. 'It's a long story. Actually, no – it's not long at all. It's just not a particularly interesting or unique one. My father died and left me some money at about the same time that a long – very long – relationship finally fizzled out. I realized I was about to hit forty with nothing to my name but what would fit in my dad's old car. I was looking through my parents' photo albums as I packed up their house. They'd done a driving tour of Scotland for their honeymoon and there was a picture of them in Crovie. It seemed such an amazing place that I looked it up online, and that's how I found the Fishergirl's Luck. I bought it on impulse, because after selling Mum and Dad's place I could afford it without a mortgage and I needed somewhere to live. I vaguely thought it would be a fresh start . . .' She looked up at Pat with a lopsided smile. 'Not the best idea I've ever had, either.'

'Ach, don't say that,' Pat said. 'You've not even been inside yet. Bren loved that place and I for one will be glad to see it occupied again.'

'Bren,' Anna said. 'Was she the previous owner?'

'Oh yes. No one else has ever lived in the Fishergirl's Luck, until now. Converted it herself decades ago – bought the building from her father out of the money she saved as a herring lassie in her younger days. Well, that's how she told it, although if you were inclined to listen to Douglas McKean he'd tell you that she cheated him out of it some-how. She was a remarkable woman. Lived there alone all her life. Died – oh, it'd be five years ago now. Ninety-five, she was, and looking after herself perfectly well right until she went to sleep and didn't wake up. The place has been empty since then. I don't think Old Robbie could face letting go of it really, to tell you the truth. They were close.'

There came the sound of the 'tradesman's' door opening and closing.

'Ahh, here's Frank,' Pat said, standing up as a figure appeared in the kitchen doorway.

Frank Thorpe turned out to be a tall, well-built man in his mid-sixties, with the sort of face that looked as if it were laughing even when it wasn't. He was carrying a curtain pole in one hand and a drill case in the other, and when he saw his wife he grinned as if the sight of her was something he'd been looking forward to for weeks. Anna went to stand up, and the smile took her in too.

'Ah ha!' he exclaimed. 'So the visitor is ours! I wondered whose car it was.'

'This is Anna, Frank. The new owner of Bren's place,' Pat told him, as Anna got to her feet.

Frank leaned the curtain pole against one of the cabinets before taking her hand and shaking it. 'Very good, very good,' he said, with a bright enthusiasm. 'Well then, lass, welcome to Crovie.' He held up the Makita. 'You need anything done in that little place of yours, here's where you come, all right?'

'Thank you,' Anna said, smiling.

'Poor thing's arrived just when Old Robbie's got a call out, and she can't get the key,' Pat told her husband, as she poured an extra mug of tea and set it down for him.

'Well, I can pick the lock for you, if you like,' Frank suggested, his eyes twinkling as he sat and pulled his mug towards him.

Anna blinked. 'Oh. I—'

'Oh, Frank, behave,' Pat chided. 'The poor woman doesn't want to know that her nearest neighbour counts that as one of his skills, does she?'

'It's only a hobby, promise you,' Frank told her. 'I've done it before for Bren, as it happens – a few years back she dropped her key in a squall and whoosh! Off it went over the sea wall, and you can forget about getting a locksmith around these parts, at least before kingdom come. So I let her in until Old Robbie could arrive with a spare.'

'Robert MacKenzie,' Anna said, seizing on a safer subject,

'he's who I bought the place from. I suppose he must have been a relative of Bren's, if he inherited?'

'Her nephew once removed, or some such,' Pat said. 'Relations around here are tangled and mysterious. Everyone's related to everyone else in some way or other.'

'I think I'd better wait until he can get here himself,' Anna said. 'I don't want to offend anyone else.'

'Douglas McKean,' Pat said, in answer to the eyebrows that Frank raised at her across the table.

'Ahh, that old gasbag,' Frank said. 'Ignore him. You've got nowt to worry about where Old Robbie's concerned – he's one of the good ones. Do anything for anyone, he will, hence him still being on the lifeboat despite the fact that it's long past time he mustered out. He'll not fret if I get that door open for you. And anyway, the Fishergirl's Luck is yours now, in't it? Do what you like with the place.'

'Don't let him niggle you into it, Anna love,' said Pat, getting up to flick the kettle on again. 'Frank's looking for an excuse to show off, that's all. Fancies himself as a criminal in a past life, when he's really softer than whipped cream.'

Frank grimaced and rolled his eyes at Anna before further taking advantage of his wife's turned back by reaching for a handful of biscuits.

'You needn't be making that face, Frank Thorpe,' Pat said. 'And if you think you're eating all of those before dinner, you've got another thing coming.'

Frank sighed extravagantly. 'Once a teacher, always a teacher, eh? Eyes in the back of your head.'

'No choice with you around, is there?'

Anna listened to this exchange with a smile on her face, though a curious pang had worked its way into her heart. It felt familiar, though it wasn't the sort of relationship she and Geoff had ever had. Anna found herself going back to her early years, when her mother had still been alive and her father had been young. They had been happy, her parents, right up until the blip on the hospital screen that had reduced first her mother's life expectancy and then, eventually, her father's optimistic nature. Anna stared at her fingers as they gripped her mug. She was older now than her mother had been when the cancer had taken hold, and what did she have to show for it? A career that had been permanently truncated in favour of a man who had never loved anything but himself, and the deeds to a house no larger than a shoebox, in a place she had no roots.

She became aware of silence and glanced up to see Pat and Frank looking at each other, as if they'd been speaking to her and received no response.

'Sorry,' she said, rubbing a hand over her face. 'I zoned out there for a moment. It's been a long few days.'

'I bet it has,' Pat said sympathetically.

'You know,' Anna went on, looking up at Frank. 'Maybe I will take you up on your lock-picking offer. If you really don't think it'll offend Mr MacKenzie?'

'It won't,' Frank said confidently. 'We'll call Barbara and let her know you've managed to get in so he doesn't have to come over when he lands. He'll be relieved, I bet.'

Three

Shortly afterwards, Anna stood by as Crovie's answer to the Pink Panther fiddled with the lock on her new front door. There was no sign of any other human movement in the village at all. The wind was getting up as the light began to tip towards dusk, dashing foamy waves against the sea wall so that they split against the stone with a noise somewhere between a hiss and a sigh. Overhead the gulls cried and cried, circling on air currents as turbulent and as unseen as a riptide. Anna's gaze followed the staggered line of houses until they curved out of sight, melding with the rock. The grassy cliffs were changing colour in the early evening sun, turning to gold as the light trembled against them, making shadows out of all their ragged edges. Crovie seemed to her as if it were caught between two tides, and the cliffs were not cliffs at all but another wall of water, about to crash down to meet the sea at the exact point where she now stood.

'Gotcha!' Frank exclaimed, and the door of the Fishergirl's Luck popped open with a slight metallic twang. He looked up at her with a beam on his face.

'Thank you so much,' Anna said, relieved beyond belief.

'You're welcome. Can I help you with your boxes?'

'There's really not much to move. I'll be fine now. I'm just going to ... explore for a bit, first.'

Frank nodded and stepped back, apparently understanding her need to cross alone through a door he knew but she didn't. 'Well then, give us a knock if you need anything. We'll be away to bed at around eleven, but any time before that, all you have to do is shout. A hand, a hammer, tea, chocolate, wine, whisky or company – whatever you need. All right?'

Anna smiled. 'Thank you – again. I didn't expect to meet such lovely neighbours so quickly.'

Frank shrugged. 'No call to be any other sort now, is there? We're glad you're here, love. If this place needs anything, it's new life. Why don't you pop over for breakfast tomorrow? Nine thirty. If we see you, we see you. If we don't, that's fine too.'

He left her then. Anna stood on the step of the cottage, one hand on the open door. She took a deep breath and pushed at it, stepping inside and then closing it behind her. Directly inside the door was another, forming a tiny vestibule, the walls of which had been built from pitch pine. Behind her, she could still hear the wind, but ahead of her the air was still, the hall space acting as an airlock against the weather outside.

Anna pushed open the second door and a waft of stale air rolled out to meet her. The space beyond was gloomy, though a faint light was being cast by the small windows.

21

She fumbled for the light switch and flipped it on, frozen in the doorway as she looked around in the harsh glare from overhead. Even from where Anna stood it was obvious that no one had been inside the Fishergirl's Luck for quite some time. Dust eddied in the air and had settled on every available surface, leaving a grey film that made everything dull.

She had paid the asking price on the understanding that she could keep the furniture and fixtures, because she had none of her own and the impracticalities of Crovie's geography made buying anything new a challenge. The solicitor had warned her that the Fishergirl's Luck would need 'updating', but at the time Anna had thought it was the best way to deal with the situation. Now, though, she saw that it meant she'd been left with a load of old junk. The main room – the living area – spread out to her left. Beneath the window that looked out onto the path was a saggy two-seat sofa in coarse blue fabric, stuffing pluming from the ends of its worn arms, and in front of that was a pine coffee table, grubby with dust. Two lumpy-looking armchairs stood the other side, upholstered in orange and brown fabric that looked as if it might have been fashionable in the 1970s. All this was arranged side-on to a hearth built into the far left wall, which housed a tiny wood burner. The staircase Anna remembered so vividly from the photographs was stuck in the far corner, next to the hearth and disappearing up to the second floor against the wall that backed on to the ocean. As Anna regarded it now, it seemed a lot less like a cute and quirky architectural feature and a lot more like a death trap. Under her feet was a threadbare blue carpet that didn't quite match the colour of the sofa, even though it seemed about the same age.

Directly in front of her, beginning under the low reach of the stairs and finishing at the cottage's right external wall, was the kitchen. Anna had checked the listing, and knew that the Fishergirl's Luck had an oven, a sink and a fridge, all arranged on a tiled oblong of floor. At the time, that was all she had cared about – when she'd walked out of Geoff's life she wasn't sure she'd ever want to go back into a kitchen at all, at least not beyond making herself toast or the occasional microwave meal. Now though, she was taken by surprise at her sense of dismay as she contemplated the space. Sure, there were shelves and cupboards. There were worktops, and even a 'dining table', if that was the right term for a little pine bench built to fit under the slope of the stairs with two stools pushed beneath it. But the whole was so very tiny that it would have slotted into the lift back at Geoff's place, and as she looked at it now Anna couldn't imagine even wanting to make toast here, let alone anything else.

To her right, a second door slanted away at an angle and joined another sturdy wooden partition, cutting off the corner between the hallway and the external wall. Inside was the bathroom: a tiny corner power shower, a sink and a white toilet, all of which mercifully seemed clean – in fact, it seemed a lot more modern than the rest of the house – but was still covered with a film of dust.

Closing the bathroom door again, Anna turned round and crossed the floor in something of a daze. It took less than six paces for her to fetch up against the old Belfast sink of her new 'kitchen'. Above it was the only window in the entire building that looked out towards the sea. It was barely bigger than a 10x8 photo frame, with small shutters that were presumably meant to guard against wave damage. Anna gripped the cold porcelain, feeling the grit of more dust beneath her fingers, and looked out at the green-grey waves.

'Oh God,' Anna muttered. 'What have I done?'

Come on now, my girl, said a familiar voice in her head. *Don't write it off yet.*

Her eyes filled with tears. *Dad*.

It was what he'd said to her on the day he'd helped move her into her digs for her first job out of catering college. That was almost twenty years ago now, but still remained vivid in Anna's memory. They had arrived to find, not her dream of an airy apartment that looked out into the bustle of London, but a hot, cramped attic room stuck right at the top of the West End hotel. The only window was an ancient skylight that she could barely reach even standing on a chair. The room came free with the job, though, which Anna had thought would be perfect. Her dad hadn't really wanted her to take it, she'd known that – but she'd already been following Geoff, even then.

'Do your own thing, darling,' he'd said, when she'd told him about the commis chef position in the kitchen. 'Don't choose this job because he'll be there. What about that place in Lancaster, that chef who told you he'd have something good for you when he opened? It sounded like you'd be doing more than scrubbing carrots all day if you went there.'

'But it's *London*, Dad,' she'd argued. 'Geoff says—'

'Anna, I don't care what Geoff says. Last month he was a student, same as you. Why should he know any better?'

'He's so talented,' Anna remembered saying. 'He's going to be a star. I know he is.'

'And what about you, Anna?' he'd asked her. 'When are you going to get to shine?'

Anna had rolled her eyes. 'Winning some little competition doesn't make me the next big thing, Dad,' she'd said.

'Did Geoff tell you that, too?' her dad had asked. 'Because you beat him in that competition. I remember that, even if he'd rather everyone else forgot. And "Young Chef of the Year" doesn't sound too little to *me*, Anna.'

'You don't know anything, Dad,' Anna said. 'This is in *London*. Anyway, I love Geoff, and Geoff's there.'

I should have listened to you, Anna thought, wiping her eyes. Her dad had tried to present another perspective right up until she'd point-blank told him she was going, and that was it. After that, he'd supported her all the way. He might not have agreed with her choice, but once she'd made it he'd been her rock, the same as always. He'd always tried to help her see her way through, to make the best of all her decisions.

You're here now, he might have said, had he been standing there with her in the Fishergirl's Luck. *Might as well see the rest of it, eh?*

Anna climbed the stairs gingerly and with a distinct sense of apprehension, but it seemed they were far sturdier than she had thought. The top two steps turned towards a small open space, partially taken up by a wardrobe that had been built against the gable wall over the stove below. There was a little window that overlooked the path outside, allowing in a bit of light. To the left of the last step, a wall divided what Anna assumed would have once been an open loft. Beyond the door in its centre, a single bed took up the right-hand side of the space. She was surprised – and puzzled – to note that on top of the bed was a new mattress, still wrapped in its plastic covering.

On the left was a low set of drawers that had been built to run the short length of the tiny room, providing shelf space on top. At the end, in the gable wall, was the biggest window the Fishergirl's Luck possessed, arched to fit the space and barely an inch above the floor. This, too, had shutters. It also had an old muslin curtain that softened the gleaming light of the dipping sun. Other than that, the room was empty of anything but dust.

Anna sat on the edge of the bed, feeling the mattress and its plastic crackle beneath her. How could she live here? She'd done exactly the same as with that horrible room she'd spent three years in when she'd first moved to London – she'd daydreamed something that didn't exist. Of course it didn't! How did she imagine she could pay the pittance that she had for this place and end up with anything better? It was exactly as Geoff had often said, she had no grasp on reality. *Stop writing cheques your brain can't pay for. Accept your limitations for once, why don't you?*

She'd spend one night here, Anna decided, because she

was too tired to go and find somewhere else to stay, but that was it. At least there was a fresh mattress for her to sleep on, and the one thing she had bought before coming was a new duvet and pillows.

As Anna walked back through the village she noticed that outside some of the houses was a kind of low wooden barrow, with two wheels and handles for pushing or pulling it along. Each had a number painted on it that corresponded to the house number to which it belonged. When she got to her car, she saw an area at the back of the small parking space, beside the recycling bins, that held more of these little vehicles. Right at the front was one painted with the name of the Fishergirl's Luck. It was to make transporting goods along the sea wall to each house easier, Anna realized. Another ingenious invention that made living somewhere so inaccessible a little more manageable.

She didn't bother pulling her barrow out. After all, she only wanted a few things from the back of her car. The rest could stay there, because otherwise she'd only have to put everything back in again when she left tomorrow.

Anna found the box with her bedding in it and pulled it out. Then, after hesitating for a second, she found another box – they were all carefully labelled, even though she'd had so little to pack – and slit it open. There, on the top, was a photograph in an old silver frame, a gateway to a happier past. She'd been about four when it was taken, during a family holiday on a beach somewhere, probably in Wales. She was on her father's shoulders, chubby white legs dangling down over his chest. Anna was holding an ice cream, which had melted all over her fingers and was about to drip into her father's hair. Her mother was trying to catch it, gripping her husband's arm with one hand as she stood on tiptoe, stretching out an open palm to stop the drip. They were both laughing, and it had always struck Anna that it said a lot about them as a family, that this was the photograph her parents had chosen as worthy of a frame and a place on the mantelpiece. It had been the first thing she had reached for when she went in to clear the house in the wake of her dad's death. It spoke to her of a simple happiness she had not yet attained in adult life, and now doubted she ever would.

Taking the photograph, her bedding and a bag of groceries, Anna went back to her tiny house. She dumped the shopping on one of the worktops, climbed the stairs and propped the photograph beside the bed. She took off her shoes, and then tugged open the plastic that covered the mattress. Sinking onto it, she pulled her duvet to her, not caring that she was still in her clothes, the bed was not properly made and that she had not eaten since breakfast. She fell asleep to the sound of the waves crashing around the feet of the Fishergirl's Luck.

Four

Anna woke to darkness, disoriented and hungry. For a moment she had no idea where she was. Then the sound of the sea brought her back to Crovie, to the Fishergirl's Luck and to herself. She got up to turn on the light, stumbling from beneath the tangle of duvet, her bare feet touching the chill of the wooden floor. She searched the edges of the unfamiliar door-frame until her fingers found the switch, then blinked blindly in the stark light until she could focus enough to read the watch still on her wrist. It was almost five o'clock in the morning.

Downstairs, the cottage was cold, but there was no wood for the burner (and besides, she hadn't any matches). Although there was an electric heater under the staircase and another upstairs in the bedroom, Anna wasn't yet awake enough to work out how to turn them on. She shuffled into the kitchen instead, collecting the bag of groceries she'd dumped there the night before. It was only the basics: bread, tea, milk, butter, jam, cheese, eggs, salt and pepper. Anna stared at the oven with distinct misgiving, wondering how bad it would be inside. When she finally opened the creaking door, though, she was relieved to find it nowhere near as in need of cleaning as she had expected. Anna lit the grill and pushed two slices of bread beneath it. Then she went to make tea and realized she didn't have a kettle. Or a mug, for that matter. Water would have to do, if she could find something to put it in and the pipe wasn't coming straight out of the sea. Toast made, Anna sank onto the sofa and ate mechanically, staring at the ceiling, feeling blank and unreal.

Anna realized that the double wooden beams above her head had been turned into storage space. In between each of the struts that held the second floor in place was a uniform five-inch gap, and in one corner there was still a book tucked into the space, lying lengthways on its cover. Anna stood and reached up to pull it out. It was an old notebook, bound in soft brown leather, and Anna opened it to discover page after page of recipes in cramped, neat handwriting. She wondered if it had belonged to the previous owner, Bren, and whether it had been left there deliberately when the MacKenzie man had cleared the place of the old woman's belongings, or if it had just been missed. After all, her own grandmother's recipe book was a precious thing, made even more so by the memories Anna had of the times she had spent with her mother as a young child, cooking recipes from its pages. Every time she used it now, Anna felt as if she knew a little more about her grandmother, who had passed before Anna was born. It helped her feel close to her mother, too, though she'd been gone for most of Anna's life.

Bren's recipe book should be a similar heirloom, and Anna made a mental note to make sure it made its way back to 'Old Robbie'. Perhaps he had children and grandchildren who could cook from it together and in so doing remember the woman who had owned the notebook. It seemed a shame that recipes compiled so carefully should be lost. In some places there were little sketches that must have been done by Bren herself, and in others, tiny notes in an even smaller, neater hand, annotating the recipes. The notebook was a beautiful thing, and deserved to be looked after. Anna put it on the coffee table and finished her toast.

Feeling drained and fuzzy but aware there wasn't much chance she'd sleep again, Anna decided to go for a walk. The front door would be fine on the latch for ten minutes, which was all she was going to need to traverse the length of the village and back again. Besides, the inner door had a key that she could turn and take with her.

Outside, Anna paused on the step and let the brisk wind snatch at her face and hair as she decided whether to start left or right. Left was what she chose, on the basis that it led to the end of Crovie she had yet to visit. The morning light, which in London would be a dirty, cloying grey even this early in the day, was crisp and bright, though half the village was still in the heavy shadow of the cliff. The tide had come in and was lapping high against the sea wall, tinted somewhere between azure and turquoise, its power shrouded in the quiet wash of waves. Anna took a deep breath, filling her lungs with the salted air, and struck out. She had always been an early riser, a fortunate trait in her line of work. She looked at her watch again and realized that in that other life she would have been on her way to the restaurant by now, ready to spend another long split-shift at her station, the only glimpse of the outside world the infrequent five-minute breaks snatched in the alley where they kept the bins. But she wasn't there, and never would be again.

Anna took in the houses as she passed, surprised to realize that in a few places where the rise of the cliff was less precipitous, concrete steps staggered up between dwellings to reach additional homes built close behind. There were gardens, too, spaces where the grasses had been left to grow, creating soft slopes where the wildflowers prospered – the blue heads of harebells; the hardy white of daisies; the purple of vetch and thistle; a cheery little yellow flower for which Anna had no name. The houses altered as the far end of the village narrowed towards the encroaching cliff. Here they were smaller, mostly single-storey dwellings, or with additional windows built into the attic space. Their open faces turned towards the unforgiving ocean instead of towards each other. They were still bigger than the Fishergirl's Luck, but not by much, and Anna tried to imagine what they must have been like inside when they were first built. Poky, cramped, cold, damp. *It is amazing what people get used to,* she thought. *Amazing what people can survive.*

No one seemed to live in any of these properties now, or at least not full-time. Most of them had signs or posters in the window, advertising them as holiday cottages to curious tourists who, like her, had wandered far enough to see them. The cliff reared up behind them, pressing in like an unsavoury stranger in a crowd. There was something else, too – an absence she could not put her finger on until she looked up and realized there were no gulls wheeling about overhead. Even the seabirds were staying away.

She caught the faint smell of dank decay. Looking up at the cliff again, Anna saw that here it was smeared with scars, old marks where the grass and earth overlying the sheer rock had shifted and slipped. Some of the houses below had obviously been affected. One had the unnaturally dark windows peculiar to abandoned dwellings. Another had curtains at its cobwebbed windows, and a blue tarpaulin was secured over its rear wall, its edges fluttering slightly in the dawn breeze. A piece of rusted guttering hung loose beneath it, torn away from its original position.

At the very end of the village, where the cliff jutted out into the bay with a curve too violent to house anything save the birds, a little open patch of grass was surrounded by a low stone wall. Three benches gave places to sit. Anna chose the one that would let her look back along the entire curve of Crovie, the village's colours brightening as the early morning sun rose. In front of her was a pole that marked the last of the village's communal drying lines. At the edge of the sea wall, thick wooden stakes had been cemented directly into the path, and between these were strung lines that, back in the day, would have served to dry the fisherman's nets, or hold them while they were mended before the season began. Now the lines were clearly used for drying domestic washing when the weather was good enough, because as early as it was, some had sheets and clothes pegged to them. As Anna sat, enjoying the smell of the sea and the lap of the outgoing tide, a figure walked towards her along the path. For one terrible moment she thought it was Douglas McKean, and her heart sank. If it was, there would be no way to avoid him, and Anna did not want to start a new day with another earful from the old man. But as the figure drew closer she saw that it was a woman with white hair that drifted around her lined face like a cloud. She was clearly on a mission, putting one foot in front of the other with determined speed. When she reached the little park where Anna sat, she smiled a brief hello, but didn't slow. Instead she stretched out one gnarled hand to grasp the washing line support and then walked around it in a tight circle, twice.

'It's tradition,' the woman declared, as round she went, and then pointed at something painted on the pole. 'See? South Pole. North Pole. Got to go around twice.'

'Oh, I—' Anna began, but before she had a chance to say anything else the woman smiled again and marched away, back the way she had come.

Anna looked at the stake and realized that yes, it was painted on one side with the words 'North Pole' and on the other 'South Pole'. Though Anna still didn't know why it would be necessary to circle either twice.

By the time she turned her gaze back to the wall again, the old woman had vanished. Anna began to walk back herself at a much slower pace, soon passing out of the shadow of the cliffs. The early morning sunlight caught the colours of the flowers in hanging baskets and half barrels set beside doors and windows, their blooms flourishing despite the salt air. Behind one of the houses she saw a raised deck with a beautiful pink rose spilling over the surrounding fence.

Ahead of her, Anna heard the splutter of an engine. A motorboat was pulling away from the pier. There were two people standing in it, one of them the old woman who had circled Crovie's north and south poles twice. At the controls was another figure, too distant to be distinct, but as the boat headed towards Gardenstown it turned, raising one hand in a wave. Anna didn't know whether the gesture was for her, or some other, unseen recipient, but she lifted a hand and waved back anyway.

When she got back to the Fishergirl's Luck, she found that a wicker basket had been left on the doorstep. It held a bottle of red wine, a brown paper bag holding four scones, a tin containing a candle, and a sealed envelope. Inside the envelope was a brass key, and a short note.

Dear Ms Campbell,

Welcome to Crovie and the Fishergirl's Luck. We are so sorry that you didn't get your key last night, and also that you arrived before we had chance to properly clean the place. Time got away from us! We had hoped to do more than just replace the mattress.

Here's your key, and a little basket we had meant to leave as a welcoming present. Please accept it with our best wishes and the hope that you are settling in already.

Best wishes,
The MacKenzie family

*

'Well then,' said Frank Thorpe a couple of hours later, as Anna sat down at the kitchen table in the Weaver's Nook. 'How was your first night in the Fishergirl's Luck?'

'Oh,' said Anna. 'Fine. It was . . . fine.'

'That doesn't sound too good,' said Pat, topping up Anna's mug with fresh tea. 'Did you not sleep well? The sea can take a bit of getting used to if you're new to it.'

Anna smiled at her hostess over a plate of breakfast larger than anything she'd eaten for years. 'It wasn't that. I actually liked waking up to the sound of the waves. But . . . I realized *very* quickly that I've made a terrible mistake. I should never have bought the place.'

Pat looked at her in alarm. 'Oh no, love, don't say that! You've not been here five minutes!'

'I know, I know. But the house needs so much work. And it's so small! I mean, I knew it would be, but now that I've actually seen it . . . I really don't think it's for me.'

'What sort of work does the place need?' Frank asked. 'I thought it was pretty solid. You haven't got a roof leak, have you?'

'No, it's nothing like that – or at least, not that I know of,' Anna said, tucking that new worry away to examine later. 'But it's very dirty, and everything is . . . well, old, I suppose.'

'Ah,' said Pat. 'Yes, I imagine it's pretty dusty in there by now. It had been on the market so long and no one had really shown an interest in it. Old Robbie did say he was going to come and give it the once-over before you moved in, though.'

Anna smiled. 'He said.'

Pat looked up from her breakfast. 'Ah! You two have met now, then?'

'No – I went out this morning and came back to find a welcome basket on my doorstep, with a note and my key. It was a very kind gesture. And honestly, I didn't expect to walk into a show home,' Anna said, although even as she said this, she wondered if that *was* what she'd expected, without even realizing it. Everywhere she had lived with Geoff in the last fifteen years had been minimalist to the point of feeling sterile, because neither of them were ever at home long enough to create clutter and anyway, that's what Geoff liked. Perhaps she'd forgotten what an actual lived-in home felt like. 'It's not even about that, really. I don't know what I was thinking, coming here like this in the first place. It was ridiculous.'

Frank turned to Pat. 'Remember that first day we woke up here?'

Pat chuckled against the rim of the mug she held. 'I was thinking exactly the same thing.'

'We thought we'd made a terrible mistake too,' Frank said to Anna. 'It didn't help that a bad storm blew in the night we arrived. It was as if we'd woken into the middle of the apocalypse. Pat cried, didn't you, love?'

'I did,' Pat admitted. 'I came downstairs to the kitchen – that was before we'd redone it and put the extra WC in – to put the kettle on, and there was a draught coming under that door that made it feel as if I was descending into the Arctic. The floor was wet, too, because rain had come in through the same gap. The rug smelled like wet dog, I couldn't get the wood burner to light,

37

and the electricity was off. I ended up sitting on the bottom step in damp slippers, sobbing my daft heart out. I thought then that we'd wasted all our savings on a mess of trouble.'

'I didn't feel much better, I'll tell you that for nothing,' Frank added. 'No, it took us time to fall in love with this place, and with the village too. But we did. I bet you will too, Anna, if you give it a chance.'

Anna smiled again, but privately didn't think she'd ever be able to fall in love with the dirty old shed that was currently all she had to call home.

'Give it a few weeks, at least,' Pat advised, as if she'd read Anna's mind. 'Spend some real time in the place – make it feel like your own. It's bound to feel strange when it's still full of someone else's things.'

'Yes,' Anna admitted. 'That is odder than I thought it would be, it's true.'

'We can help with that,' Frank told her. 'If you've got stuff to move in or out, let me know – I'll be happy to lend a hand.'

'Thank you,' Anna said, genuinely touched at how welcome the couple were trying to make her feel. 'To be honest, I think the first thing I need to do is clean. Could I borrow a floorcloth, a scrubbing brush, some spray and a bucket?'

After all, she reasoned to herself as she speared another piece of bacon, whatever she was going to do with it – the vague thought of a holiday let had passed through her mind, although who would want to rent a shed with nothing but a single bed in it, she couldn't imagine – the Fishergirl's Luck would need a good scrub.

Five

Anna started with the kitchen, because the idea of a dirty work surface upset something fundamental in her chef's brain. In one of the cupboards she found an old dustpan and brush, with which she swept the tiles in preparation for later mopping. Then she attacked the worktops. Anna was surprised at how well the old slabs of oak came up beneath her attention, the wood's curving grain a natural mirror of the shape of the waves she could see through the tiny picture window over the chipped enamel of the sink. The sea was gentle today, and she wished she could hear it more clearly as she worked, but soon discovered that the window had not been designed to be opened. It was no doubt another safety feature to guard against the weather, and it made Anna wonder about the storm that Pat and Frank had mentioned. What it would be like to experience one, especially from inside the tiny confines of the Fishergirl's Luck?

Anna had always liked storms. The first house she had lived in had an old lean-to conservatory on the back, and one of her earliest memories was of her dad waking her one night long after she'd been put to bed. There had been a storm rolling closer and he'd wanted Anna to see it. Her mum had been alive then, and when her dad had carried Anna downstairs she'd been in the kitchen, making them all hot chocolate. Her father had pulled the cushions from the old wicker sofa and arranged them on the floor, adding blankets to make a sort of nest so that the three of them could lie looking up at the storm crashing over their heads through the mottled glass of the conservatory roof. Even now Anna could still remember the rumbling bellow of the thunder as it drew closer, the blue-white crackle of the fork-lighting that had split the night sky above them, the taste of the thick hot chocolate, the murmur of her dad's voice as he'd explained to her the science behind each strike, even though she'd been far too young, then, to really understand the words.

Anna paused in her scrubbing to watch the waves out of the window. *Dad and Mum would have loved it here*, she thought. *In fact, I already know that they did, don't I? They must have gone to so many places on that honeymoon trip, and not all of them would have ended up in that album. But Crovie did.*

Was it grief that had prompted her to buy this place? Loneliness, a need to regain a connection to something fundamental and now lost to her forever? Anna supposed it must have had something to do with it. She cursed herself as an idiot again. As if a place could make up for how alone she felt in the world, take her back to a time she had felt connected, safe, wanted. How she wished she could talk to her dad about this place now.

Tell me what to do, Dad, she thought. *I can't live here, can I? I can't. There's nothing for me here. What was I thinking?*

She went back to scrubbing so that she wouldn't have to listen to the silence.

The oven and its tiled surround supplied its own surprise. Removing the dust revealed a splashback of beautiful dark green glaze that shone in the late morning light. Anna tried the extractor and found that, though slow to start up, it worked just fine, and that the hood itself only needed a polish to bring it back to gleaming health. Bleach did a reasonable job of returning the old Belfast sink to its former glory, although there were a few chips and cracks in the bottom that no amount of scrubbing would set right.

Next were the cupboards and drawers, all of which had already been emptied but definitely needed a refresh. Then the fridge, which did not smell nearly as awful as Anna had been expecting, then the little pine 'dining table'.

By the time Anna was finished in her quest to clean the kitchen, she was tired, hot and, despite the huge breakfast she'd had courtesy of Frank and Pat, hungry again. Her clothes, towels, most of her toiletries and all of her kitchen equipment were still in the car. Anna realized now that she was going to be here for at least one more night, so she may as well bring more of her belongings into the Fishergirl's Luck, if only so that she didn't have to keep returning to the car every time she needed something.

The village was still quiet as she walked back through it again, for which Anna was grateful given the sweaty mess she had become in her quest to clean. When she reached the old Fiat she saw that something had been pushed beneath one of her window wipers, a square of white paper that fluttered in the breeze blowing off the North Sea. Anna pulled out a note and saw that someone had scrawled on it in untidy letters that matched a brief, unfriendly message.

Parking is for RESIDENTS

Anna looked around as she held the note in her hand, but there was no sign of anyone who might have left it there. If she'd had to guess she would have said it was the work of Douglas McKean, but he already knew that she owned the Fishergirl's Luck, so where would be the sense in leaving a note like this? She scrunched it up in her hand and then shoved it into her pocket, but the note's advent left an unpleasant feeling lurking in her gut.

Don't worry, she said silently to whomever might be watching and wishing her gone. *I won't be here long.*

This time she used the barrow to cart her boxes along the seafront. She passed a couple of people, who nodded and said hello, suggesting that neither of them were responsible for the note, but then, who ever really knew what was going through someone else's head?

Anna gave the miniature bathroom a wipe down, and then tried the shower. The water was mercifully hot, the pressure not bad. She came out of it feeling refreshed, and pulled on a pair of sweatpants, a sweatshirt and the comfy boot slippers that Geoff had always condemned as ratty and cheap-looking.

When she stepped out of the bathroom, Anna was caught by surprise at how good the kitchen looked in its newly clean state.

All Anna could be bothered to make was an omelette, which was fortunate considering the meagre ingredients she had brought with her. She located her favourite copper-based frying pan (the one she had proudly bought herself with her first-ever paycheque and had looked after meticulously ever since) and turned on the gas hob, smiling to herself as she whisked the eggs. An omelette. It was the first thing she had learned how to make at catering college, even though she, as with every other student there, had scoffed at the idea that they didn't already know this simplest of recipes – which was, of course, the point. Everyone thought they knew how to make an omelette, but to be a good chef meant first acknowledging that you didn't know as much as you thought you did, and moreover that the basics were not beneath you. Because, maintained Madame Chaubert, their tutor, if you were too arrogant to acknowledge that one required a foundation of these basics on which to build, one could never achieve greatness. In her philosophy truly great chefs, even those at the top of their game, would always recognize that there was still much for them to learn. Therefore, learning to learn was the most important first step in a chef's career, and what better place to start than with the ultimate simplicity of breaking eggs into a bowl?

Geoff, she remembered, had refused to make that first-day omelette, declaring that his parents hadn't spent a fortune on college tuition for him to be taught something he'd been making perfectly since he was six, and threatening to take his complaints to the dean if Madame tried to force him. Then, when she'd told him he was welcome to do so, he had made an omelette faster than the tutor and ignoring all her advice, just to prove a point. It was one of the things that had drawn Anna's attention almost immediately – his utterly unshake-able sense of self-importance. She'd been appalled by and attracted to it in equal measure; she, the quiet little mouse from nowhere who had arrived at the college with promise but the full belief that there was still everything to learn. That moment had turned Geoff into the king of the class and given him an infamy that defined his career, right from that early moment. Everyone knew who he was, and he loved it.

She should have known better, Anna saw now, than to be so easily dazzled by the shallow theatrics of ego.

Having eaten and wanting to avoid the dark grip of rem-iniscence, Anna found a renewed burst of energy. When the knock at the door came she was busy hoovering the carpet, having discovered that the threadbare patches weren't all that bad, really. They could easily be hidden by a bit of strategic furniture placement and a new rug, certainly enough to sat-isfy the demands of Anna's theoretical future tenants.

'My goodness!' Pat said, as Anna waved her visiting neighbour into the Fishergirl's Luck. 'You have been busy. It spruces up nicely, doesn't it, this little place?'

'Yes,' Anna admitted, looking around the room, into which was shining a cheerful amount of sunlight. 'It does, actually.'

'Well, I don't want to hold you up,' Pat said. 'It's only that Frank and I were thinking we might have a few friends over on Saturday night. It'd be the usual suspects from Crovie and Gardenstown and the like. You should come, it'll give you a chance to meet some new faces. They're all good people, our friends.'

'Oh,' Anna said. 'Well – that's really kind of you, but . . .'

'It wouldn't be anything grand,' her neighbour added. 'There's usually something going on at one or other of our houses on a weekend. It might help you to feel less like a visitor passing through if you knew more people, that's all. It can't hurt, can it? Even if you really do decide you don't want to stay.'

'The thing is,' Anna told her, 'once I've got this place straightened up and taken some photographs, I think I'll try putting it on Airbnb until I can work out what to do with it more permanently. I'm not sure I'll still be here at the weekend.'

Pat smiled, though a little sadly. 'I see. Ah, well, that's a pity.'

'I'm sorry,' Anna said, feeling inexplicably guilty.

'Don't be, love,' Pat told her. 'You have to do what's right for you. But look – if you change your mind in the next couple of days, you'll still be welcome to join us. Any time after seven. Just knock and come in.'

Hey selkie lass,

Dolphins are the latest thing, have you noticed? He's drawn them all over his schoolbooks, in the margins, on the covers, everywhere. Should we worry about how obsessive he gets? Does it mean something? Is it normal? Is encouraging him a good idea, or not? Last week it was geology, wasn't it? The bathroom is still full of rocks. Maybe I should give Miss Carmichael a call. Why don't kids come with manuals? Everything else does and nothing else is nearly as complicated. Or expensive.

They're too easy to get wrong.

Love you.

PS: Yes, there is more beetroot. Just don't ask me to open the jar. Love will carry you so far and then it'll smother you in the fumes of a pickled beetroot. I'm not falling for that one.

PPS: I can't call Miss Carmichael. I think she fancies me. Can you do it?

Six

The next day Anna drove along the coast to Fraserburgh with a list of items she wanted to find for the Fishergirl's Luck. Chief among them was a rug to hide the bald patches in the carpet. She also wanted a new muslin curtain for the bedroom and had borrowed Frank's tape measure to take down the size. A kettle, that was essential – she'd have plenty more to buy for the kitchen before she put it up for rent, but for now, something she could make tea in while she worked on the place would be enough. She also needed a way to make the old armchairs a bit less garish . . . the list had lengthened exponentially as she'd added to it the evening before.

As Anna wound her way out of the village her phone found its first hint of reception in several days and beeped at her. She pulled into a lay-by and listened to the message Cathy had left the day before.

I know you're probably busy and out of signal in the back of beyond, said the woman who had been her closest friend for too many years to count, *but do give me a ring when you re-enter civilization, won't you? Just so I know you're alive.*

Smiling, Anna held the phone to her ear as it rang out.

'My goodness,' said Cathy's familiar voice, 'if it isn't Kensington's answer to Scott of the Antarctic. I was beginning to think you'd discovered that the Earth is flat after all, and fallen off the edge.'

'Close, but not quite,' Anna laughed. 'I'm fine. Sorry – this is the first time I've had a signal.'

'I thought as much. Glad to hear you, though. So – how is it all? Or is it too soon to tell? Tell me about Crovie. How have your first couple of nights in the cottage been?'

Anna detailed the events that had happened since she'd arrived in the village, correcting her friend's pronunciation from *Crovie* to *Crivvie*. It felt good to offload on someone who knew her almost as well as Anna knew herself. Anna had met Cathy in secondary school and they had been friends ever since. In fact, Cathy was really the only friend that had survived throughout the Geoff years. Any others Anna had had slowly faded from her life through lack of the nurturing that all friendships require. Anna knew she was to blame for that as much as anyone, just as she knew she had Cathy's determination to thank for the fact that they were still close.

'Anyway, long story short, I'm an idiot and I knew at once that this was a ridiculous misadventure,' Anna told her, as Cathy listened with quiet attention.

'You've hardly been there two days!' said her friend. 'It might not be quite what you expected, but honestly, Anna, it's been a while since I've heard you sound as enthusiastic about something as you have been about this move. Besides, where will you go if you don't stay there?'

'I don't know,' Anna said, 'but somewhere I at least have the hope of getting a job.'

'But I thought you were going to take the time to work out what you really want to do from this point?' Cathy asked.

Anna sighed and rubbed a hand over her face. 'I was.'

'Look,' said her friend. 'It sounds to me as if you need to take a breath. You're so used to that crazy kitchen, it's bound to feel weird to have such a sudden change of pace on top of everything else that's happened in the past few months. Why not take a few weeks – as a holiday, if nothing else. You deserve one. I think you *need* one.'

'I should have gone to Spain, like you said.'

Cathy laughed. 'Knowing you, you'd have been just as restless there, too. Take some time out and ... *stop* for a while. The place is yours. You're not going to lose any more money on it if you keep it to yourself for a bit, and it'll mean not having to outlay more money for something else, won't it?'

Anna chewed her lip and looked out at the glint of sun on sea. 'I suppose so.'

'Either way, it sounds to me like a sound investment as a holiday let,' Cathy pointed out. 'Quirky places to stay are the in thing. And this couple you've met, Pat and Frank – they sound lovely.'

'They are,' Anna agreed. 'They've invited me to a party at the weekend, to meet some new people.'

'That's great!' Cathy said.

'Is it?' Anna asked.

'Of course it is,' said her friend. 'Meeting new people is always great.'

'I think I've forgotten how,' Anna admitted. 'I can't remember the last time I had a night out without Geoff. And every time I went somewhere *with* him, he was the one everyone wanted to talk to, not me.'

'Exactly,' Cathy said. 'And you're not standing in his shadow anymore. Even if you don't end up staying there permanently, where's the harm in getting to know your neighbours?'

Cathy was right, Anna realized. She needed to remind herself how to make new friends, new connections. Crovie was as good a place to do that as any – especially, actually, if she wasn't going to stay permanently after all.

Start saying yes instead of no, she told herself. *Don't close yourself off. Be open to everything, or try to be, and especially while you're here.*

'You're right,' Anna said. 'I do need a holiday, and I do need new friends. I can stay a bit longer. It'll give me time to get the place properly sorted out. I'll be spending all day today shopping for new things for the Fishergirl's Luck.'

There was a pause. 'Word of advice, then,' Cathy said, carefully. 'Avoid the magazine racks, especially the celeb rags.'

Anna's heart did a curious backflip. 'Oh?'

'The new series starts next week. He's been doing the rounds. Interviews everywhere, alongside that smug face of his. In case you want to avoid them.'

Anna sighed. 'I will. Thanks.'

There was another pause.

'You're okay, aren't you?' Cathy asked. 'Leaving was the best thing you ever did, Anna. Even if you did follow it up by disappearing off to the back of beyond.'

Anna hummed. 'I know. Still—'

'Yeah,' Cathy said softly. 'Still. But it'll get better. I promise. You know you've always got a room here with us if you need it. But for now, make the most of where you are. This party sounds like a good start. Wear something swish and knock 'em all dead.'

Anna laughed again. 'Not that kind of party, really. Not that kind of *place*. And I'm definitely not ready for that anyway.'

'Let your food do the talking for you then,' Cathy said breezily. 'I mean, they'll all love you, obviously, but especially if you do that thing with the peppers. Dammit, I miss your cooking. And you. Horribly.'

'I miss you too,' Anna said, around a smile. 'I'll call you, okay? Love you. Give Steve a hug from me. He'd love it up here, by the way. What isn't farmland is a golf course. You can be the first people to stay in the Fishergirl's Luck when I rent it out, if you like.'

They said goodbye but Anna remained where she was for long minutes, lost in thought, watching absently as a stray crisp packet danced across the wind-blown tarmac. She'd been an idiot to imagine that Geoff couldn't follow her here. She wondered whether he'd had any moments like this, lost in a memory of her. It was doubtful. If she knew Geoff, one of those tabloid photographs would be a pap shot of him leaving some achingly hip nightclub with a baby-faced model on his arm. It would not, after all, be the first time, or even the second or third.. The thought stabbed a pang through her chest and Anna took a breath, trying to dispel the sudden pain. It wasn't worth dwelling on. That wasn't her life any-more; it had nothing to do with her.

She restarted the car and turned out onto the road. Anna wasn't sure she really wanted to cook for the get-together. She'd been thinking that she'd pick up a bottle of wine or two, maybe some fancy crisps, that was all.

Hours later and with the car stocked to the gunnels, she drove the twenty miles back to the village along the coast road, enjoying the green of the fields and the flash of light dancing on the water. There were only a handful of villages along the route – none were as precariously placed as Crovie, but all of them were small, with a slightly desolate sense of clinging to their existence by force of will alone.

She negotiated the road down to the harbour more easily this time. As she dragged her bags out of the boot and into her cart she saw a figure in the distance. Hunched over a cane, a flat cap pulled down over his eyes, it was clearly Douglas McKean. Anna slammed shut the hatch and headed for the cottage, studiously ignoring his glare.

Anna spent the next couple of days deploying her pur-chases around the house. The beautiful wine-red throws she had found were strategically tucked over the sofa and armchairs, followed by new cushions. At some point she'd probably have to replace the sofa, but actually it was surprisingly comfortable and the throw disguised the ageing fabric perfectly well. Meanwhile, the wool rug in a similar colour with blue and cream accents covered the worn patches in the carpet and tied the whole together. Upstairs, Anna wrestled the new muslin curtain into place, pausing to watch the light dancing on the waves, the sun so warm and bright through the glass that she thought she could probably lie on the floor and sunbathe in it.

Since she'd decided to stay a while longer, Anna also unpacked the last few boxes of her belongings. Her clothes she tidied away into the wardrobe and drawers upstairs. As her kitchen equipment found its way into the cupboards downstairs, Anna realized that her initial dismay at the general grubbiness of the space had blinded her to how well it had been designed. Yes, it was tiny, but it was beautifully laid out, with everything positioned exactly where Anna herself would have put it had she been fitting it out herself.

She unwrapped her chef's knives, secure in the sturdy wrap her father had proudly bought her when she'd graduated. The thick linen was tired now, but she'd carry on using it until it fell apart, or until it was too threadbare to protect the blades within. For much of her life, right up until she'd signed the contract on the Fishergirl's Luck, the knives had been the most valuable possessions Anna owned. She knew the weight and feel of each as if it were an extension of her own hand. Working with them felt like home. As she checked them over, Anna realized that she was looking forward to cooking in her new kitchen after all. And, for the first time in a long while, there was no faintly derogatory running commentary from Geoff about her ideas. He hadn't followed her inside this space. The kitchen in the Fishergirl's Luck, cramped as it was, was hers and hers alone. The thought lit an unexpected glow in her chest.

As Saturday drew nearer and Anna slowly became more comfortable with her new surroundings, Cathy's assumption that she'd make something to take with her to the party kept popping back into mind. The thought of cooking had started familiar cogs turning in Anna's head. She could do a few bits and pieces, couldn't she? Nothing too labour intensive, but delicious, nonetheless. It might even be fun to try out her 'new' kitchen properly. Gradually, Anna's thoughts of Geoff were replaced with thoughts of food: *her* food, not his. She never had to cook another bloody Geoff Rowcliffe recipe in her life. The thought made Anna smile.

After toying with a few ideas, Friday morning saw Anna driving back to Fraserburgh for provisions. Back at the Fishergirl's Luck, the kitchen filled with herbs, spices and oils as she unpacked and found homes for everything she needed and the additional items that had simply taken her chef's fancy. Standing amid the rows of fresh fruit and vegetables, Anna had rediscovered the pleasure of shopping for produce, of finding the unexpected and thinking spontaneously about flavours and textures. Sure, a megabrand supermarket wasn't a patch on standing in the middle of Borough Market on a Friday morning. But then even Borough Market had lost its magic, the rough-and-ready nature that had sustained it for a century replaced by hipster brands relying on tourist curiosity and city workers more interested in picking at bits and pieces than in cooking themselves.

By late that evening, the fridge was full, because once Anna had started she hadn't wanted to stop. This renewed joy in cooking had come as a complete surprise. She'd thought that might be something else she had left behind in London, in her other life.

With her kitchen wiped clean and all her equipment tidied away, Anna thought she was just a little more in love with the Fishergirl's Luck than she had been before. She ran her hand up the stone wall as she climbed the stairs, thinking that the place probably deserved a fresh lick of paint.

Seven

When Anna woke the next morning to sun streaming through her new curtain, she was already thinking about food. She must have dreamed of cooking, and was left with a nebulous memory of presiding over the creation of an elaborate feast. Anna lay looking up at the low pitch of her ceiling, watching the luminous patterns cast there by the morning sun and trying to remember the details of what that shadow-self of hers had cooked. She had dreamed of food a lot when she was younger, the thrill of discovering a talent for a profession to which she aspired suffusing every moment of her consciousness. In those early days Anna's sleeping mind had conjured ideas for whole dishes so often that she had kept a notebook by her bed and developed the habit of scribbling them down before they scattered after waking. As the years had passed, though, this night-time tendency of her subconscious had atrophied, shrunken into non-existence by constant thwarting. Always working in others' kitchens meant that Anna so rarely got to cook meals of her own design. This persisted even once Geoff had become chef-patron of his own place with enough clout to listen to her ideas, had he felt so inclined. He never did.

Anna got up and went downstairs to fill her new kettle, because tea was always a good place to start. Taking the milk out of the fridge, she was reminded that, really, she'd already cooked enough. Still, she was still eager to follow this renewed seam of creativity.

I haven't made anything sweet, she thought. *I could take some dessert.*

As she leaned back against the kitchen counter, contemplating what would be appropriate, her gaze fell on Bren's recipe book. She picked it up, leafing through the dry pages, wondering if there was anything within that would work. It seemed like a nice idea to take something of Bren's along to this first meeting with her neighbours.

A recipe for raspberry and hazelnut shortbread caught Anna's eye, both because it sounded delicious and because there was a lovely little sketch of two wild raspberries still on their canes in the corner. There was a note alongside, in writing so tiny that Anna had to turn the book sideways and squint to make out the words.

Almonds good, too, but DM hates hazelnuts so that's favourite for domino night or the greedy so-and-so will scoff the lot. Nuts better chopped, not ground – June 1983

The note made Anna smile, but also wonder. DM? Could that be Douglas McKean? Either way, she didn't have any hazelnuts, but Anna had picked up a bag of whole blanched almonds with her shopping. And she hadn't been able to resist the punnets of ruby red Scottish raspberries that had been in abundance at the supermarket, and so it was that Bren's almond and raspberry shortbread joined the party.

'Well,' said Frank, later, laughing as he contemplated the array of plates and trays on their kitchen table, 'we're none of us going to starve, at any rate!'

'You really didn't have to go to all this trouble,' fretted Pat. 'You didn't have to bring anything with you at all – we *said*.'

'It wasn't any trouble,' Anna told them both. 'I was really enjoying myself, which is why I went a bit overboard. I also wanted to apologize for not accepting your invitation sooner. I'm sorry. I think this week has been a bit overwhelming.'

'You're sorry?' Frank asked. 'Don't be daft. We're just glad you're here. And would you look at all of this!'

'Everything looks delicious,' Pat agreed. 'And so pretty – it's like an art exhibit. Everything's identical too! I can't even fold a T-shirt the same way twice.'

Anna laughed, mainly at herself. 'Old habits die hard. The place I worked before I came here counted tweezers and a spirit level as essential kitchen gadgets.'

'You won't find me complaining,' Frank said, picking up a prawn on a lemongrass skewer and devouring it whole. 'Mmph. That's amazing.'

'Frank!' Pat smacked her husband's arm in outrage. 'You've left a hole, and no one else has even arrived yet!'

'Sorry,' Frank said, without a single trace of remorse. 'Right, Anna. What can I get you to drink? We've got wine in all the colours, beer, gin and tonic ... There's even some orange juice if you're so inclined, although as far as I know we've yet to have a teetotaller in the village.'

'White would be perfect, thank you,' Anna said, with another laugh. 'I could do with a drink, to tell you the truth. I'm a bit nervous.'

'Don't you worry,' Pat told her, as Frank turned away to the fridge. 'Everyone we've invited is lovely.'

'Do all of your friends live here permanently?'

'Most, but not all – or at least not yet,' Pat said. 'David and Glynn come over from Inverness most weekends, and for holidays. David's mum and dad owned their place as a holiday cottage all the way through David growing up, so he's about as much a part of the village as you can get, and Glynn loves it here too. Their plan is to retire to Crovie, but they're a ways off that yet. Rhona's originally from Fraserburgh but didn't want to go back after her divorce so she found a place in Gardenstown. Marie and Philip live in Edinburgh. They're both lawyers and always busy but they love to come up as much as they can. Terry and Susan—'

'I'm never going to remember all this,' Anna laughed again.

'No need to fret, lass,' Frank said, handing her a glass of wine with one hand and deftly sneaking a roast pepper roll with the other, 'one look at this lot and they'll all be eating out of your hand.'

By eight o'clock everyone else had arrived – David and Glynn first, bearing bottles of wine and enthusiastic hugs for

Frank and Pat. Then Rhona appeared with Marie and Philip, then Terry and Susan. They all welcomed Anna with handshakes and smiles. As time went on, she relaxed, warming to the company and the ebb and flow of chat, which soon turned to her purchase of the Fishergirl's Luck.

'It's so good to know that Bren's place will be lived in again,' Rhona said. She was a tall woman with a tanned, freckled face, hazel eyes and dark, blousy curls that she continually pushed back behind her ears. 'When I saw that Old Robbie had put it up for sale I was half tempted to buy it myself, but there would be no room for my workshop.'

'You have a workshop?' Anna asked. 'What do you make?'

'I'm a potter. Kitchenware, in the main – mugs, plates, bowls, that kind of thing.'

'It's beautiful stuff,' Susan chimed in. 'I love buying Rhona's work, everything makes such wonderful presents. I think most of our friends and family own a mug or two. We've got a whole dinner service, and we adore it.'

A murmur of assent rippled around the group, and Rhona smiled as Pat said, 'It's where our tea mugs come from, Anna, if you remember them? The ones with the blue glaze. The colour always reminds me of the sea at dawn.'

'Oh yes!' Anna said. 'I thought at the time that they were beautiful. What a fantastic skill to have.'

'Well, I'm still learning,' Rhona told her. 'I only took it up when I moved here. There was a workshop as part of the property, and I'd always wanted to give it a go, so I thought, "What the hell, Rhona, you're not getting any younger – why not give it a try?" There have been so many things I put off for some nebulous time in the future when everything would miraculously fit together like some cosmic puzzle. And I decided, it's now or never.' She smiled at Anna. 'You know how it is.'

Anna laughed into her wine glass. 'I suppose I do. That's pretty much how I ended up buying the Fishergirl's Luck.'

'It's a bold thing to do,' Terry said. 'Not just buying somewhere so out of the way, but committing to live there, too. Especially in a place like Crovie. I admire you, Anna.'

Anna made a face. 'Well, living here was the original plan, yes. But I pretty much decided on my first day that I can't stay. For a holiday, maybe, but living here permanently? I really don't think I can.'

The company gave a collective laugh that had a note of sympathy running through it.

'I completely understand how you feel,' said Glynn. 'When David first brought me here I honestly couldn't imagine coming back once, let alone to live. I couldn't see how anyone lived here at all, or even why anyone would want to. But this place has a way of getting under your skin and staying there.'

'Philip and I were the same,' Marie agreed. 'But we've owned our place here for twenty-five years now and sure, this coast can sometimes be difficult, but it's beautiful. And so are the people.'

Maybe it was the wine – she'd knocked back a couple of glasses too quickly, driven by nerves – but at that moment, Anna felt a warm buzz growing in her chest.

'If you don't mind me asking though, Anna,' said Terry, a moment later, as he held a plate of food in one hand and a beer glass in the other, 'what about your career? I assume you left your job to come up here. If you're not going to stay in Crovie, will they take you back? Or are you thinking of taking a different route entirely now?'

'The honest answer is that I haven't a clue,' Anna told them, swirling her drink around her glass. 'Originally, when I left London, I thought I was leaving cooking for a living behind, too.'

'Oh, that would be a shame,' said Susan. 'You clearly have a huge talent. Everything here is delicious.'

'Thank you,' Anna smiled. 'It's just . . . I suppose I had reached an impasse in my career, and I've no real idea of what to do next. That's another reason I ended up buying in Crovie, really. Thanks to the sale of my parent's place, I was able to buy the Fishergirl's Luck without a mortgage, and with my own savings and what Dad left me, I've got enough to live on for a year, maybe longer if I'm really careful. My plan was to use the time to figure out what I'm going to do for the rest of my life, because for years I've felt . . . I don't know, a bit lost, I suppose. As if I'm aimlessly drifting along.'

Rhona tutted in sympathy. 'Aye, hen, I know what that's like, believe me.'

'But now,' Anna gestured to the plates that Frank and Pat were offering around, 'after making my own food, exactly the way I wanted – I've realized how much a part of me it is.

It's what I do, it's what I am. It's how my brain works! So now I'm not sure. I'll have to think about it. I'll have to work out where I want to work. That'll probably dictate where I go.'

'You should reopen the Crovie Inn,' Philip suggested. 'That place has a whole kitchen sitting there, not being used.'

There was an enthusiastic chorus of 'yeses', but Anna demurred. 'Oh, I'd never be able to run my own place. I'm strictly a kitchen urchin, built for taking orders, not leading from the pass.'

'What makes you say that?' Frank asked.

Anna opened her mouth to reply and then stopped. They had been Geoff's words, she realized, never hers. She'd been hearing them for so long – her entire career – that she'd never before thought to examine the truth in them.

'I'm ... I don't have the experience,' she said, shaken by her realization. 'Or the capital, either.'

'Well, I think it's a great idea, and it's obvious that the food wouldn't be a problem. Where was it that you worked in London?' Terry asked. 'What sort of place? It must have been fine dining, judging by what you've fed us here.'

Anna gulped a mouthful of wine, the nerves of earlier returning. For a moment she wondered whether she should lie, and then decided that the truth was the only option. 'It was a restaurant called the Four Seasons.'

'Bloody hell,' David said. 'You mean Geoff Rowcliffe's place? Didn't that get another Michelin star last year?'

'Yes,' Anna said quietly. 'It did. *We* did.'

There was a moment of silence, and then Rhona laughed.

'Crovie has a Michelin-starred chef!' she exclaimed. 'Who'd have thought it?'

'Not me. It was the kitchen, under Geoff.'

Susan snorted. 'Please. I bet, like anything of that sort, all the real hard work is someone else's.'

Anna allowed herself a smile at that. 'Anyway, I'm not there anymore.'

'How long had you worked there?' Pat asked.

'Since it opened. Fifteen years, give or take. Long enough. Too long, to be honest.'

'I like his programmes,' Marie volunteered. 'There's a new one starting next week, isn't there?'

'Yes, I read a thing about it yesterday,' Rhona said, and Anna's heart sank. 'It sounds quite good. He went out and found little out-of-the-way places in the UK and learned new recipes from the owners. Pity there's nowhere here he could come, I've always rather fancied him. He's recently split up with his long-term partner too, apparently. Another opportunity lost to me! Come on, Anna, reopen the Inn and persuade him to visit, for my sake!'

Everyone laughed. Anna felt Pat watching her and kept her eyes on her glass, instead. Then the doorbell rang. She was nearest the door and saw a chance for an escape, however brief.

'Shall I – get that?'

'Sure, love,' Pat said with a smile, as if she could read Anna from across the room. 'It'll be Old Robbie. He said he was going to be late.'

She was so preoccupied with the excruciating mess of a conversation behind her that she went into the hallway and opened the door without really thinking about what was on the other side of it. She'd heard 'Old Robbie' and her mind had conjured the grizzled, weather-beaten face of Douglas McKean. So when she pulled open the door to be confronted by a man who could be mistaken for Robert Redford in his forties, standing on the step with a broad smile and a bottle of wine in each hand, Anna's mental processes ground to a complete and utter halt.

'Um – hi,' he said, his smile faltering after a few seconds of her silence. 'You must be ... Anna?' He wrestled one bottle under his left arm and held out a hand. 'I'm Robert MacKenzie. I sold you the Fishergirl's Luck?'

Anna opened her mouth but found it still wasn't connected to her brain. She closed it again, then shook his hand and finally managed to take a step back to let him in.

'Of course, sorry,' she said, in a rush. 'Sorry, sorry. Come in, they're all in the sitting room. It's nice to meet you.'

He moved past her, looking a little wary. Not surprising, she supposed, and kicked herself.

'Sorry,' she said again, feeling a need to explain herself. 'But – you're not old.'

He blinked, then frowned. 'I'm not – what?'

Anna exhaled, finally finding her way back to equilibrium and wondering whether she might have been the subject of some sort of elaborate local hazing ritual. 'Since I got here everyone's been calling you Old Robbie. And the first person

I met was Douglas McKean, who is certifiably ancient, and then Pat and Frank said you two were friends, so I ... I thought you were—'

'Old,' he finished for her, the smile back again. 'Ah, well. Some people would say I am. My son's also called Robert, and so around here, I'm *Auld* Robbie and he's—'

'Young Robbie.'

'Exactly.' Robert MacKenzie grinned again. 'Sorry for the confusion.'

Anna grimaced. 'Sorry for looking like a loon when I opened the door. So far this "getting to know your neighbours" thing is making me feel as if I should just become a recluse.'

He laughed, a deep booming sound that filled the hallway and tugged a smile at her lips. 'Oh, you don't want to do that around here,' he said. 'That really is a sure way to become a basket case.'

The noise from the other end of the hallway suddenly grew more distinct as Pat opened the living room door.

'Everything all right?' she asked. 'Robbie, you'd better come and eat some of Anna's food while there's still some left. Another five minutes and you'd have missed it all.'

The evening progressed, meandering its way between those gathered with chat about friends and families, as well as a fair bit of village history, gossip and intrigue for Anna's benefit. She laughed along with the tales of mischief accomplished by past residents still much missed, many of the stories tied to the time that the Crovie Inn had been a thriving business, and apt to sell its wares far past official closing time. There were stories of the Fishergirl's Luck, too, which were told with such affection that Anna wished she were able to turn back the clock and visit when Bren had been alive.

'Do you remember that storm we had about six months after we moved in?' Pat said to Frank. 'It rattled the tiles so fiercely we were sure it was going to take our roof right off, and we thought how much worse it must be for Bren?'

'Oh, aye,' Frank said, nodding. 'The waves were so big I was sure we'd look out in the morning and find the whole place had been swept straight out to sea. After about the third time a wave had washed up past our front door – about 1 a.m., that was – I decided to go and get her and bring her over to the Weaver's Nook. Better safe than sorry, I thought, and we had plenty of room. Anyway, I wrapped myself up and battled my way over there to bang on the door. It felt as if I'd been knocking for half an hour before she finally opened up, all snug and cosy in her dressing gown, declaring that I'd woken her!'

Pat laughed. 'We didn't bother after that. I've never known a soul as hardy as that one. Bless Bren, we still miss her.'

'I forgot to say,' Anna said, indicating the half-empty plate of shortbread, 'I found an old recipe book of Bren's yesterday and made the raspberry and almond shortbread out of it.'

'Oh, how lovely!' Susan exclaimed, reaching for one of the biscuits. 'Dear Bren and her baking. She was a whizz with a cake.'

'I meant to bring the book with me, actually,' Anna said, turning to Robert MacKenzie. 'Your family should have it back. I can go and get it now, if you like.'

Robert smiled. 'You know what? I think you should keep it. You're more likely to use it than we are, and I like the idea of it staying in the place where all those recipes were first baked.'

'Are you sure?' Anna said, touched. 'That's really kind of you.'

'She left us plenty to remember her by. I took Young Robbie out in her dinghy the other day,' he added, addressing the whole gathering. 'It's taken a while to get it up to scratch, but it's there now. I think the boy's going to be a fine seaman. Bren couldn't have given him a better present.'

'Oh, that's wonderful,' said Marie. 'Mind you, not surprising he'd take to the sea, given his blood, eh? Both his grandfathers, you on the lifeboat, his grandma, his mum, his aunt ...'

Old Robbie dragged a hand through his hair, and Anna saw the glint of gold on his ring finger. 'Well, he'll do anything to follow his beloved dolphins, this is the thing. He's got it in his head that he can use the dinghy as a rescue boat for any that run into trouble with nets and so forth. I've made him swear a solemn oath that he'll never take it out without either me or Barbara with him. He's a good boy, but he gets so carried away.'

'Is your wife a sailor too?' Anna asked. 'That must make for some great family days out.'

He glanced at her, a sharp look that was almost a wince, and Anna felt her stomach plummet with the absolute certainty that she had said something terrible. A sudden, brief silence suffocated the buoyant atmosphere in the room.

'Actually, Robbie's mum died a few years ago,' he said, his voice even but quiet. 'Barbara is his grandma. She helps out a lot. She's an exceptional sea-woman herself. She was with us on the lifeboat until a few years ago.'

'I – I'm sorry,' Anna stammered. 'I didn't—'

Old Robbie smiled and shook his head slightly. 'There's no need to apologize. Anyway, you're right – Cassie *was* a sailor – she was so much a part of the sea that I used to joke she must really be a selkie.'

Eight

The next day, Sunday, Anna joined David and Glynn as they walked their Irish setter, a great soppy beast with shaggy red fur. The windswept trio had knocked on her door as they passed and asked her to join them. Anna had accepted, touched by the ready offer of friendship and remembering her vow: *Say yes to as many things as you can while you're here.*

'Don't ask,' David said, as Anna was officially introduced to their hound, which claimed the incongruous name of Bill. 'It's all Glynn's fault. The agreement was that I got to choose the breed and he got to choose the name and I should have known that if a deal sounds too sweet, it probably is.'

'I think it's a fine name,' Anna said, as she and the effervescent Bill got to know each other, and then laughed as Glynn beamed at David in triumph.

They set off up the main – the only – track out of the village and then turned off at the car park, striking out over a stile into the fields that topped the cliff above Crovie to the east. The path wound steadily higher and steeper as the cliffs rose towards the sky. At times it came perilously close to the edge – so close, in fact, that below she could see not just the Fishergirl's Luck, but also the roofs of the houses.

Anna watched Bill charge ahead of them, his great paws galumphing along the track before he doubled back to check they were still following his lead. The wind was up this morning, tearing at hair and breath. In rain or in winter walking up here would be an even more difficult proposition. In the more precipitous parts of the track there was evidence of slippage, too – scrapes in the slopes where the grass had separated from the earth to reveal the reddish soil beneath. It reminded her of the damaged houses she'd spotted on her first perambulation of the village.

'I meant to ask last night,' Anna said. 'Has there been a landslide in the village? There are houses in Crovie that look as if they might have been hit by one.'

'Yes,' said David, 'that was terrible. It was a couple of years ago now. There was a huge storm off the coast. We got off lightly, considering – it could have been a lot worse. The council keep talking about earthworks to shore up the rest of the cliff, but no one in the village can really see how that would be possible.'

'Neither can they, evidently,' Glynn added, 'as they've gone very quiet about it for the past year.'

Anna frowned. 'That's a bit of a worry, isn't it?'

'Well, it is,' David agreed, 'and there have been other, minor landslips since. But Crovie has been here for centuries and has survived a lot worse. The great storm of 1953 washed away whole houses all along this coast and Crovie was no exception. You've probably noticed where one of them was – there's a gap next to one of the larger cottages? There used to be another house there, but it was so damaged it had to be taken down. The storm was pretty much what killed the last of the fishing in the village. They lost so many boats and it was too small a community to get back on its feet. Tragic, really.'

'The Fishergirl's Luck must have been there in 1953,' Anna said.

'Oh yes, it would have been,' Glynn nodded. 'And Bren would have been in it, too, I bet. I doubt she even noticed it knocking at her window.'

'Did you know her?'

'David more than me,' said Glynn. 'I met her a few times – enough to know she was a force to be reckoned with, though to be honest one meeting was probably enough to see that. She was already a wee old lady with silver hair by the time I knew her, but still formidable. One of those stalwart grannies you think is going to soldier on forever. I wish she had. She was one of the last links to Crovie's past, really.'

'I remember her as I was growing up,' said David. 'She never seemed to look any different. She was always smiling, always had a piece of tablet in her pockets for us children. Right up until the last few months she used to walk to the harbour to meet Old Robbie as he brought in her shopping from Gamrie. May we all be as spry as Bren MacKenzie when we're in our ninety-fifth year.'

'I'd love to know more about her.'

'Talk to Old Robbie,' Glynn suggested. 'He'd be happy to tell you stories about her.'

Anna sucked in a cold breath. 'Oh, I think I'll be avoiding Robert MacKenzie until I move on,' she said.

'What? Why? Because you mentioned a dead wife none of us had thought to tell you about?' David asked. 'Honestly, he'd never hold that against you. Why would he? Cassie's been gone for five years and I can't believe he and Young Robbie don't talk about her all the time. I don't think she's a taboo subject. I hope she isn't, anyway — that would be sad, for all of them.'

But Anna remembered the expression that had flashed through Old Robbie's eyes as she'd asked the question. It had been gone in less than a second, but still. She wondered whether there was anything more tragic than seeing a man still so clearly in love with a dead wife. Anna's father had never really got over her mother's death and although the two of them had talked about her frequently and had filled the house with as many photographs of her as they could, Helen Campbell's departure had cleaved a void in her husband's heart too deep to be filled. The look that had been in Robert MacKenzie's eyes at that second had shaken Anna because it was so familiar. She had seen it on her father's face as he'd contemplated a photograph of her mother on their wedding day. That was only a week before his own passing, and her mother had been dead for almost thirty years. Some loves last no more than a season, and others reach beyond a lifetime. Each could be as powerful, Anna knew, which was one of the many inexplicable geographies of the human heart. Perhaps it was because she was still feeling her father's death so keenly herself that she felt so awful about probing that hurt in someone else. Whatever the reason, it weighed on her, and she could not seem to forget that swift flash of pain that had crossed Robert MacKenzie's face.

'How did she die?' Anna asked, looking out towards the turbulent, wind-churned waves far below them. They had left the village behind now, and all Anna could see was wild, rocky coastline. 'She didn't drown, did she?'

'Cassie? Oh no, it was breast cancer. Her funeral was a sight to see. She was a primary school teacher over in Macduff and the whole school turned out, as well as plenty of former pupils and just about every resident from here to Fochabers. Cassie MacKenzie was very much loved.'

Anna thought again about the look she'd seen in her widower's eye, and didn't doubt it for a moment.

Anna spent the next week painting. She started with the downstairs living space, borrowing dustsheets from Frank and carefully rolling up her new rug. It was amazing what a difference the clean walls made. Anna had chosen a bright white paint that made the most of the light that filtered in through the bothy's few windows and helped the interior of the Fishergirl's Luck to feel bigger. It was a tiring job, though, and when the sun began to shine just as she was almost finished with the final coat, Anna took it as a sign that she should listen to Cathy and have an actual holiday, one where she wasn't constantly looking for something to do.

By the Thursday of her week-long 'holiday', however, Anna was restless. She had thought, after years of long hours and few holidays, her body would thank her for a prolonged period of complete relaxation. Once she'd decided that her sojourn in Crovie was a vacation, Anna had imagined she could catch up on all the books she'd always planned to read and had never had the time to pick up, seek out the best places on the coastline around her to swim, go for day-long sun-drenched hikes where the only time she had to worry about was when it would be too dark to find her way home. She had expected long lie-ins and lazy afternoons spent in cafés. Instead, she woke as early as ever, and without anything else to occupy her, she kept thinking about things best left behind – about her father and how she hadn't seen him nearly enough in his last years, about how much she missed him. She also kept thinking about Geoff, to whom her dad had never warmed. Why had she put up with Geoff for so long? How had he managed to convince her that a half-life with him was as good as she could ever hope to get? She found she was becoming angry with herself at the time she had wasted, the years that could have been so much better spent.

Anna's need for distraction and the enjoyment she had felt as she prepared for Pat and Frank's gathering gave her a renewed desire to cook. She supposed she should be pleased that the passion for the skill she had thought jaded beyond recovery had in fact only been on hiatus, and that her new circumstances had allowed it to flourish again. The problem was, of course, that now she had only herself to cook for.

'I've been thinking about the cookbook I used to talk about writing,' Anna told Cathy, during one of their chats via the new wi-fi that she'd had installed in the Fishergirl's Luck, on the basis that any holiday let would need one. 'Maybe I should work on that. The problem is that all the recipes I have at the moment would be ones I've cooked at the Four Seasons.'

'Then start cooking new stuff,' Cathy advised her. 'You've got a kitchen there, right? What about all these new neighbour friends you've made? I bet they'd all jump at the chance to have you make them a meal.'

Anna looked around the Fishergirl's Luck. 'The place is so small, though. There's not much room for entertaining.'

'I'm sure they'll understand if you have them over two at a time. They know how big the place is, after all. I think the cookbook is a great idea — it'll give you a chance to work out exactly what sort of food you want to cook, for one thing, won't it? That'd help when you do start looking for another job.'

'You're right, it would.'

'Of course I'm right. I'm *always* right. Don't you know that by now?'

Anna smiled. 'Sorry, I'd forgotten.'

'Pfft,' was Cathy's parting shot. 'Don't let it happen again. Oh, and please, please, please email me the recipe for the chocolate and pistachio roulade thing you make. I'm going insane without it.'

Anna asked Pat and Frank to be her first guests, both because they were the closest and because she still felt indebted to them after all their hospitality, not that they would see it as something that would need repaying. The more Anna saw of them, the more she loved them.

'Are you free tomorrow?' she asked Pat, as they sat having another of their now customary cups of afternoon tea.

'We've actually got guests arriving in the evening, would you believe it,' said Pat. 'They want a bite to eat when they get here. Sorry.'

'How about lunch instead?' Anna asked.

'Lunch would be lovely, if you're sure it's not going to put you out too much.'

'Of course not,' Anna said. 'It's not as if I've got any pressing engagements, is it? Is there anything either of you don't eat?'

'No, we're both pretty easy to please.'

'I'd like to cook fish, if that's okay with both of you,' Anna added. 'I'd rather get it from a local supplier than off a shelf at Tesco, though. Do you have any suggestions?'

Pat considered. 'Well, there's no local fishmonger anymore,' she said. 'But the Gamrie boys still ice their catches at Gardenstown before it gets taken for processing at Fraserburgh.'

Anna chewed her bottom lip. 'I think I'll take a drive over and see what I can see.'

'You could walk it,' Pat suggested. 'It's a nice day and the sea's fair. It'll be beautiful out there at the moment.'

'There's not a path between Crovie and Gardenstown, is there?' Anna asked, surprised.

'There is,' Pat told her. 'Come out and I'll point you to it. The snook, we call it. I'd come with you but I've got to get the sea-view room sorted for these visitors. Not that I'm complaining. Roll on the summer season, that's what I say.'

Nine

The path from Crovie to Gardenstown – known locally by its old name, Gamrie – had been built along the cliff that jutted out into the bay between the two settlements, forming a narrow passage above the tideline. To get to it, Pat said, Anna needed to walk down through the car park. There she would find a narrow path, which was just visible from the front door of the Fishergirl's Luck. Further on, as it rounded the cliff, this became a more formal concrete walkway.

'It's about a mile or so, straight into Gamrie,' Pat said. 'Wear good walking boots – at high tide the waves will splash across the path, and at the other end the beach is rocky. But it's a lovely stroll.'

The day was blustery but warm as Anna set out, the early April weather showing promise. On one side the path was edged by the sheer weight of the cliff and on the other by thin chains strung between slim metal fenceposts, rusted red by the salt wind. Below, uneven rocks jagged the shoreline, slick with moss and seaweed, scenting the air as it decayed. Sea birds screamed on the wind above her head, a sound to which Anna was surprised to find herself becoming accustomed, despite the harsh and plaintive pitch of the gull's piercing calls.

As the path rounded the promontory, Gardenstown opened up ahead of her. The oldest part of the town was closest to the water, built as Crovie had been by farmers cleared from other, richer lands further from the coast. As soon as she was on the other side of the cliff, the wind dropped to no more than a fresh whisper, and Anna realized how much more protected the larger village was compared to the exposed lip on which Crovie perched. Still, Gardenstown's harbour was enclosed by sea walls built to give more protection than even the natural shelter of the bay provided, which probably explained why there were more boats moored within its confines. Most of them were pleasure boats, but two or three looked to her untrained eye as if they could be small fishing trawlers.

Anna checked her watch – it was coming up to three in the afternoon. She had a chef's knowledge of how the British fishing fleet worked, having been on shopping runs to Billingsgate fish market on numerous occasions. Working with the tides, out at night, back in the ultra-early morning, the fish for purchase there came from all over the UK, but not, she suspected, from tiny Gardenstown on the Moray Firth. Still, their fishing hours were likely to be similar. With any luck, Anna would arrive in time to find one of the crew to talk to before they set out for the night's catch.

The harbour was quiet as she reached it, but voices carried to her across the water. Three men kitted out in knitted sweaters worn under heavy-duty waterproof dungarees were hefting nets on the deck of one of the trawlers. The rest of the place seemed to be deserted. As she walked along the harbour wall towards them they looked up at her with brief nods and then away again, resuming their conversation.

'Hi,' Anna called. 'Can one of you spare a moment?'

They stopped talking again, looking at her and then at each other before one of them dropped what he was holding and came closer. He leaned on the trawler's rail with a smile. Anna estimated him to be in his late twenties, with dark hair cropped short above a tanned face and square, stubbled jaw. His eyes were the colour of a turning sea under eyebrows thick enough to make him seem intense. It was the kind of face, Anna thought, that probably got younger women into a lot of trouble: a lot of younger women, frequently.

'What can I do for you?' he asked, as behind him the other two men finished their task and disappeared below deck.

The lack of Scots burr took her by surprise, as did the presence of a very different kind of accent.

'You're a long way from home,' she said. 'Kiwi, right?'

He smiled again. 'Right. Good ear. Most people say Australian.'

'I don't want to hold you up,' she went on. 'Someone mentioned that you might be able to sell me some fish.'

He shifted against the rail. 'Our stock's all for Fraserburgh.'

'Okay. Is there any other boat coming into the harbour that might be able to help me? I'd rather use a local supplier than schlep over to Fraserburgh to buy something wrapped in plastic.'

He turned his head and looked out over the water for a moment, contemplating. 'I don't think so. I mean, you could charter someone to take you out, if you wanted . . .'

Anna shook her head. 'Too much money, not to mention time. I'm only looking for enough for three lunchtime meals.'

'What fish?'

'Whatever's good and fresh out of the water.'

He watched her from the deck, studying her as if trying to work her out. 'You're Anna Campbell,' he said, after a moment. 'The chef that's moved to Crovie.'

She was floored. 'How do you know that?'

He grinned. 'It's a small place.'

'Yes, but I don't live here. I've never even been to Gardenstown before. I've only been in the area a few weeks!'

He shrugged one broad shoulder, grin still present and a glint added to his eye. He had the easy manner of a man who knew he was good to look at and had never had trouble making the most of it. 'Very pretty woman moves in, people take notice. Very pretty woman with knife skills moves in, people talk. Very pretty woman turns up looking for fresh fish, a Kiwi puts two and two together.'

Anna narrowed her eyes, trying to stop the smile that was attempting to find its way onto her face. 'Don't flirt with me, Kiwi. You're almost young enough to be my son.'

He laughed at that. 'Not unless you're a lot older than you look, Anna Campbell. Tell you what: I'll bring you something from the catch tomorrow, and you can cook me one of your Michelin-starred dinners. Fair deal?'

'No deal at all,' Anna said, laughing too. 'For a start, I don't know who you are. Also, my table is already full. If you know who I am, you know where I live, and you know I'm not lying on that score.'

'You should get a table for outside,' he told her. 'That'd give you more space.'

'Yes,' she said, wryly, 'I can just see me wrestling a picnic bench into my car and then along the sea wall to the Fishergirl's Luck. That'd be the talk of every town on this coast for years, wouldn't it?'

'You need a big strong man to do it for you,' he suggested, with what she thought (hoped) was his tongue firmly in his cheek.

'I've had plenty of big strong men, thanks,' she retorted, 'and in my experience they're all a disappointment.'

He grinned again, one eyebrow cocked. 'Then I guess you haven't met the right one yet, Anna Campbell.'

She sighed and shook her head with mock annoyance. 'All right. Well, thanks for nothing, Kiwi. I'll find my fish somewhere else.'

'Wait,' he said, as she started to walk away. He hopped over the boat's rail and up onto the harbour wall. 'I can bring you some of the catch. It won't be until about 6 a.m. tomorrow though. Will that work for you?'

'Yes,' she said, 'but you don't have to do that. I'm happy to come here and get it.'

'It's no bother,' he said. 'And it'll be easier for me.'

Anna frowned. 'It won't be nicked, will it?'

She was pretty sure his outrage was feigned. 'Do I look like a pirate?'

'Not far off, actually.'

'It will be completely above board. Promise. You want me to gut it for you first?'

'I believe we've already established that I'm the one with the knife skills.'

'True enough,' he agreed easily. 'All right. I'll see you tomorrow, *avec poisson*.'

Anna was about to ask him what his name was, and then decided that it was more fun not to know. 'Cheers, Kiwi.'

He laughed. 'You're welcome, Anna Campbell.'

'Ahh,' said Rhona. 'So you've encountered the wonder that is Liam Harper. Sight for sore eyes, isn't he?'

'Hmm,' said Anna, 'and doesn't he know it.'

Rhona laughed. 'That he does. He's sweet with it, though. Has a way of giving you his full attention when you're speaking, no matter what else is going on. That's a surprisingly rare trait, I've discovered.'

Anna was standing in Rhona's workshop, having realized that since she was in Gardenstown anyway, she could drop in. Rhona owned one of the two-storey houses that stood on the village's main zig-zagging hill street. The 'workshop' doubled as her showroom and was really a converted garage that opened directly onto the thoroughfare. It was perfect, as Rhona herself pointed out, for attracting the attention of passing tourists during the high season.

'Everything is so beautiful, Rhona,' Anna said, admiring a shallow bowl that had been washed with a pale glaze flecked in blue, ochre and sea green, recognizable as the colours of a sandy beach at low tide. 'I can't believe you've only been doing this a few years.'

Rhona smiled. 'It's funny, isn't it, when you find the thing you should have been doing all along? Slide right in like coming home and you wonder how you didn't get there sooner.'

'I'm going to have to take some of your dinner and side plates, and bowls too, if I can carry them,' Anna decided. 'I wish I could invite you for lunch tomorrow too, but I don't have the room. Will you come next?'

'Don't fret – I couldn't have come during the day. And of course I'll come – I'll look forward to it, but there's no hurry. I think you're doing amazingly well considering how long you've been at the Fishergirl's Luck. When I moved in here I was in chaos for months.'

Anna thought about this. 'Hmm. It definitely does feel as if I've been here a lot longer than three weeks. I suppose that means I'm settling in.'

Rhona smiled. 'Maybe a sign you should stay after all?'

Anna laughed. 'I think that's going a bit far. But I might extend my stay for another couple of weeks. Maybe a month. We'll see. It's not as if I've got anywhere else to go.'

'Are you in a rush to get back?' Rhona asked. 'Or could you stop for a gin and tonic? The sun's well over the yardarm and I'm not driving anywhere tonight. Seems a pity not to make the most of this beautiful weather. It can change in an instant here, you know.'

'I can't remember the last time I had a drink in the afternoon!'

'Then you definitely have to have one. Besides, it's near as dammit early evening, I'd say.'

They drew chairs to the edge of the workshop, where the sun spilled over the step and onto their shoulders and laps.

'I watched the first episode of that new Geoff Rowcliffe series,' Rhona volunteered, after they'd been chatting long enough to be on their second drink. 'It wasn't bad. Pretty as he is, though, he does come across as a bit of a dick.'

Anna nearly choked on her drink and spluttered a surprised laugh.

'Well, I'm sorry, but he does,' Rhona insisted, laughing too. 'And I owe you an apology. I think I probably put my foot right in it when I blathered about him that night at Frank and Pat's.'

'What?' Anna asked. 'No, of course you didn't.'

Rhona shrugged slightly. 'It has occurred to me since that the fact that Crovie has suddenly acquired a top chef might have something to do with another top chef where she worked before coming here splitting up with his unnamed partner of twenty years.'

Anna made a face. 'I should call you Sherlock.'

Rhona held up a hand. 'I don't want to pry. Still – I'm sorry. For being so insensitive.'

Anna snorted. 'I think if anyone was that, it was me. Poor

Old Robbie, having some woman he doesn't know from Adam slap him around the face with his wife like that.'

'You weren't to know.'

'Still—'

'In any case,' Rhona added, 'it's time he moved on. He's too lovely a man to be on his own forever. Cassie wouldn't have wanted that. Maybe you came along at the right time, Anna.'

Anna eyed her new friend, wondering if she was really saying what Anna thought she might be. 'Oh, *hell* no,' she said, emphatically. 'I've just got out of a complicated long-term relationship, there's no way I'm getting straight into another one.'

'It wouldn't *have* to be complicated.'

'Of course it would be!' Anna laughed. 'He's got a child, he was married to someone that everyone around here knew, he's part of the fabric of this place. I've recently bought a house here. What's the saying? Don't foul your own door-step? We'd not be able to move two steps without everyone knowing our business. Regardless, it's a moot point. I'm not staying, and he's still in love with his wife. I'm not getting into the middle of *that*, thanks very much.'

There was a moment of silence. 'Seems like you've given it some careful thought,' Rhona said.

Anna opened her mouth and then shut it again, feeling her cheeks flush. 'No! I—'

'I'm only teasing, hen!' Rhona laughed. 'You're right on all counts. Far more sensible than I would be if Robert

MacKenzie ever looked at *me* across a room for a second or two longer than necessary.'

Later, Anna walked back along the coastal path with her new flatware carefully wrapped and packed in the canvas bags Rhona had lent her. The weight felt good, like anchors keeping her at rest. Shooting the breeze with Rhona, talking rubbish while the sun blazed overhead – it wasn't something she'd done for a long time, or had ever really had time to do at all. Geoff hadn't liked her going out without him, even on the rare occasions that she'd had an evening off, and he often hadn't wanted her with him when he went out, either. It seemed crazy to her now, how she'd simply accepted it as the way their relationship worked. That it had somehow seemed perfectly normal that her entire life had been moulded to fit around what worked best for him at any given moment.

Never again, she thought. *Whatever I end up doing now, it'll be because of what I want, not what's best for someone else.*

Anna breathed in, a fuzz of happiness hazing around her along with the faltering light of dusk. The fishing trawlers had gone from the harbour. There was no sign of them on the horizon, either. Anna imagined what Liam Harper might be doing at that moment, and then told herself that was a gin-thought, not a real one. She pushed it back towards the nowhere it belonged, and should most definitely stay.

Ten

Saturday morning dawned fair and found Anna waiting at the pier well before 6 a.m. She wasn't the only person up and about, either – she passed Douglas McKean coming the other way as she left the cottage. Anna risked a smile and a quiet 'hello', but the old man ignored her. She thought the energy required to be so contrary was probably draining for one of such advanced years, and wondered why he found it necessary to be so dour. Part of Pat's explanation – that he was the only original Crovie blood left in the village – made a kind of sense, she supposed, but still seemed to Anna to be a spurious reason. After all, if not for those who had chosen to make a life here – even a part-time one – Douglas McKean would be alone in a village crumbling to ruins. It must be more to do with the other aspect that Pat had mentioned, that McKean somehow thought he had a claim over the Fishergirl's Luck.

Robert MacKenzie would be the one to ask, of course, and for several reasons – not least of which was Rhona's teasing the day before – Anna was resolved to stay as far away from him as possible.

Her thoughts were interrupted by the whine of an

on-board motor, and a couple of seconds later a small rear-powered skiff took a wide arc around the promontory and slowed as it angled into Crovie's pier. Liam Harper saw her waiting and gave a broad smile.

'Hope I'm not late,' he called, as he killed the engine and threw her a tether. She wound it around the nearest post and, without any idea of how to tie an appropriate knot, held the free end while he climbed out to join her, carrying a white plastic crate.

'Right on time,' she said. 'Thanks again. What have you brought me and how much do I owe you?'

'Well, I hope this is all right, but it's langoustines, not fish,' he said, setting down the crate.

'Perfect,' Anna said. 'Thank you.'

'That's a relief,' he grinned as he took the end of the rope from her and tied it off. 'I didn't want to be another disappointing male in your life. And I've brought you something else too, but you'll have to give me a hand to get it out of the boat and down to the bothy.'

He turned and nodded at the skiff, and Anna saw that what she'd thought was an old wooden crate resting in the base of the boat was actually a picnic bench tilted on its side.

'What's that?' she asked, astonished.

'It's a table, for your garden, like we talked about. Remember? Come on, give me a hand.' Liam leapt back down into the boat and hefted the bench around.

'What are you doing buying me a picnic bench?' Anna asked, as together they began to wrestle it onto dry land.

'Ah, well – first confession,' he said. 'I didn't buy it. It's been lying around the harbour for ages, waiting to go out with a load of scrap. I checked it over and I reckon all it needs is a good scrub. So I asked if I could take it and was told I could.'

'And the second confession?' Anna prompted, as she held on to the bench while he clambered out of the boat again and helped her drag it sideways onto secure ground.

Liam leaned his weight on the bench with both hands, a quick grin on his face. 'Well, it's kind of a bribe.'

Anna raised one eyebrow. 'Oh? And what kind of bribe is it, Kiwi?'

He laughed. 'I still want you to cook me dinner, chef lady.'

She crossed her arms and shook her head. 'What if I say no and leave you here to get it back into the boat on your own?'

'You won't do that.'

'Sure of yourself, aren't you?'

'You're not the first person to say that.'

'I bet I'm not.'

He smiled again. 'So, what do you say? It doesn't have to be fancy, or take forever to prepare. It could be an omelette, for all I care. And I'll bring the wine.'

'If it doesn't have to be fancy, why do you want me to cook it? Cook it yourself!'

He glanced down at his hands, for a moment looking strangely self-conscious. 'Ah well, that's the third confession.'

'Oh?'

He looked up at her, eyebrows knitting together briefly

and with an expression in his eye that turned her heart over right there in her chest.

'It's not really about the food. It's about the company.'

She refused to look away. He could play whatever games of flattery he liked. It probably worked most of the time. 'You can't cook, can you, *Liam*? That's the truth.'

He grinned. 'Someone's been doing some research of their own, eh?'

She shrugged. 'It's a small place.'

'It is that,' he agreed. 'Come on. Let's get this down to the bothy. I've got to get back and you've got langous-tines to cook.'

Anna steamed the shellfish, then separated the delicate flesh and set it in the fridge to chill. She put the empty shells into her pressure cooker and added onion, garlic, carrot, celery and plenty of white wine, then set them to simmer. She knocked back the soft white dough she had made earlier, shaped it into baguettes, slashed the tops with a knife and set them to prove again.

Anna made notes as she went along, listing ingredients, quantities and timings, because what she had told Cathy had been true – Anna had once dreamed of creating a cookbook of her own. She'd helped Geoff with the first of his, in fact, because he'd declared himself to be an ideas man, with no interest in the actual practicalities of how one described the cooking process so that a home cook could follow along with ease. That book had been timed to coincide with the first TV series, and it had been a lot of work that she'd had to fit in around her usual shifts at the restaurant. When the proofs had come in for them to check, there had been a note from the editor, suggesting that Geoff include an acknowledgement page. Her name had been one of the last in the short paragraph. 'Thank you to my girlfriend Anna for her support', was what it had said. After that, when the show had been such a success and it was clear there would be as many more books as he could churn out, Geoff had insisted that he be given a 'proper' ghostwriter. From then on, the publisher had paid someone to do the job that Anna had done for nothing. She had looked at the acknowledgements of the second book, simply out of interest. Her name had not appeared at all. She hadn't asked Geoff about it, thinking badly of herself for feeling that it should have been. After all, when it came down to it, she was only his girlfriend and a sous chef at his restaurant, wasn't she? Why should she expect any thanks?

Cathy hadn't held back her anger on Anna's behalf.

'But it's like Geoff always says, isn't it?' Anna had told her friend. 'There is no "I" in team.'

'Oh, come off it!' Cathy had told her. 'In my experience, people who fall back on that phrase do so specifically so they can ignore the equally important adage "credit where credit's due".'

When it came time for her to make a dessert to go with lunch, Anna turned to Bren's book again. This time she was fascinated by a recipe and a note accompanying it that had been added in 1938, when Anna realized that Bren would have been just seventeen. It was for 'broonie', a version of a gingerbread made with oats and using buttermilk and molasses as well as ground ginger.

Mrs Towrie at Stromness brought us this for pieces while we were at the herring, said the note that accompanied the neatly written recipe. *Asked her if she would tell me the makings and she did. Best left a night afore cutting. Keeps well for a week a'more. July 1938.*

Reading this made Anna feel as if she were only understanding half of the words. She reached for her iPad to search for information about herring in Orkney and soon found herself looking at old black-and-white photographs. In them she could see lines of women in heavy wool dresses and shawls leaning over long wooden troughs set on busy docks, the sharp knives in their hands catching the strong northern sunlight as they gutted thousands of herring. The women were known as herring lassies or 'quines', Anna learned, and in season hundreds of them would travel around the coasts of Scotland, Ireland and England, gutting and salting the huge numbers of herring that were landed by the fishing fleets every day.

Anna pored over the photographs, wondering whether one of them was Bren. Maybe even on the day that Mrs Towrie brought the gutting teams her gingerbread as a 'piece' to eat. Some of the money the young Bren earned there had helped to buy the shed that had become the Fishergirl's Luck.

Half an hour later, Bren's broonie was in the oven. Anna wouldn't have time to leave it overnight before cutting, but after reading the note and looking at those photographs, Anna had been determined to make the cake. To serve she would whip soft double cream and drizzle with heather honey.

Once the cake was in, Anna washed her hands, took off her apron, and went outside to examine the bench. By now the sun was fully up and a light breeze, though not too strong, was filtering through the village. The North Sea seemed to be behaving itself, merely teasing the sea wall with its waves, as if it were playing a game of knock-down-ginger with the village's edge. Anna checked the tide times and predictions and decided that it was worth the risk. The sky was too blue and the sun too warm not to take advantage of Liam's gift, even if she and her two guests would be sitting on a blank oblong of grey concrete. She wished for tubs of flowers, the flashing scarlet of bright, hardy begonias, but she had no time to search any out, and so the table itself would have to do.

Anna filled a bucket with hot soapy water. An hour later she had scrubbed the worst of the grime from the bench's sturdy wood and decided it was still strong enough to take the weight of her and her guests. It looked, in fact, as if it could go another fifty years without sagging under the strain. It dried quickly in the sea air, and she laid it with a white tablecloth weighted with silver cutlery that she buffed as she set down, Rhona's plates, water glasses and wine glasses turned upside down to avoid wind-blown sand and inquisitive bugs.

'My goodness, how beautiful,' Pat exclaimed, when she and Frank arrived. 'I feel as if I've come to the most exclusive restaurant in the world.'

'You don't do things by halves, do you, lass?' Frank laughed, as she seated them at the table and poured them all a crisp white New Zealand Sauvignon Blanc. 'Where did you find the bench? What a wonderful idea.'

The story of her encounter with the Kiwi came out as they ate their starters – a salad of smoked salmon and cucumber lightly pickled with dill – and by the end of it both Pat and Frank were laughing.

'The cheek of him!' Pat said. 'So what are you going to do?'

'Not sure yet,' Anna told them. 'But I think he'd probably be good company for an evening. And I made myself a promise when I got here. I've spent too many years with no opportunity to experience new things. So while I'm here, I'm going to say yes to as many things as I can.'

'Ooh, dangerous words,' Frank chuckled. 'I wouldn't let him know that. Or any other bloke in these parts, for that matter.'

'Frank,' Pat scolded.

'Ach, you should have some fun, Anna,' he went on, 'he's been here since last summer. Took off over winter to see a bit of Europe, then came back again. He'll be gone for good in another few months. Once the season's over he's off home again. Talk is that he's got to take over his parents' farm as his old dad is ailing. This trip of his was a last chance at a few months of freedom before he settles in to that.'

'I'm sure,' Anna said with a faint smile, 'that Liam Harper has *plenty* of fun.'

They moved on to the bisque, which was met with rapturous approval. It was very good, Anna had to admit. Even at the great Four Seasons, despite its Michelin stars, the langoustines would have been a few hours older than the ones Liam had hoicked out of the sea and brought to her doorstep.

As they ate and talked, a couple passed them, nodding and smiling. They were clearly tourists out for a stroll, and Anna wondered if they had known that Crovie was here or whether they had followed the signpost on impulse and discovered it by accident.

'Oh, you'll find a lot of tourists find their way down here in the summer months,' Pat said quietly, as Anna remarked on the couple. 'Most don't stay long, but they walk down the road and do a circuit of the village all the same.'

The three of them were still eating as the pair walked back the other way. Anna saw them pass and then pause, before the man turned back and leaned over the fence.

'Hello,' he said. 'I'm sorry to bother you – but is there anywhere to eat nearby? Is there a café or restaurant in this village, perhaps? This looks so idyllic, and the food smells so delicious. It's making us hungry, and we didn't really plan our day out too well.'

'I'm sorry, there isn't anywhere in Crovie,' Anna said.

'The Garden Arms at Gamrie would be closest,' Frank said, smiling at the visitors. 'Otherwise it'll be the Pennan Inn, back the other way, or at Portsoy, towards Macduff.'

The man smiled. 'Thank you, and apologies for interrupting your lunch. It really does smell exquisite.'

'Well,' Anna said hesitantly, looking at Pat and Frank. 'If you two don't mind – I do have more. You could join us, if you like.'

'Oh no,' said the man, as the woman with him – his wife, judging by their rings – moved closer. 'We don't want to impose.'

'It's no bother for us,' Frank said, as Pat nodded her agreement. 'It's Anna's table, Anna's food.'

'Please,' Anna said, standing up. 'Come and join us. I don't want it to go to waste.'

The couple looked at each other, and the wife smiled.

'Then we'd love to, if you're sure,' she said. 'How extremely generous of you.'

So it was that Liam's bench – which Anna kept calling it in her head, despite telling herself not to – gathered another two visitors into Anna's garden. She served two more bowls of bisque, brought out another still-warm baguette and poured more wine. Over the next hour they learned that her additional guests were Anthony and Rose Linden, who were staying in Portsoy for the week but lived in York.

'This really is delicious,' Rose said again, as she finished her bisque. 'And your bread is divine.'

'And what a perfect setting,' Anthony added. 'Honestly, Anna, you could fill a dozen tables every lunchtime if you lined them up along this wall. Even if you only served this you'd be rushed off your feet.'

'One of our friends thinks she should reopen the Crovie Inn,' Frank said. 'I think it's a top idea.'

'I've only just got here,' Anna protested. 'Besides, I don't have the capital for that.'

'Start small then,' Anthony suggested. 'There must be plenty of people like us who visit the village, especially in summer. Give them a reason to stay a bit longer. Even if it's only at this table.'

'It's a nice thought,' said Anna, 'but I'm not sure how sustainable that is, and I'm not planning to stay here permanently.'

'Well,' said Anthony, 'take it from me. We'll be telling everyone we possibly can about this magical experience we had at a superb chef's table in the village of Crovie.'

'We will,' Rose agreed. 'I'll be dreaming about that bisque for weeks. I'd ask you for the recipe, but I already know I'd never make it the way you do.'

They sat at Liam's bench until long past four o'clock. Finally, wine finished, Bren's broonie devoured and coffee drained, the party slowly broke up. Pat and Frank helped Anna carry the detritus into the kitchen, and when they came out again Anthony discreetly slipped her a fold of notes.

'Thank you for your hospitality,' he said. 'It really has been wonderful – and, I think, a real privilege – both to meet you and to eat at your table, Anna.'

'I can't take this!' Anna said, pushing the money back towards him without looking at it. 'You were my guests, and you were very welcome.'

'No, take it,' he insisted, as Rose came up behind him, smiling warmly. 'That was the best meal we've had all week. I know what effort went into it, and how much it should have cost.'

'Please,' Rose added. 'We've had an experience here that we couldn't have got anywhere else.'

Defeated, Anna accepted the cash. 'Well, thank you,' she said. 'It's been wonderful to meet you both. Maybe you'll come back and visit us again sometime?'

They shook hands, and Rose pulled her into a brief hug.

'Trust me, Anna,' Anthony said. 'The minute we hear that you've opened the Crovie Inn as a going concern, we'll be booking one of these holiday cottages and a table in your restaurant every night.'

Eleven

The weather changed over the next few days – the wind got up and squalls of rain marauded along the coastline beneath an increasingly leaden grey sky. Anna watched Pat's bed and breakfast guests from behind the muslin of her bedroom window as they walked first one way and then the other along the sea wall, dodging the waves big enough to breach its height. She wondered what had brought them here: whether they had found what they had been looking for.

Having hidden away indoors for a week, working on her cookbook, on Sunday Anna braved the wind and rain for another cliff walk with Glynn, David and Bill. Once back in Crovie she invited them into the Fishergirl's Luck for a warming lunch of soup and fresh bread, which they ate on their laps while Bill spread out in front of the hearth. Outside, Liam's bench stood firm, already hardened against the worst that Scottish weather could bring as it waited patiently for another day bright enough for guests.

Anthony Linden's words stayed with her. *Give them a reason to stay a bit longer, even if it's only at this table.*

Could she do it? Should she? There was more warm

weather coming, so the forecast said, and there wasn't really any rush for her to leave. She could stay through to the end of summer, couldn't she?

By that evening the wind was howling around the Fishergirl's Luck, rain throwing itself against the walls of the cottage in a blind fury. It might have been past winter further south, but Anna was glad of the stock of wood and kindling she had bought.

'I actually kind of like it,' she told Cathy, as she lay curled up on the old sofa beneath a blanket, phone in one hand and a mug of tea in the other. 'It feels as if the whole world could be crumbling outside and this place would still be standing.'

'Rather you than me,' said Cathy. 'I can hear that wind from here. It sounds as if all the hounds of hell are circling your front door.'

'Maybe they are, but they can't get in. An incomer's home is her castle. I've locked the gates and barricaded the door.'

'Nutter,' Cathy said affectionately. 'Well, at least you sound more sure of yourself.'

'I think it's the cooking,' said Anna. 'I've made something every day since Pat and Frank came over for lunch. I've always been most at home in a kitchen and it feels good to be in command of my own. I've never actually had that before.'

'Your lunch party did sound idyllic,' Cathy said, with a wistful sigh. 'Fresh food – *your* food – good wine, the ocean – what could be more perfect? I wish I'd been there. I can easily imagine how lucky those people felt to stumble across you.'

'It's given me an idea, actually,' Anna admitted.

'You're thinking of taking over the Crovie Inn after all?'

'No. But do you remember that "supper club" thing that went on in London a few years back? Pop-up dining rooms in people's houses? I knew a few chefs who did it because they couldn't afford their own premises and they wanted to start building a reputation around their food.'

'Yeah, Steve and I went to a couple, they were great. You want to do that at the Fishergirl's Luck?'

'I wouldn't do evenings, and it would be weather dependent, but I thought it might work for lunches a couple of days a week. I can only fit eight people around the bench, and I'd probably limit it to six so there's plenty of room and I'm not stretching myself. But I think it could work.'

'Do you think you'd get enough custom?'

'Pat says Crovie gets a lot busier in season. I think it's worth a try. If it doesn't work, at least it wouldn't use up too much of my savings. And it'll give me a way to develop more of my own recipes.'

'How many courses?'

'Three, I think. A simple starter, a main and a dessert. I'd try to source local produce as much as possible, keep things seasonal, that kind of thing. It'd be great to see what comes in on the boat each morning.'

'That'd make the most of your tame fisherman, too, eh?'

Anna laughed. 'I suppose it would.'

'Speaking of which,' Cathy went on, 'tell me again how he turned up with the perfect gift on what was only your second meeting and then asked for a date?'

'Stop it,' Anna scolded. 'I told you, he's the local flirt. Besides, he's far too young for me, even if he were genuinely interested, which he absolutely isn't. And even if he were, I wouldn't be. All right?'

'All right,' said Cathy. 'We'll revisit this at another time.'

'No, we won't.'

'I guarantee we will,' Cathy said, merrily. 'As for the other thing, it sounds like a fine idea to me. Have at it. Want me to do you a poster?'

'It's a bit early for that,' said Anna. 'Although I won't lie and say that the thought hadn't crossed my mind . . .'

Cathy laughed. 'Of course I'll do one. Drop me an email with whatever you want on it – when you know – and I'll get to work. I can already see it, actually. It'll have to be hand lettering all the way for "Lunch at the Fishergirl's Luck".'

'I knew being mates with the best graphic designer south of the Watford Gap would come in useful one day.'

'Flattery will get you everywhere. So what's on the agenda for the rest of the evening?'

Anna listened to the weather outside and pulled the blanket more firmly around her. 'Oh, I don't think I'm going anywhere apart from to the kitchen for more tea. And maybe a chocolate biscuit. I'm sitting here going through recipe books I haven't looked at in years. Making notes, jotting down ideas. That sort of thing. I've been going through some of my mum's old recipes, and I'd like to try to work in some of Bren's recipes, too. I like the idea of making sure she's part of it somehow.'

'It really does sound as if you're inspired,' Cathy said. 'I'm glad. Right, I'd better go. Love you. Email me.'

Anna had just put the phone down and was contemplating swapping her next mug of tea for a glass of white wine and wondering what to make herself for supper when there was a hard knock at the door. She struggled out from beneath the blanket and went to open it, expecting to find Pat or Frank coming to check on her in the storm. Instead she was faced with a drenched Liam Harper.

'Liam!' she exclaimed, pulling him in over the threshold, where he promptly started dripping onto the floor. 'What on earth are you doing out in this? What are you doing *here*?'

He held up both wet fists. In one was a bottle of wine, in the other was a carton of eggs. 'The boat's stuck in dock,' he said, as rivulets of water ran down his face. 'So I thought I'd come and see about that omelette.'

Anna stared at him. 'How did you get here? You didn't bring the skiff?'

Liam shook his head, showering the walls – and her – with spray. 'Not likely. I walked. It was quite . . . bracing.'

'Kiwi, you're an idiot.'

'You know, it's not the first time someone's suggested that.'

'You surprise me. And it wasn't a suggestion. You'd better come in. Take your coat off first or you'll flood the place. I'll stoke up the fire.'

She gave him a towel and a glass of the wine and then went into the kitchen to make them both dinner as Liam dried himself off in front of the wood burner. His hardy fisherman's coat had kept his core dry, but his legs were soaked. His cargo pants were the sort that turned into long shorts and so he zipped off the legs and laid them on the hearth. Anna watched out of the corner of her eye as he scrubbed the towel over his dark hair and tried not to notice quite how tanned and muscular his bare calves were. She told herself she should probably be annoyed that he'd put her in a position that meant she couldn't in all conscience turn him away.

But she wasn't.

'It's not that I don't love New Zealand, or my parents, or even the farm,' Liam said. He was sitting on the floor, his back against one of the armchairs, one leg bent at the knee, one elbow resting on it as he stared at the flames dancing in the wood burner. 'But I'm not sure I'm ready to be a farmer for the rest of my life. Our place – it's big, and it's remote. There won't be much "popping to the pub for a quick half" once I'm back there.'

'Is it North or South Island?'

'South, in Central Otago.'

'I bet it's beautiful.'

'It is. Have you been?'

'Yes,' Anna said. 'Only the South Island, but I loved it. We went mainly for wine country – my ex was filming part of a series there. I remember thinking I'd happily live there permanently if it weren't so far away. My dad was alive then, but it would have been too far for him to visit.'

Liam nodded. 'Yeah. People say that a lot.'

'So this trip around Europe is a last bout of freedom before settling down?'

He grinned. 'Something like that. It was my mum's idea, actually. She wanted me to see the world. I think she was worried that if I didn't, I'd regret it later on.'

Anna smiled. 'You ended up in a pretty tiny corner of it.'

'I know,' he laughed. 'I don't even know why I came back for this season. I could have stayed on the Continent. The fishing suits me, I guess. I'm better at being outside. And there are good people here.'

'There are,' she agreed.

'Good cooks, too.'

'Oh yes, I can break eggs with the best of them.' She poured him more wine.

Liam sighed and leaned back against the chair. 'I always loved this place from the outside. I'm so glad it's as cute inside, too.'

They were quiet for a few moments. Anna watched his face, at the way his eyes studied the bookcases in the ceiling, the colourful spines of her many cookbooks. He had surprised her by being better – and quieter – company than she'd anticipated. She'd expected him to be fun – and he was, he'd made her laugh a lot. But here, in the Fishergirl's Luck, he seemed more contemplative, more serious, somehow. Part of her wondered if that was deliberate, as if he were trying to show her a different side of himself, and if that was the case she was surprised he would bother, or think it necessary.

Liam moved, caught her watching him and raised an eyebrow, his dark eyes laughing at her. Anna smiled and looked down at her glass.

'I'm trying to work out what you're doing here, Liam Harper, taking up space on my floor.'

He looked at his watch. 'I guess it's late. Should I go?'

'That's not—' she paused, then smiled again, aware of how what she was about to say would sound. 'That's not what I meant. You don't have to go. I just ... I don't know why you're here at all.'

'I like you, and I got the impression you liked me,' he said, simply. 'That's all. I wanted to know you better.'

'You could have asked me to go out for a drink with you instead of turning up at my door in a gale.'

'Yes,' he agreed. 'But both of the nearest pubs will be full of people who know me and know of you, and I didn't think you'd be too comfortable sitting in a corner chatting with half the coastline listening in. I didn't tell anyone where I was going tonight and the gale means it's unlikely anyone saw me arrive at your door.'

Anna opened her mouth and then shut it again. 'I suppose so.'

'I also figured, given what you seem to have left behind in London, that gossip might be something you'd like to avoid.'

'You're not wrong there,' she admitted.

'Besides, you would have said no, because it would have been too much like having to make a deliberate choice to go out with me, and for some reason you've decided that would be a bad thing to do. So I thought what you needed was to get to know me behind closed doors. Has it worked?'

Anna laughed. 'Seriously, have you so exhausted the choice of women in the area that you needed to grab the first new one to move in?'

'No,' he said. 'But I'm going home in three months. And I ... am not planning to take anyone home with me, put it that way. And you ... don't want to start anything that might actually be the start of anything, because you're not planning to stay either, and you've recently come to the end of something long and painful. Am I right?'

'Hmm,' she said, watching as he put down his wine glass. 'You are, as it happens.'

'There you go then,' he said, his eyes fixed on hers. 'Perfect for each other, that's us, right now.'

Anna again laughed and gulped more wine because actually his argument was a pretty decent one and besides that, he was gorgeous and seeming more so by the minute. Dammit.

'There is another reason,' he said, as he moved closer, still on the floor, eyes still locked with hers.

She took a breath, cleared her throat and put down her wine glass. 'And that is?'

Liam stopped, kneeling beside where she sat on the sofa. He reached up and touched her cheek before stroking his fingers through her hair. 'You're beautiful.'

Anna couldn't stop looking at his mouth. Her good sense seemed to have abandoned her completely and her heart was in overdrive. 'Flatterer,' she said, her voice distinctly uneven.

'It's true,' he whispered, and then his lips were against hers, his hand was in her hair, and her insides were in the most delicious kind of freefall.

'I don't know,' she murmured, a minute or so later, 'if I think this is a good idea.'

He let her go and sat back on his haunches, looking up at her. She felt the separation like a chill wind. 'All right. That's fine. I'll go.'

Liam went to get up but she stopped him, one hand against his cheek. *Say yes,* she thought. *While you're here, say yes to as many things as you can.*

'No,' she said. 'Don't.'

Twelve

Anna woke before it was light the next morning, just as Liam was slipping out of bed. When he saw she was awake he leaned down to kiss her.

'I was trying not to wake you. Go back to sleep,' he said quietly. 'The storm's blown itself out. I'm going to make my way back before anyone's up and about out there.'

She ran her fingers through his hair, then tugged gently at one dark lock. 'You don't have to, Kiwi.'

Liam smiled and then kissed her again, the touch lingering. 'I'll write down my number and leave it on the table. Call me any time – if I can answer, I will. If I don't it'll be because I'm working.'

Anna shifted under the covers, watching him pull on his boxers. The rest of his clothes were still downstairs. 'I hope you managed to get some sleep. It's been a long time since I slept in a single bed with company.'

He laughed. 'It wasn't so bad. I spend a lot of time in bunks, remember? Right. I'm going.' He kissed her again and was gone.

She listened to him moving around downstairs as he

dressed. There was a couple of minutes' silence, then more footsteps. He came back up the stairs, quickly, and a second later he was pressing her into the bed, kissing her hard, the roughness of his knitted sweater scratching against her breasts, the fervent nature of the kiss making her laugh against his stubble. Then he was gone again, his feet loud on the stairs. The door of the Fishergirl's Luck clicked shut behind him.

Anna stared up at the ceiling for a few minutes. Her body was pleasantly heavy, drowsy in all the right ways. She thought about getting up, but felt her eyes closing instead.

When she woke again, dawn light was edging through her window. Downstairs, the Fishergirl's Luck held a new kind of stillness, the sort left in the wake of activity. Liam's note was on the coffee table, scrawled in an uneven hand: his number, and a brief message.

I had fun. Hope you did too. Call me.

Smiling, Anna put the note back down on the table and went into the kitchen to make tea. Through the window the sea looked like tumbled green glass, its rough edges sanded smooth. Suddenly what she most wanted was to be outside, in fresh air.

The track was wet with the recent downpour, the grass either side of it bent over and glistening with the weight of rain. The wind was still brisk, plucking at Anna's hair and jacket, scattering the bright yellow petals of the storm-battered gorse before her as she walked. It was the first time she'd been up on the cliff alone, and without Bill's big paws stampeding ahead and Glynn and David to chat to, it seemed like a foreign landscape. Everywhere was green, from the ocean stretching choppily into the brightening horizon to the earth beneath her feet.

Anna pulled in huge lungfuls of air and pushed on, enjoying the buffet and rush of the damp air, thinking of nothing and everything. It wasn't until she glanced down and saw that the route she was walking had dwindled into not much more than a rabbit track that Anna realized she must have stepped away from the path. Looking behind her she also saw that she'd come much closer to the cliff – over the edge of it, in fact, and had begun to make her way down a sloping dip that descended the cliff face itself. She stopped, considering her options. Ahead of her the route got steeper, dropping down towards the water, but it didn't seem impassable. Besides, although it was overgrown and narrow, there clearly was a track that had been trodden by feet other than hers. She thought it probably led around the promontory towards Troup Head and Pennan, and wondered if it were possible to walk all the way around the edge of the cliff. Might there be a walk like the one that led from Crovie to Gardenstown?

She decided to push onwards a little further, enjoying the blast of wind in her face and the new view of the cliff. Crovie had vanished behind her and it felt as if she were teetering on the edge of the world. Anna walked on. The path grew steadily more broken and precipitous. In places she had to descend with one hand braced against the wet brush to find her footing, until finally the path disappeared altogether beneath the tangled weight of a gorse bush that had grown right across it. It was frustrating, given how close she now was to the water – close enough that she could see the waves dashing themselves into white churn against the rock, which here was black rather than red. Anna could see a tiny beach, too, a miniature cove sheltering beneath the overhang, bounded by the verdant growth of a plant she thought was probably sea purslane.

Looking back up the way she had come, it occurred to Anna that she had descended much further and on far steeper a route than she had realized as she'd walked.

In for a penny, in for a pound, she thought, and stepped off the track to circumnavigate the voluminous gorse. *I've come this far, I might as well see if I can get to the purslane.*

Anna had almost reached the sand when she heard a shout. It came, not from the cliff, but from the water. She was in the process of negotiating a particularly steep and slippery bit of rock and stopped, twisting her head over her shoulder. Bobbing on the waves was a wooden dinghy painted in stripes of turquoise blue and white and bearing two figures, one of whom she recognized as Robert MacKenzie.

'Hi!' she called.

'What are you doing?' he called back.

Anna jumped down onto the narrow spit of sand so that she could face him and saw that the other person in the boat was a boy of about ten. He had a mop of sandy hair that closely resembled Robert's, and could only be his son. He also wore a miniature version of Old Robbie's yellow fisherman's jacket and had a pair of serious-looking binoculars around his neck to match the serious look on his small face.

'I'm taking a walk,' she shouted.

'Down the cliff?' Robert asked, his incredulity clear despite the noise of the waves and the wind.

'I didn't meant to come down it, I just—'

A gust of wind stole her words, throwing them to the sky. He held up a hand to cup his ear. She started to yell again, and then gave up, holding up her arms in an expansive shrug. Anna expected him to wave a goodbye and carry on, but instead she saw that they were bringing the boat onto the shore. Its pilot came close to beaching it and jumped out, the water up to his thighs as he dragged the dinghy up onto the sand. Young Robbie jumped out after him.

'The cliff isn't safe,' Old Robbie said, as they got nearer. 'Especially not after a storm like that. Look.'

He pointed up and Anna followed the direction of his outstretched hand to see fresh signs of scarring where the shallow earth had slipped its tether and slid down the underlying rock. In places it had obscured the narrow path she'd been on – she just hadn't noticed as she'd picked her way along it. From her viewpoint it had looked like the natural bearing of the cliff.

'Did that happen last night?'

'Some of it. The erosion is getting worse every year.'

'Right,' Anna said, feeling slightly queasy as she realized what a fall on the cliff would have meant. 'Okay. Well, lesson learned. Thanks. I guess I'd better be careful going back up.'

'You can come in the *Silver Darling*.' The voice came from the boy, his face still solemn. 'We'll take you. It'll be safer.'

Anna smiled at him. 'That's very kind. Thank you.'

The boy didn't smile back, only nodded and pushed his glasses up his nose. His dad looked at his watch.

'We'd better go or you're going to be late for school. We're cutting it fine as it is.'

'I can't be late again, Dad!'

Old Robbie laid a hand on his son's shoulder, propelling the boy back towards the boat. 'Well, whose idea was it to drag me out on dolphin patrol before breakfast, eh? I was all for pancakes, but no, it was all about the dolphins, wasn't it?'

'Hang on,' Anna called after them. 'Two seconds, I want to—' she dashed over to the purslane, bending to snatch a few handfuls. It was easier said than done, the stiff stalks refusing to break easily. After a few seconds in which she waged a pathetic losing battle with the local flora, a shadow fell across her and a hand appeared over her shoulder, holding out an open utility knife. 'Thanks,' she said, taking it and cutting at the plant. She stood up and turned, closing the knife and holding it out. Robert was watching her with an amused expression. It crinkled the lines around his eyes like the ripples on a sea on its way to becoming unsettled.

'Dad!' Young Robbie called out, behind them. He was already in the dinghy. 'Come *on!*'

Old Robbie helped her into the boat and then pushed off, hauling himself from the water and over the side without even seeming to lose a breath. Anna settled herself on one of the narrow benches and then they were off, the older MacKenzie manning the rudder with practised ease. Anna sat facing him, his son beside her, and watched as the boy pulled a rolled-up exercise book out of his pocket. The words 'Dolphin Patrol Notes' had been written with felt pen in haphazardly bold lettering on the front. Young Robbie retrieved a pen from the pocket of his yellow jacket and bent over a new page. After writing the date at the top he began diligently making notes.

'Did you see any this morning?' Anna asked him. When he nodded, she added, 'That's wonderful. I've never seen a dolphin.'

He looked up at that. 'What, never?'

Anna shook her head. 'Not in the wild. I'd love to, though.'

'You will,' the boy said confidently. 'There's a pod in the bay at the moment and I think they're going to have at least one baby.'

'A baby dolphin! Now that I would like to see.'

'That's why we came round to the cove,' Young Robbie went on. 'It's on their route and we needed to check for nets.' He chewed his pen for a minute, eyeing the bushy bunch of purslane in her hand. 'What's that?' he asked.

Anna held up the leaves. 'This? It's called sea purslane. You can eat it.'

The boy wrinkled his nose. 'Really?'

'Yes. It's very salty.' She snapped off a leaf and ate it as he watched with fascination. 'Want to try?'

Young Robbie hesitated, looking at his dad. Old Robbie smiled and nodded. 'Anna knows what she's about,' he said. 'She's a chef.'

The boy picked a leaf and gingerly put it between his lips, nibbling carefully. A surprised look came over his face. 'It tastes like the sea!'

'It does,' Anna agreed. 'That's why it goes well with fish and other seafood.'

'What are you going to make with it?'

'Don't know yet. I just thought I'd better grab some. After all, that's the last time I'm going to be on that cliff.'

'It's all right,' Young Robbie said. 'When you want to pick some more we can take you in the boat, can't we, Dad?'

Anna looked over at Old Robbie, who was still smiling. 'Sure. Of course we can.'

'This is my boat really,' Young Robbie explained. 'Auntie Bren left it to me. But I'm still learning how to use it.'

'It's a fine boat. And you can do your dolphin patrols in it, too.'

The boy smiled for the first time. 'You can come on one of those, as well, if you like. We get really close sometimes. Not too close, though. We don't want to disturb them, just observe them.' He said this as if it might have been a mantra learned from somewhere.

Anna smiled back. 'I would love to. Thank you.'

They rounded the cliff and swung into Crovie's little harbour. Old Robbie coasted easily up to the jetty, keeping the engine running as Anna got up to climb out.

'Thank you, kind gentlemen,' she said to them both. 'For rescuing a damsel who hadn't even realized she was in distress.'

Old Robbie smiled. 'Not so much distress as blissful ignorance.'

'It's funny how often adult life is made bearable by that very combination, isn't it?' she said, and he laughed.

In that moment, Anna wanted to say something about Cassie – how sorry she was for their loss, and also to apologize for the way she had mentioned her so bluntly when they'd first met. But how could she, with their son there, sitting in Bren's boat and looking up at her so attentively? Then there came the sudden crunch of footsteps behind them, accompanied by the sound of a familiar, bitter old voice.

'You're tae late, Auld Robbie,' said Douglas McKean. 'Saw the foreign lad sneaking out of Bren's bothy nae four hours hence. Field's already ploughed.'

Anna felt her face burn scarlet with an equal combination of humiliation and rage as she registered the meaning of the old man's words. She opened her mouth to bark a response, but Old Robbie beat her to it.

'Well, that wouldn't be my business now, would it, Dougie, any more than it is yours,' he said, his face giving away no hint of emotion, though his eyes were flinty cold. He turned his attention to Anna, ignoring the old man completely. 'Razor clams do you?'

Her head was still so buzzing with rage that Anna couldn't fathom the question. 'I–what?'

Robert MacKenzie nodded at the bunch of leaves in her hand. 'To go with the purslane. Razor clams.'

'Yes,' she said. 'Razor clams would work perfectly.'

'All right. I'll take you to collect a bucket later. Now I've got to get this one to school.'

Anna barely watched them leave, the sound of the revving motor echoing around the cliff. Douglas McKean was watching her with dark, narrowed eyes. She looked at him in disgust and shook her head, not trusting herself to speak for fear that her words would be laced with rage. Anna walked away, the purslane clutched in her hand so tightly that it left an impression of leaves across her palm.

Thirteen

Pat was hanging up washing as Anna came back along the narrow path.

'Morning,' she said, cheerfully, and then saw Anna's face. 'Oh – is something wrong?'

Anna shook her head. 'It doesn't matter. I'll get over it. Have you got time for tea? I've got *plans* – with a capital P – to tell you about.'

'I can't this morning, I'm afraid. Frank's got a hospital appointment and I'm going with him to do some shopping in town while he's there.'

'Oh?' Anna asked, worry immediately clouding her thoughts. 'He's all right?'

'Just a check-up, love, on his pacemaker.'

'I didn't realize he had one.'

'Ah well,' said Pat, with a sigh, 'he'd prefer to pretend he doesn't. He had a heart attack two years ago. You'd think that'd be a wake-up call for him to slow down a bit, but no, not our Frank. Likes to think he's still thirty and tries to act like it, too.'

'Oh Pat, I'm sorry. That must be a worry.'

Pat reached out and squeezed Anna's arm. 'Old age, love. Gets to us all in the end. He's mostly right as rain, and who knows? Perhaps the doctor will be able to talk some sense into him.' Her neighbour nodded at the overflowing basket of washing. 'Give me a hand and you can tell me all about these plans of yours as you do.'

Most of Anna's anger had evaporated by the time the last of Pat's sheets were pegged to the North Sea wind.

'I think a pop-up restaurant is a fine idea,' Pat said, picking up the empty basket and resting it against her hip. 'Anything you need from Frank and me to make it work, let us know.'

'Well – and do say if this is too big an ask,' Anna began, 'but I wondered whether it would be possible for any customers I do have to use your downstairs bathroom during my service period? I'd worry that if I let people use mine I might get them wandering into the kitchen. Not something health and safety would approve of if they were ever to turn up.'

'Not to mention that you don't want to be worried about strangers nosing about in your home,' Pat agreed. 'Let me check with Frank, but I don't see why not. We can always turn the key to the kitchen if we need to.'

'Thanks, Pat,' Anna said, relieved.

'No problem, dear. Let us know if you think of anything else.'

'You can be early standby customers!' Anna said. 'I'm planning to make sure the table's full of friends, if no one else.'

'Oh, I don't think filling your table will be a problem,' Pat said, heading indoors. 'Look at the customers you had without even trying. Pop over later for a tipple if you fancy it.'

Anna spent the rest of the morning and early afternoon making notes and lists of tasks she would have to accomplish before the lunch club could open. The kitchen would need some reorganization. She needed a complete set of matching flatware – from Rhona, of course. There was cutlery to think about, too, glasses, napkins – a multitude of considerations beyond the food itself.

She was so engrossed in her plans that she completely forgot Robert MacKenzie's early morning declaration about razor clams until he banged on the door at two o'clock that afternoon. Anna opened it to find him in his customary yellow jacket, hands on his hips.

'Tide's heading out now,' he said, by way of greeting.

'Oh!' Anna was momentarily flummoxed. 'Yes – of course. Thanks. What do I need to bring with me?'

'A coat, your wellies and yourself.'

'I don't have any wellies.'

He shrugged, 'Boots will be fine, then. The ones you were wearing earlier?'

Anna pulled her coat from its peg and shoved her feet into her boots. She hesitated on the step. 'Give me a second,' she said. She dashed back inside, scrabbled around for a moment and then dashed out again, pulling the door shut behind her and turning the key, feeling entirely unprepared.

Her embarrassment of earlier returned as they walked to the harbour in a silence that felt intensely awkward. She wondered if she should say something, but what, exactly, could she say? And anyway, why should she feel obligated to say anything?

The boat that waited for them at Crovie's pier was not the skiff she had seen that morning, but a larger boat clearly made for fishing. It was about six metres long with an open cabin over the steering wheel and an enclosed prow. It was navy blue and white and on its side, painted in red and gold, was its name: *Cassie's Joy*.

Less than five minutes later and for the second time that day, Anna found herself speeding over the waves, the coastal cliffs rearing into the cloud-specked sky.

'We're not going far,' Robert said, once they'd taken a long, wide curve out of the bay and left Crovie behind. 'There's a cove out towards Rosehearty, beyond Pennan, that's usually full of them. Have you ever harvested razor clams before?'

'No,' Anna shouted back, over the sound of the outboard motor and the ubiquitous roar of the wind. 'I've cooked with them, but that's it.'

He nodded. 'It takes some muscle.'

'And some salt.'

Robert looked over at her, surprised. 'You do know a bit about it, then.'

'I know the theory of many things,' she said, 'but the reality of very few.'

He smiled, the first such expression she'd seen on his face since he'd knocked at her door. 'Sounds familiar,' he said.

The hop around the headland was brief. The cliff here was another monolith of sheer rock, reaching skyward in ragged clefts. Anna noted that there had been landslides here, too – signs that she was beginning to learn. They looked like shallow channels in the rock and mud, almost like stream-beds run dry.

Robert tied off the boat, though there was still a foot or so between the *Cassie's Joy* and the beach, and Anna could see why he'd recommended wellington boots.

'Right. Grab that,' he said, pointing to a galvanized bucket near her feet. 'The salt's in the box inside. Bucket, salt, and over the side. Okay?'

In the next moment, he had hopped into the water, holding out a hand for the bucket. She passed it to him and then clambered inelegantly into the cold North Sea. The water splashed up to her knees, soaking the walking trousers she was still wearing from her earlier walk.

She waded after Robert, who had reached the shore and turned to wait for her. He waved at the wet sand beneath their feet.

'Just a few here to choose from.'

In ridges of sand left by the outgoing tide were hundreds of holes. Some had piles of ejected sand beside them, but others – small circular indentations that disappeared beneath the shallow film of brine caught by the motion of the tide – were clear, denoting the hidden clam's air holes.

'There are so many!'

Robert nodded. 'I'll pour, you catch.'

He opened the box of salt as Anna pulled out her gloves. They were gardening gloves that Geoff had given her years ago, despite the fact that she'd never actually had a garden of her own. At the time she'd had the feeling that it was some kind of barbed statement concealed as a joke at her expense. She was glad now that she hadn't thrown them out.

Robert looked at her with amusement as she put them on. 'Don't tell me the hardened chef is a wee bit squeamish?'

Anna grinned, pushing her hair back behind her ears to stop it dancing wildly in the wind. 'I want to be prepared, that's all. I've never done this before.'

He nodded, then crouched over one of the air holes. 'I'll let you into a secret,' he said. 'Neither have I.'

Anna laughed, astonished. 'What? But—'

He looked up at her with a quick grin. 'Theory, not reality, right? Anyway, what is it the kids say? Fake it 'til you make it?' He jutted his chin at the sand. 'Ready?'

She gave him a thumbs up and he tipped some salt into the hole. They watched in silence for a few seconds as it dissolved. Then came the reaction: a sudden bubbling of water being expelled before a tower of shell erupted as the creature tried to clear its airway.

'Quick,' Robert exclaimed, leaning back to give her space, 'grab it!'

Anna wrapped her fingers around the shell and pulled. The clam resisted, but she dragged it from the sand and held up the fat shellfish, watching the foot search for purchase and finding none.

'It worked,' Robert said with surprise, and then laughed, the most heartfelt she'd yet heard him give: a good sound, alive and free. 'Well, would ye ken that?'

Anna dropped the clam into the bucket, laughing too, although as she watched the animal still searching for its home a familiar feeling of guilt washed over her, followed by a swell of sadness in her chest. *Poor thing*, she thought, watching it struggle.

'Hey,' Robert reached out, touching his fingers to her arm. 'You all right?'

She looked at him, at the way the wind had dealt so roughly with his sandy hair, at the concerned look blooming among the lines on his face, at how right he looked here, now, in this place he knew so well. 'Yeah. I guess you could say I'm a sentimental chef, rather than squeamish.' Geoff certainly would have – had done so frequently, in fact.

Robert looked down into the bucket. 'It's not sentimental to care,' he said. 'Not even for something that's going to end up in the cooking pot. I can do this, if you like.'

'No,' she said. 'They're for *my* kitchen, *my* cooking pot. It's my responsibility.'

He said no more about it.

'How did you find this beach?' Anna asked, an hour or so later. They were sitting on a rock, sipping coffee from a flask that Robert had produced from the boat's cabin. The full bucket was stowed away.

'I didn't. It was Cassie. She knew this coast like the back of her hand. She loved this place.' Robert smiled, a lopsided gesture as he looked up to stare out over the waves. 'We came here on one of our first proper dates. She borrowed her dad's boat after school one day to bring me here – she could already handle it like a pro, even at fifteen. I'd sailed past this place myself since I was small, but I'd never noticed it enough to bother exploring. She was like that, though. Noticed everything. *Interested* in everything.'

Anna looked over at the boat they'd come in; at the name so proudly painted on its hull. 'The *Cassie's Joy*,' she read, again. 'This was your wife's boat?'

Robert MacKenzie nodded. 'I bought it as a wedding present. We couldn't afford a house but I bought Cass a boat of her own,' he shook his head as if in wonder at his youthful foolishness. 'We were out in it every spare moment we had.' His face took on an uncomfortable expression and he glanced at her. 'Sorry.'

'Sorry? For what?'

'Here I am going on about my dead wife.'

'I was the one who asked,' Anna pointed out. 'I've been trying to find a way to apologize to you, anyway, for bringing Cassie up the way I did when we first met. I didn't know that you had lost her. I'd never have been so insensitive if I had.'

Robert shifted beside her, their shoulders brushing together. 'It wasn't insensitive. You didn't know.'

'Still,' Anna said. 'I'm sorry. And I would never stop you talking about Cassie, if you wanted to. Talk about her as much as you like.'

He gave a slight smile. 'Be careful. That's a big thing to offer.'

'Is it?'

He looked out at the water again. 'It's a difficult thing to listen to, isn't it, other people's grief? People want to believe they can, but ... usually they find it's too much. Besides, Cassie's been gone for five years. Most people around here think I should be over it by now. That I should have moved on.'

Anna watched his profile for a moment. 'What do people mean,' she asked, 'when they say you should be "over it"? Over what? The fact that you loved your wife? That's not how it works, is it? Are you supposed to somehow forget that feeling? I don't think you ever do that. All you can do is learn to make it a part of your life. How and when you manage to do that isn't down to anyone else. There's no time limit on grief. There's no road map to guide you through it, either. Everyone deals with loss differently.'

He turned to look at her. 'How did you get to be so wise?'

She looked away.

'I'm sorry,' he said quietly. 'Now I'm the one putting my foot in it. You've been through it yourself.'

'It's not that long since my dad died,' Anna admitted. 'I hadn't lived at home since I went to college, and thanks to my ex I hadn't spent nearly enough time visiting as I should have in the past few years. His passing has hit me really hard. I miss him such a lot. It keeps catching me out when I least expect it. The realization that I'm never going to see him again. It was only the two of us for so long.'

She wasn't looking at him, but from the corner of her eye, Anna saw Robert nod in understanding.

'It's brought back how I felt when Mum died, too,' she went on. 'I saw my dad go through what you've experienced. She died when I was ten and my dad ... I don't think my dad ever got over her passing. Not really. They were the way I think you and Cassie must have been – perfect for each other. That's not to say he was never happy after she'd gone. He was, often. But it took years, and most of his time was taken up with me. He put everything into raising me, and I'm not sure that left him enough time for himself. He was so young when she died, really. Looking back now, I do wish he'd met someone else. But I never would have told him that he had to leave my mother behind to do that. I don't think he'd have been able to even if he'd tried.'

Robert nodded. 'My problem is that I don't know how to be without her,' he said. 'We'd known each other since we were children. We grew up together, we shared all our friends ...' He shook his head. 'There is still so much around here that reminds me of her. Every place I go, I remember her being there. It sometimes makes me forget that she's ... not still here. Robbie, too. Sometimes I look at him and all I can see is her. Without Robbie I might have sunk completely. Having him meant I had a reason to get up every day. If it had just been me ... I'm not sure I would have bothered. It must have been the same for your dad.'

They lapsed into silence, finishing their coffee.

'I'm also sorry about this morning,' Robert said, a few minutes later, in a tone that suggested he'd been trying to work out how to bring it up for a while. 'About Douglas McKean, I mean. That was unforgivable.'

'It wasn't your fault.'

'No, but . . .' He shrugged, uncomfortable again. 'What he was suggesting . . . that's not why I said I'd bring you out here. I don't want you to think I'm sniffing around looking for . . . Well. You know. That's not – *me.*'

'I know.'

He tipped up his coffee cup, letting the dregs drip onto the sand. 'McKean's a cantankerous, misogynistic old bastard. There's no excuse for how he spoke. But he's got troubles that aren't of his own making.'

'Right.' Anna did not feel inclined to care about Douglas McKean's troubles, whatever they were. This must have been clear in her voice, because Robert MacKenzie smiled slightly and gave a nod. His words did make Anna think about the Fishergirl's Luck, though, and what Pat had said about its ownership. 'Is it because of the Fishergirl's Luck?' she asked. 'Pat said something about him always complaining that it should have belonged to him.'

'Ach, that old chestnut,' Robert laughed. 'That's what he'd have everyone believe if he could, but there's no truth in it. Bren owned that place fair and square. She had no brothers, you see. Only a sister, and she died young. Bren's father was a fisherman. To hear Barbara – that's Cassie's mum – tell the story, they were herring lassies together as young girls, but

131

Bren always wanted to be out in the boats with the men, doing the fishing instead of the gutting.'

Anna wrinkled her nose. 'Can't say I blame her.'

'Nope,' Robert agreed, with another smile. 'But women gutted, mended nets and tended home. Men went out to fish. That was the way of things. Anyway, Bren's dad might have been willing to leave her the boat – from what Barbara's said it sounds as if he might have been pretty forward-thinking for his time. But though she might have been able to own and manage it from shore, there was no man who'd crew it with Bren aboard, and without that it would have become even more of a money pit. When her dad got sick, he sold the family home and the boat to Douglas McKean to clear the last of his debts so that Bren wouldn't have to deal with them herself. McKean's family were spread between Crovie and Gamrie, and owned several boats. They were doing well for themselves.'

'Was this before Bren converted the Fishergirl's Luck?'

'Oh yes. Back then it was storage for the family's fishing clobber.'

'Let me guess,' Anna said. 'McKean thought he was getting the shed in with the bargain.'

'Got it in one. But Bren had already got her dad to put it in writing that the place belonged to her. She'd even paid him for it out of the money she'd earned from the herring, to make sure there could be no dispute. The deed should be with the solicitor – you've never seen it?'

'I never thought to ask for it. I should – I'd like to see it.'

'Bren left it with them for safekeeping. Just in case.' He

laughed at her expression. 'Not necessarily because she thought Dougie would try to steal it. I don't think even he would go that far, and it can only ever have been about a point of principle. But so many lost boats and property in the 1953 storm. I think Bren wanted to make sure it would be easy to find in case the place was ever badly damaged by another event like that.'

Anna looked out over the water, shaking her head. How she wished she could have known Bren MacKenzie. Even this brief description had painted in her mind a picture of a woman who knew exactly what she wanted and had no intention of ever being talked out of it.

'She started converting the place bit by bit way back in the 1940s,' Robert went on. 'First using her own savings from the herring and then what her father had left her. She bought her own boat – it was only a small dinghy, but still, it meant she could fish for herself in-shore if she wanted. She'd have been in her late twenties, early thirties then. Barbara says everyone saw it as a bit of a joke at the time. They always expected Bren to give the place up and finally get married, even though she was an old maid by that point. But she never did. I think, actually, that accounts for some of Dougie's bitterness. I think he might have asked her at some point.'

'What? To marry him?'

Robert nodded. 'Not that he's ever told me that, or ever would.'

'Maybe he'd thought that being given her dad's property meant he'd get Bren too.'

'Maybe. Anyway, neither of them ever married. When Bren died I actually offered to let him move into the place. His needs so much work, and he can't keep up with it. It's getting worse every year. But he point-blank refused. "I'll not set one foot in that harpy's hovel" were his exact words.'

'"The Fishergirl's Luck",' Anna mused. 'Even the name sounds defiant to me now. Do you know why she called it that?'

Robert smiled. 'I think even that might have been a bit of a dig at Dougie, to be honest. He was one of the men who'd taunted her for wanting to be out fishing. But in the end, Bren's dinghy was the only boat left in Crovie harbour, and she went out fishing from it until she was well past eighty.'

Anna shook her head. 'I wish I could have met her.'

'I think she would have liked you,' Robert said. 'And I think she'd tell you to ignore Douglas McKean in exactly the same way she did all her life.' He looked at his watch. 'And now we should start back,' he said. 'Robbie's at an afterschool club but he'll be home soon. I'm with the lifeboat tonight so I'll have to bunk at Macduff. I want to be there for supper so I can have some time with him first.'

'Who looks after him when you have to work?'

'Barbara. She lives two doors down.'

'I think I've met her, you know,' Anna said, thinking of the woman who had marched towards her to circle Crovie's north and south poles on that first morning she'd been in the village. 'She seemed a force to be reckoned with.'

'She's a wonder,' said Robert, 'and without her I'd be in even more of a mess than I am.'

Anna smiled as they headed for *Cassie's Joy*. 'You don't seem to be in a mess at all.'

Robert MacKenzie gave a snort. 'Don't you believe it.' He stopped and looked back at the cliff, as if contemplating something for a moment. Then he turned to Anna. 'I've got something I want to show you. Come on.'

He took off back across the sand, towards the cliff. Anna followed, only hesitating when she saw him start to climb, fitting the toes of his boots into crevices he seemed to know were there. He reached a wide lip in the rock and turned, crouching to offer her his hand. Anna hesitated.

'It's all right,' said Robert. 'Trust me. It's worth it.'

She slipped her hand into his and pushed her toes into the same crevices she had seen him climb. Robert's hand gripped hers hard and pulled her up. Once she'd found her footing he let her go and turned back towards the cliff face right in front of them.

'Look,' he said.

For a moment she was confused. There seemed to be nothing worthy of attention there at all. Then Robert stepped forward, placing one large hand flat against the stone with his thumb and fingers splayed to create a right angle.

'There. You see?'

Anna peered closer. Inside the space roughly encapsulated by his hand she could make out a series of marks, too deliberate to be caused by erosion or element.

'They're petroglyphs,' said Robert.

'But – how?' Anna said, astonished. 'Who left them there?'

Robert moved out of the way to let her take a closer look. 'There are examples all along the coast. There's a cave at Covesea that's full of them. There aren't any more here, only these. I've never heard anyone else mention them either. I don't think anyone knows about them but Robbie and me. And now you.'

'I can't believe you found them at all,' Anna said, her eyes tracing the fading shapes. 'How did you ever see them in the first place?'

Robert was silent for a moment. When Anna looked over her shoulder at him, he was looking away from her, but then he turned back with a faint smile.

'I didn't. It was Cass. She always did have eagle eyes. Spotted those that first time she brought me here, while I was down on the beach, shaking wet sand out of my shoes, shouting at her to be careful and wondering if she was ever going to kiss me.'

Anna turned back to the shapes. She reached out, pressing a gentle fingertip to the marks in the cold cliff face, trying to make sense of them. They lined up close beside one another: thin, deep scrapes at angles to each other. Below the first group was a second, and between them a single symbol.

'What are they?' she asked. 'Do you know? What does it mean? Are they words?'

Robert moved closer again, his bulk cutting out the brisk wind as he leaned over her shoulder.

'Cassie wanted to believe that they're names.'

'Names?'

He reached out, touching his fingers to where Anna's had been only a second before. 'When I was fifteen – actually, the week before that first date – I carved my name next to hers on the apple tree in my parents' garden,' he said. 'With a heart in between.'

Anna realized what he meant. 'She thought this might have been two lovers, doing the same?'

'The thought always made me sad, to be honest.'

'Sad? Why?'

He dropped his hand and stuck it into his pocket. 'Because they couldn't possibly have known,' he said quietly. 'They couldn't possibly have known, when they were carving it, that this was all that would survive of them. That this is all they would leave behind.'

The wind was rising, whistling around them as it buffeted against the cliff, which was huge and eternal, made of age itself and carrying with it the only aspect of humanity that is as ageless, the only indelible thing that cannot be corrupted by time or infirmity.

'But they have survived,' Anna said. 'Here they are, in the stone, whoever they were. They were here, together. They were loved and they loved in turn. What else does survive of us, whoever we are and whatever we leave, in the end?'

Robert didn't look at her, even when she turned her head, even though he was close enough that the wind had spread her hair across his shoulder. She saw him swallow, instead, and take a breath as if suddenly the wind had stolen his air.

137

'Cassie said the same thing,' he told her. 'She loved this place so much. I should have carved our names up there, beside these. I should have made us both a part of this cliff. Maybe then—'

Robert stopped himself and in the next moment had moved away. Anna continued looking at the rock, at the short series of marks that seemed so inconsequential but had come to mean so much.

'Well, would you look at that,' Robert said behind her a moment later. 'The dolphins have come to see you.'

Anna turned and looked out over the water. There, in the depths beyond *Cassie's Joy*, was a pod of dolphins, sleek grey commas leaping in curving splashes up, and up, and up again.

Sweet selkie lass,

   The boy and me met the woman who's taken Bren's bothy. Bren would like her, I think. And I think you two would be friends. Robbie wants us to take her out to meet his dolphins.

   Love you.

PS: No beetroot. I got home and it wasn't in the bag.

PPS: I'll call Miss Carmichael myself, then?

PPPS: How does a chef called Anna wash up here of all places, on our wild and narrow shore?

Fourteen

As April faded into May, the weather set fair again, the longer days warmed by a sun that seemed to shine without pause from dawn until dusk. Over the bank holiday weekend, Liam's bench hosted its largest gathering yet. Finally, with somewhere larger than her miniature front room to entertain, Anna could invite the entirety of the group that Frank habitually referred to as 'the Usual Suspects'. Though Anna saw Rhona, Pat and Frank regularly, and still had her customary walk along the cliffs whenever David and Glynn were in residence, she hadn't had the chance to get to know Marie and Philip or Terry and Susan very well at all.

'I love the planters you've put out,' Marie said, admiring the old terracotta chimneys that Anna had dragged back from an antiques place she'd found in Portsoy and filled with bright pansies and scarlet begonias. 'And the strings of fairy lights, too.'

'It looks great,' Philip agreed, over the hubbub that had enveloped Anna's garden beneath the tiny glittering lights she'd strung up above their heads. 'I've always thought this bit of concrete was something of a lost cause, but you've transformed it.'

'Rhona's been telling us about the lunch club,' Susan added. 'Have you heard about this?' she asked the rest of the gathered friends. 'It sounds like a brilliant idea.'

Anna explained again about her plans for Liam's bench, and was relieved that the idea seemed to be met with universal approval.

'When are you going to start?' Terry asked.

'All being well, the fifteenth of May,' Anna said, 'so two weeks from now. I've got quite a lot to organise before I go ahead.'

'Tell me about it,' laughed Rhona. 'I'd better get a move on, eh? I left four plates glazing in the kiln before I left but I've still got a ways to go.'

Rhona had been the beneficiary of Anna's razor clam harvest. Over dinner and wine the evening she and Old Robbie had brought them back, Anna had explained her plan. Rhona's enthusiasm had been touching, as had her insistence on making a set of plates and dishes especially for the table.

'I'm gutted that we won't be around,' David said, as Glynn nodded. 'We're away down to Manchester for a wedding that weekend. Although you don't want us cluttering up your table, I suppose – we'd edge out all the real customers!'

'I'm not even sure there will be any such people,' Anna said. 'I've already got Pat and Frank on standby in case I have no takers.'

'That's not going to happen,' Rhona said, with total confidence.

The sound of laughing voices reached them from the path.

It was Robert MacKenzie and Liam Harper, making their way towards them from the harbour. Anna was pleased to see Liam – when she'd left him the message earlier the invitation had been as casual as she could make it, and she hadn't been sure he'd turn up. He looked up and raised a hand with a smile when he saw her watching.

Since that first evening, Liam had become a regular visitor to the Fishergirl's Luck. In fact, in between the nights he was out with the boat, Anna wasn't sure he'd spent a single night in his own lodgings. Not that she was complaining. It was, as he'd written in his note that first morning, fun.

When the two men reached the party, Liam surprised her by bending down and kissing her on the lips. It wasn't that she minded public displays of affection in front of her friends, but somehow she'd imagined Liam might be reticent about pegging out a flag about their relationship, given how casual they'd both agreed it was.

Robert kissed her too, a fleeting touch on the cheek, his hand on her shoulder. 'Thanks for the invite,' he said. 'The wee lad's at a sleepover and it's too nice an evening for housework.'

She laughed. 'Too right. Did you two come together?'

'I hopped in Old Rob's ride,' Liam said. 'Seemed daft to bring both.'

'I owed him,' his captain added. 'He's been putting up with Robbie's endless questions about the bloody dolphins every morning.'

'Ach, I don't mind,' Liam said, as Anna poured them both

a drink from the table. 'He's a cute kid. Smart, too. You've got a budding cetologist there, mate.'

'Aye,' said Robert MacKenzie, nodding his thanks to Anna as he took the glass she passed him. 'I think you might be right. Although I guess we'll see if he's still getting up at 5 a.m. to pester the lads on the dock when he's a teenager . . .'

The evening continued, a pleasant bubble of chat and laughter surrounding the Fishergirl's Luck as the sun slowly sank below the horizon. Once, looking along the path towards the cliff, Anna saw a dark figure lurking in the gathering shadows. *Douglas McKean.* She glanced at Robert, remembering his comment about the old man's problems. She should probably show willing and invite him to join them for a drink and a bite to eat. But Anna still hadn't forgiven him for his vile rudeness at the harbour that day. Besides, the next time she looked, he had melted away.

'This is great,' Liam said, later, as he looked at the email on Anna's iPad, which displayed the poster Cathy had created for the first lunch club. 'It manages to be really elegant and perfectly legible at the same time.'

'She does them all by hand, too,' Anna told him, busy unwrapping the sample flatware that Rhona had brought over earlier. 'I'm surrounded by talented people. Look at these, aren't they beautiful?' She held up one of the dishes she'd just unwrapped. The glaze on it was almost black, though a closer inspection revealed a gradient of dark to lighter green moving towards the centre. 'These belong in a gallery, not on my little table.'

It was late and the rest of her guests had gone home, but Liam had stayed. It had been a subtle agreement and no one had batted an eyelid when Old Robbie had left without him. Anna had been relieved, and then wondered why. There wasn't any reason to suggest any of 'the Usual Suspects' would be prudish about her choices. Still a hangover from the encounter with Douglas McKean, she supposed.

'So a week Saturday's the day, eh?' Liam asked, getting up from what had become his customary seat on the floor and coming over. 'I'm really sorry but I'm not going to be around.'

Anna put down the plate and reached up to give him a quick kiss. 'Oh?'

He caught her around the waist before she could move away any further. 'I'm off that weekend. But I'm booked onto a group dive up in Shetland, to a wreck called the SS *Glenisla*. I've been meaning to go up there ever since I got here, and well . . .'

'You're running out of time,' Anna finished for him. 'I'm glad you've got yourself booked on one, then.'

'You're not upset I won't be here?'

'Of course not. Why would I be?'

He grinned and pulled her back in for another kiss. Anna smiled against his mouth, his stubble scratching against her chin.

'Well,' he murmured, backing her slowly across the room towards the stairs. 'Since we're both going to be busy for the next while . . . how about we make the most of me being here right now?'

'Hmm,' Anna hummed, between kisses. 'Seems like a reasonable idea to me.'

'Next thing I know, you'll be moving to New Zealand,' Cathy said with an elaborate moan as they talked on the phone the following day. 'Maybe you'll keep moving further and further away until you really *do* fall off the edge of the world.'

'Nope,' said Anna. 'Not going to happen. That's not even on the cards and honestly, I really wouldn't want it to be. We're having fun, that's all. It's an interlude.'

'Fun,' Cathy echoed, wistfully. 'I'm not sure I remember what that's like.'

'Don't say that,' Anna said. 'You and Steve are still happy, aren't you?'

There was a pause. 'Of course we are,' Cathy said. 'It's just life, isn't it? We probably need a bit of pepping up, that's all. I envy you, Anna. You chucked it all in to start over and you're really making a go of it. That's a rare thing.'

Anna leaned back against the sofa. 'I wouldn't have done it if things had been different, you know that. I thought I was going to spend my life with Geoff. I thought we'd eventually have a family, settle down, all that stuff . . . Now here I am, knocking forty and on my own with no partner, no kids, no career and home is a glorified shoebox that I don't even think I can live in full-time.'

'You're not on your own. You've got the hot Kiwi, at least for another few weeks. And I thought you were beginning to love the Fishergirl's Luck?'

'I am. I do! But this isn't where I thought I'd be, especially not at this point in my life.'

'Yeah, I know. Sorry.'

'Anyway, it's fun right now, but that can't last.' Anna bit her lip, trying not to ask but needing to. 'Have you . . . heard anything? About Geoff, I mean? Whether he's . . .' she trailed off.

'Anna,' Cathy said. 'You don't really want to know, do you?'

Anna rubbed a hand over her face with a sigh. 'No. Except . . . I don't know. I still find myself thinking about him.'

'That's not surprising. You were together a long time. And he always made sure you thought of him before anything or anyone else, even yourself.'

She dropped her hand and looked at the poster again. 'He'd probably laugh at me for the lunch club,' she said. 'He always used to hate the idea of supper clubs. Said they were only for second-rate chefs who couldn't get a real gig.'

'Yeah, well,' Cathy said, darkly. 'You know the truth about Geoff Rowcliffe?'

'What?'

'He really is a dick.'

Anna laughed.

Fifteen

The day of the first lunch club rolled around quickly. Anna had pinned the poster to her door on Friday morning, hoping that some of the tourists that made it as far as the Fishergirl's Luck would be intrigued enough to make a return visit.

'I'm sorry I can't be here,' Liam told her again, as they stood at the harbour early on Saturday morning after he'd dropped off the fish she'd asked for.

'It's fine,' she said. 'I wouldn't have expected you to be. I hope you have a good time. Be careful up there.'

He kissed her. 'Text me,' he said. 'Let me know how it went.'

'I will. Now go,' she said. 'You've got places to be and I need to prepare this fish. Have a great time, be safe, and I'll see you sometime next week.'

Anna listened to the growl of the skiff's engine as she hefted the crate up, ready to walk it back to the Fishergirl's Luck. As she turned she saw an efficient-looking woman in a dark blue suit and low heels with a clipboard under one arm walking cautiously down the road into the village. She saw Anna and smiled.

'Good morning, I wonder if you can help me. I'm looking for a place called the Fishergirl's Luck.'

'Oh,' Anna said, in surprise. 'That's me. I mean, that's my house. Is it me you're looking for?'

The woman looked her up and down, her gaze landing on the crate Anna carried. 'My name is Belinda Turner,' she said. 'I'm the health and safety examiner responsible for eateries in this area. We've had a report of an illegal restaurant operating in Crovie. At the Fishergirl's Luck.'

Anna's stomach turned over and then sank into her toes. 'Oh, God. That isn't – it's not a *restaurant*.'

'But you are selling food?'

'No – not really. People aren't obligated to pay if they don't want to.'

The woman gave her a steady look. 'But you do invite donations?'

Anna's mouth ran dry. 'I – well, I was planning to, to help to cover costs. Look, I know what I'm doing. I'm a trained chef, I have all my personal health and safety documentation up to date.'

'That's good,' Belinda Turner said. 'I'd like to see that, if I may. And the areas in which you'll be serving and preparing food. I'm sure you understand – we've had a complaint, I can't ignore it.'

'Of course.' Anna began to walk along the sea wall, feeling as if she were heading towards the gallows.

'My goodness,' the woman said, when she saw the Fishergirl's Luck. 'Is it this place? I've seen it on visits to Crovie before and always wondered what it was like inside!'

Anna backed in through the doors, holding them open so that her visitor could follow. She put the crate Liam had given her onto the nearest work surface.

'Feel free to look around,' Anna said, as she opened a cupboard and took out one of the tubs she had bought specifically to store seafood. 'I'm just going to get this fish sorted and into the fridge. My papers are in there.' She pointed to a plastic ring binder on the bench beneath the stairs.

'You're planning to make the meals you want to sell from *this* kitchen?' Belinda Turner asked, looking around before she reached for the binder.

'My idea was to serve lunch on the bench outside a couple of times a week to whomever happens to be passing,' Anna explained.

'How many covers?'

'No more than six. I couldn't do more than that comfortably in a kitchen this size.'

Turner nodded as she turned the pages of the records Anna had already begun to keep. A lifetime in professional kitchens meant that checking daily fridge temperatures and logging her cleaning routines came as a natural reflex, and Anna had been doing it since she'd first considered the idea of the lunch club.

'Can I look at the fridge?' Turner asked.

'Of course.' Anna stood aside as the woman sifted through the impeccably clean and perfectly organized shelves.

Belinda Turner took her time. Anna watched as she shifted things here and there, opened drawers and cupboards, examined worktops and the oven. The woman's demeanour was calm, her face entirely neutral, and yet the more time she spent looking at her kitchen in miniature, the more Anna's anxiety grew.

'What about bathroom facilities?' the inspector asked.

'I thought it would be better to ask my neighbours, who own the bed and breakfast opposite, to let guests use theirs instead of mine,' Anna said, intensely glad now that she'd had this idea. 'It's inside the door directly on the other side of the path.'

'That's a sensible solution. What about the serving area?'

Anna took her outside and showed her the picnic bench. 'I haven't dressed it yet,' she said. 'But I can show you a photograph of the last time I had friends over for dinner, if you like – I'll be setting up the same.'

'I don't think that's necessary,' said Belinda Turner. 'Look, it's clear that you know what you're doing, and honestly, I've been asked to rate kitchens that aren't a patch on yours for cleanliness and organization. You're clearly conscientious enough to keep your own rigorous checks. But here's the thing. That sink really needs replacing. It's badly cracked and even though I can see you're fastidious about keeping it bleached clean, that's still something that prevents me, in all conscience, from giving you the highest rating. You know as well as I do that you should have two washing areas – one for food, one for utensils.'

'Yes,' Anna said, 'that's why I've got the washing-up bowl, so that I can keep them separate.'

'I understand that, Ms Campbell, and ordinarily I would accept that as a solution. But with the sink beneath as it is . . .'

'That's not a total strike out for a rating though, surely?' Anna asked.

'No, it's not,' Turner agreed. 'It'd take you down to a four instead of the full rating of five. But I do think you should consider replacing the sink before you start this lunch club. With that, I'd be happy to give you the highest rating. You could operate with a four, you know that. However, I'd strongly advise you not to give whoever is out to meddle any further opportunity to make trouble.'

Anna's heart sank. 'Right.'

'I want to help you, I really do. And frankly, I don't like people who are out to stir up trouble.' She dug into her bag and pulled out a card. 'Think about it. If you decide to make the changes I've recommended, call me. I'll be out the same day if I can. But for now . . .'

Anna nodded. 'I understand.'

Belinda Turner shrugged. 'As for today – you could ask your friends at the Weaver's Nook if you can serve from their kitchen. I did the rating for their B&B myself, I know it's up to scratch.'

'That's a good thought. Thanks.'

The two women said their goodbyes. As the inspector walked away, the front door of the Weaver's Nook opened and Pat and Frank appeared on the doorstep of the tradesman's entrance.

'We know her!' Pat said in a stage whisper. 'She's the health and safety woman! What was she doing here?'

Anna turned to look at the door of the Fishergirl's Luck, on which was pinned Cathy's beautiful poster for the lunch club. She reached out and took it down. 'Telling me I can't serve today.'

'What?' Frank said. 'But why—'

'Someone reported me for running an illegal restaurant.'

'No,' Pat said, appalled. 'Who would do that?'

'Do you really need to ask?'

'Dougie, you mean? I doubt it,' said Frank. 'He's spiteful enough, for sure, but I can't see him working out who to call at the council and then going through with it.'

Anna sighed. 'Well, whoever it was, they've got what they want.' She rolled up Cathy's poster. 'There'll be no lunch club here.'

'Oh love,' Pat said. 'I'm so sorry. What can we do?'

Anna briefly considered telling them what Belinda Turner had suggested, about her serving from their kitchen, but dismissed the idea. It was supposed to be 'Lunch at the Fishergirl's Luck', not 'lunch made somewhere else and carried to a bench that happens to be beside the Fishergirl's Luck'. Anna had been looking forward to serving out of the tiny puzzle box that was her own kitchen, not suddenly having to adjust to use someone else's. Besides, if someone around her besides Douglas McKean was upset enough about her plans to stoop to such sabotage, did she really want to provoke them further?

'Yes,' she said, forcing a brightness she did not feel. 'You can help me round up the Usual Suspects for dinner at the bench later. I don't want all the ingredients to go to waste and I can't eat everything myself. We'll have our own dinner party instead.'

That evening, Anna served the meal she had been intending to give her first guests to Pat, Frank, Rhona, Robert and herself.

'I'm so sorry, Anna,' Robert said, his forehead furrowing into a deep frown once she'd filled in him and Rhona. 'Maybe I should go and have a word with Dougie?'

'We don't know for sure it was him,' Anna told him. 'Frank seems convinced that it couldn't have been.'

'It doesn't seem his sort of thing, complaining to the council,' Frank said, with a brief shrug. 'It's not as if he's a fan of bureaucracy in any form, is it?'

'True,' Robert agreed, 'but he wouldn't be above stirring up trouble. You know what he's like once he's got a bee in his bonnet, and he really seems to have one about Anna moving into the Fishergirl's Luck.'

Anna paused in the motion of refilling his glass. 'What do you mean?'

Robert grimaced slightly. 'I didn't want to tell you about it if I could avoid it. He's been griping about the ownership of the place again. Firstly to me, and when I told him to knock it off, to anyone else he thinks might listen. Barbara said he'd called her the other day.'

'Oh, for Pete's sake,' Rhona said. 'Daft old coot. So any one of the people he's been bellyaching at could have taken up the cause and used the lunch club as a way to put the boot in?'

'I suppose so,' Robert admitted. He glanced up at Anna again. 'Did you get the solicitor to dig up the deeds?'

'Not yet,' Anna said. 'I didn't really see what good they would do. I mean, what am I going to do, tack them up in the window? But it sounds as though I'd better before I put this place up as a holiday rental. Otherwise I can see the same person – or people – making trouble online. You know how word of mouth and rumour works in the hospitality business. A couple of malicious reviews and I'll be scuppered before I've even had a chance to establish the place. Besides, I'd hate to think that anyone staying here would be harassed for it.'

'What about the lunch club?' Pat asked. 'You are going to try again, aren't you?'

'Yes,' Frank said. 'What you've served us today was absolutely delicious, Anna. And I can fit a new sink for you, no problem. It sounded as if this Turner woman would be willing to do a quick turnaround once it's in. If we get the measurements written down and head up to Inverness first thing on Monday, I could have it in for you by Monday evening.'

'Yes!' Rhona said, with full enthusiasm. 'Today wasn't a cancellation, it was a postponement. Lunch club can start next weekend, instead, can't it?'

Anna sipped her wine and shook her head. 'Oh, I don't think so. It was a daft notion in the first place. No,' she said, holding up one hand to fend off the instant protests from her friends. 'I'd rather just cook for you lot. Really. Rhona, I'm sorry you went to the trouble of making me all this beautiful flatware, but believe me – I'll make it a feature on the rental listing and I'll take some of it with me wherever I end up.'

Rhona shook her head. 'The lunch club wasn't a daft idea,' she said. 'It was a great one, and I'm sorry someone made you feel otherwise.'

Anna reached out and covered her friend's hand with hers. 'Thank you,' she said, as Rhona squeezed her fingers. 'To all of you. It means a lot that I've made such supportive friends here. But I don't want to go to war. Not over something that was only ever going to be for a few weeks. It really isn't worth it.'

Sixteen

Liam surprised her by arriving at her door on Monday morning. She answered a knock to find him standing on the step of the Fishergirl's Luck with a curiously pensive look on his face.

'Hello,' she smiled, as she held the door open to usher him past her. 'I didn't expect to see you so soon. Surely you only got back last night?'

'Yeah,' he said, bending down to touch his lips to hers in a brief kiss as he squeezed past her. 'But you didn't text.'

'Ahh,' Anna shut the door and followed him into the living room. 'Well, that's because I didn't have anything to tell you.'

'What do you mean? What about the lunch club?'

'Didn't happen,' she said. 'Do you want a coffee? I was about to make some.'

'Hang on,' Liam said, catching her by the wrist and turning her towards him. 'What do you mean, it didn't happen?'

Anna explained the events that had led to the cancellation of lunch club, watching the look on Liam's face grow darker by the second.

'I'm sorry,' he said, brow knitted together in a frown. 'That was low.'

She shrugged. 'Who knows? Maybe they genuinely thought they were doing the right thing. Anyway, it's done and I need to move on. Tell me about your trip,' Anna said, as she headed for the kitchen. 'Did you have a good time?'

There was a slight pause before he said, 'Yeah. It was good.'

Anna looked over at him as she filled the kettle. 'You don't sound too sure about that. What's wrong?'

He smiled, but she could tell it was strained. 'Nothing. Everything's fine.' He stuffed his hands in his pockets, hunching his shoulders. For a moment he looked very young. 'Can we sit outside with the coffee? It's such a lovely day.'

'Sure,' Anna said, a sudden weight inexplicably attaching itself to her heart. 'I'll bring it out in a minute – why don't you go and sit in the sunshine?'

By the time she followed him out he was sitting at the bench, staring out to sea, his fingers restlessly picking at the wood's grain.

'Okay,' he said quietly, as she sat down beside him. 'To be honest I did come here to talk to you about something. But it can wait, especially after the weekend you've had.'

Anna began to pour the coffee. 'Liam. Whatever it is – you can say it. I'm a big girl. Okay?' She pushed his coffee mug towards him and he wrapped both hands around it.

'All right. Well, you remember, when we started . . . this,' he said, waving a finger between them, awkwardly. 'We said it would be … you know, a relaxed thing. No strings. No permanent attachment.'

Anna sipped the strong coffee and watched his restless fingers, thick and calloused by his work, skin tanned darker still by the sun. 'Yes,' she said, 'I do.'

'And it always had an end date, what with me going home at the end of summer, and you not planning to stay here either …'

She looked at the anxious frown on his face. A look of worried concentration creased crow's feet around his eyes.

'You want to end this – us – now,' she realized.

'No.' Liam looked her in the eye. 'But the thing is, I kind of … met someone.'

She watched him. 'On the dive?'

He nodded, shifting uncomfortably. His gaze flicked away from hers again, endlessly seeking the ocean. Perhaps it represented escape, to him: a passage away from whatever dogged him on land and that could not follow him to sea.

'Look,' Liam said quietly. 'I'd like to … see her. You and I always said that we'd be casual, didn't we? And we never agreed to be exclusive. I really like you, Anna, we have a lot of fun and I don't want to stop seeing you. But I know the guy you were with before was a cheater, and I don't want you to feel that's what I'm doing to you by seeing this girl as well. So … I thought honesty would be the best policy. Before … well. You know.'

Anna laughed at that. 'Yeah. I know.'

Liam sighed. 'I don't want to be a rat. You deserve better

than that. And maybe if we were both going to stay here permanently ... things might be different? But the rest of our lives are somewhere else, so ...' He shrugged, cutting himself off.

'We have had fun,' Anna agreed. 'And we both knew it was going to end sooner or later.'

'It doesn't have to end,' Liam pointed out. 'Not yet. We can carry on exactly as we have been until I go home, or until you leave yourself, whichever comes first. I just – didn't want you to find out from someone else and be upset by it, that's all. People around here—' He rolled his eyes. 'Well. You already know what they can be like.'

Anna smiled. She looked at the coffee eddying in her mug for a moment, contemplating. It wasn't that she'd expected Liam to be exclusive. But she couldn't help thinking that from now on, if they did carry on as they had been, she'd find herself wondering where Liam was when he wasn't with her, what he was doing and with whom. She had a feeling it would be easy to get caught in that mental eddy again, being sucked down into a whirlpool of hurt that would have nothing to do with this relationship and far more to do with the fact that really, she was still recovering from the harm Geoff had caused her over the years. Her time with Liam had been good – great, even – and so far he'd shown her more respect than Geoff ever had. That's how she wanted to remember him.

She reached over and squeezed Liam's fingers. He turned his hand over so that he could grasp hers.

'I don't feel badly about you wanting to see this girl at all. But I think it would be for the best if we call it a day before you do,' she told him. 'This is a cliché, but . . . it's not you, it's me. You've been honest, and I appreciate that. And you're right, we've had a lot of fun, and I won't ever regret the time we've had. But I think it's run its course. Let's leave it at that, shall we?'

The shadow of disappointment crossed Liam's face. He looked down at their twined hands, and then lifted her fingers to kiss them, briefly.

'Are you all right?' he asked.

'Yes,' she said, smiling again. 'I'm fine. Really. Come and say goodbye before you go back to New Zealand. We'll sit at this bench and have one last glass of wine.'

Liam smiled at her. 'I'll do that.' Then he reached out his free hand to brush her hair back from her face and leaned in to kiss her. The touch was warm, but didn't linger. When their lips parted, so did their hands.

Anna watched as he walked back along the path in the day's fading light. They didn't say goodbye, but it was enough of an ending. Then she turned to face the water. Slowly she probed the throb in her chest, checking gently for damage. There was a feeling of loss, of regret, but she had never expected Liam to be a permanent fixture in her life. As handsome as he was, she hadn't wanted him to be, either. Her heart was aching, yes, but Anna didn't think it was really him she was aching for. It was for a connection lost. She was alone again.

She leaned back against the bench and looked at the Fishergirl's Luck, standing as steadfast as it ever had. Solid and of itself; alone yet never lonely.

A movement at the far end of the village caught Anna's eye. She looked up to see Douglas McKean halfway down the sea wall, leaning on his walking stick as he watched her with a baleful eye. Anna stared back, a defiant kind of fury growing in her chest. Whether it was him that had made the call or not, it was Douglas McKean who had scuppered lunch club. What right did he have to meddle in her life aside from a ridiculous delusion that the Fishergirl's Luck should really belong to him? As if it would be as it is now if he had. It was Bren MacKenzie who had looked at this tiny shack and seen that it could be lived in, Bren MacKenzie who had poured her hard work and earnings into making that idea a reality. And now this place was Anna's, fair and square, just as it had belonged to Bren before her, and she could do what she liked with it. Bren hadn't let McKean bully her, not for a second. Why should Anna put up with him, or the cronies that had joined in his bitter quest? She didn't need McKean's approval, nor anyone else's either. She'd already wasted too much of her working life trying to scale that particular mountain.

Leaving the coffee tray where it was, Anna went to knock on the door of the Weaver's Nook.

'Frank,' she said, when he answered with a mug of tea in his hand. 'Could you spare me a bit of time this week? I need your plumbing expertise.'

Seventeen

By the end of the week, Anna was in possession of a brand-new sink and a five out of five rating from the health and safety branch of the local council.

'Very nice,' said Belinda Turner, when she saw the excellent job that Frank had done of fitting the double Belfast and swing tap. 'I'm so glad that you're going to go ahead with the lunch club,' she added. 'I think it's a wonderful idea. I'd like to come along myself. Are you going to start tomorrow?'

'No, I'm going to wait until the bank holiday weekend, at the end of the month. That'll give me time to prepare and will hopefully also mean there'll be more visitors around,' Anna told her. 'First come, first served, first course ready at 1.15 p.m. It'd be nice to see you.' Anna was no fool. Having the health and safety officer willing to eat at her table was an optic she could get behind. *Stick that in your pipe and smoke it, McKean.*

'I'll be away, sadly. But perhaps sometime further down the line.'

'Ah,' Anna said. 'Well, let me get through this one first before I commit to any more!'

'Good luck,' Turner smiled, as the two women shook hands in parting. 'I'll have my fingers crossed for you that the weather holds fair, at least.'

Anna spent the next week making sure she knew exactly what she was going to be doing when lunch club finally went ahead. The Usual Suspects were all delighted to hear that she was giving it another shot, as was Cathy, who lovingly revised the poster she had designed for the first one. Anna pinned this up on the Friday before the long weekend, taking a step back to admire the way it looked against the cornflower blue of the Fishergirl's Luck's front door.

Bring it on, she thought. *This time, it's happening, Douglas McKean be damned.*

For a moment, Anna imagined Bren standing beside her, grinning, and smiled to herself.

Next morning, Pat appeared on Anna's doorstep, declaring that she had come to provide help with prep.

'I'll be your kitchen urchin!' she said, arms held wide as if she could hug the world, and Anna had no doubt that this woman would do it too, given the chance.

'Thank you,' Anna said, with a laugh. 'Although I'm not sure there'll be room for both of us.'

'We'll make it work, love,' said Pat, as she came inside. 'Needs must, and all that.'

The women moved around each other in the small space with efficient ease as Pat followed Anna's instructions. Her friend's steady, warm presence reminded Anna of cooking with her mother when she was young – it was a different energy from being in a professional kitchen and one that Anna hadn't realized she'd missed so much until that moment. The knowledge shocked her, spun into her heart with a powerful physical pang as it occurred to Anna anew how very alone she was in the world. For all her new friends and new life, for all the fun moments she'd had with Liam, she had no family left. Pat couldn't hug her in quite the way her mother used to. Her father wouldn't come barrelling into the kitchen, making them all laugh as he lifted her out of the way to steal a biscuit, still warm from the oven.

Dad.

Anna looked out of the tiny window onto the ocean waves that were churning gently in the sunlight, her heart suddenly a heavy, thumping mass. She'd been so busy in recent weeks that her thoughts had turned to his loss less frequently, but now there he was, surfacing unexpectedly, his hair as untidy as ever, smile still in place.

She swallowed hard against the threat of tears, and then found herself thinking about Robert MacKenzie. How could anyone expect him to simply move on from his wife, whom he had loved so completely, however many years it had been since her passing? She couldn't even let her father go easily. Anna herself knew so well, now, the hopeless ebb and flow of grief – the inevitable, inescapable undertow that carried one helplessly from anguish to guilt, from the temporary buoyancy of memory to the flat exhaustion of absolute depression, all in the space of minutes and often in the middle of some-thing entirely unrelated.

'Are you all right?' Pat asked, apparently picking up on Anna's change in mood.

Anna forced herself to shake off the sudden flood of grief. 'Yes,' she said. 'Thank you so much for your help, Pat, you've been wonderful. I think I'll be fine on my own now, if you want to get back?'

Pat took off her apron and pulled Anna into a warm hug. 'Try to enjoy yourself, love,' she said. 'This is what you do! You're so good at it. I know whoever you end up serving today will love your food as much as we all do. Pop over later and tell us all about it,' her friend added, giving her a final squeeze. 'I've put a bottle of bubbly in to chill for the occasion.'

Once Pat had gone, Anna threw herself into the work, the hours slipping by in deep concentration. She'd chosen a risotto for the main course and was checking the seasoning when there was a knock at the door. Anna glanced up at the clock, which told her it was almost one o'clock.

Anna went to open the door and found a young couple in their twenties standing on the step.

'Hi,' she said, smiling. 'Are you here for lunch?'

They both smiled and indicated the poster. 'Yes! We were hoping to be, anyway,' said the man. 'It says first come, first served – does that mean we're still in time?'

Anna ignored the sudden fizz of nerves. 'It does! You're my first guests.'

'Wonderful,' said the woman. 'I know we're early, but can we sit down now?'

'Of course you can,' Anna said. 'I won't be ready to serve for another quarter of an hour, but if you take a seat, I'll bring you some drinks. I can't serve alcohol, but—'

'Water would be fine. Thanks!'

She left the door open as they headed for the garden, and was filling a jug with water for her guests when another much younger and very excited voice called to her from the step.

'Anna!' called the voice. 'Anna, Anna, Anna! Guess what?'

Young Robbie MacKenzie was standing in the doorway, clutching his Dolphin Patrol exercise book in both hands and looking as if he were about to explode.

'Robbie! What are you doing here?'

'Dad said we were coming to yours for lunch. We've seen the pod – and they've got the baby with them!'

'Robbie, stop yelling,' came his father's voice. Robert MacKenzie appeared beside his son and rested a hand on his excited head, looking through the door at Anna with an apologetic smile. 'Sorry. It's been quite a morning.'

Two more figures appeared beside him – another boy of Robbie's age and a man that Anna assumed was the child's father.

'This is Fraser and Jamie. We've all been out on dolphin patrol, as you will have gathered,' Robert MacKenzie explained, 'and I thought we might be in time to join your lunch club. Have you got room for four hungry mariners?'

'I – yes,' Anna said. 'Yes, there's still space.'

'You don't mind?' Robert asked. 'Maybe you'd prefer to keep it for new faces . . . ?'

'Of course not,' she told him, smiling. 'It's lovely of you to come. Take a seat, I'll be out in a moment. There are two guests already there.'

Anna went back to the kitchen and picked up the water jug, adding it to a tray of glasses and a plate of gougères she'd made in case she needed extra time in the kitchen. Carrying everything out into the sunlight, she saw that Robert and his friend had seated themselves opposite each other in the middle of the bench, as a kind of buffer between her two other guests and the two boys.

'Hello, everyone,' she said. 'Welcome to lunch at the Fishergirl's Luck.' She put the tray down in the centre of the table. 'Please help yourselves. Lunch will be served shortly.'

'Anna,' Robert said, 'let me quickly introduce Fraser.'

His friend got up and held out a hand with a warm grin. 'Pleased to meet you, Anna,' he said. 'I hear you've got a bit of an adventurous spirit, which always goes down well with me. Can't wait to try this food of yours.'

'Oh – thank you,' Anna said, slightly taken aback at this characterization. 'You're local too, then?'

Fraser sat down again, grinning. He was a big man, broad-shouldered with a hugely square jaw and a dark mop of wiry black hair. 'Born and bred in Macduff,' he nodded at his friend, 'grew up with this reprobate. We live in Elgin now, though – it's easier for my wife, she commutes to Inverness every bloody day.'

'Dad!' Jamie exclaimed, digging him in the ribs with a sharp elbow.

'Oops, sorry,' Fraser said, putting a finger to his mouth but smiling behind it all the same. 'Don't tell Ma, all right? I'll be in the doghouse.'

Jamie squinted up at him. 'What's it worth?'

Robert laughed. 'He's got you there, Fraser.'

The young couple at the other end of the table laughed along too and Fraser turned to them with a dramatic, long-suffering sigh.

'We should introduce ourselves as well,' he said, holding out a hand to the young man, 'since we're eating companions. We promise not to be too rowdy. Well, the kids won't be, anyway. I'll try to keep Old Robbie in line but he's a wild one at heart . . . Here, have one of these cheese things, they're amazing.'

As Anna went in and out to the table, she gathered that the young couple were called Nathan and Kate. They lived in Aberdeen, but had come over to Rosehearty for an impromptu night away. The conversation had made its way around to occupations by the time she came out to clear their plates.

'You're really a cooper?' Nathan asked Robert. 'There aren't many of you guys left, are there?'

Anna looked at Robert, interested herself. When she'd learned that he was on the lifeboats, she'd assumed that was his main occupation.

'There aren't,' he agreed.

'Which distillery are you at?'

'Macduff.'

'I didn't even know there *was* a distillery at Macduff,' Kate said, surprised.

'There's no reason you would,' Robert told her. 'It's not a single malt producer anymore. Production is only for blends. And though I'm based there, I move around.' Anna took his plate and he looked up at her, smiling. 'Thank you. That was the best thing I've eaten for a long time.'

'Yeah,' his son agreed. 'Dad's a rubbish cook. He even burns beans on toast.'

Fraser gave a loud belly laugh that rippled around the table as Anna went back to the cottage to serve dessert. Her gaze was drawn to the figure slowly making his way towards them along the path. It was Douglas McKean. Her stomach did a sick spin. He wasn't usually out and about at this time of day.

She busied herself with the lemon possets, taking them out of the fridge, unwrapping them and putting them on plates with the buttery shortbread she'd made alongside ramekins of fresh raspberries. Then she heard Old Robbie's voice, slightly raised.

'Douglas,' he said. 'How are you doing?'

There was an answering grumble that sounded like thunder gathering on a hot day. Anna went outside to see that McKean was leaning over the fence. She could feel his eyes on her as she passed, heading for Nathan and Kate at the far end of the table.

'Why don't you join us, Mr McKean?' she asked. 'I made

extra desserts and there's coffee on. You're welcome. I can bring out an extra chair for you.'

The old man didn't even acknowledge that she'd spoken. His eyes were fixed on Old Robbie, instead.

'The shame,' he said, his accent thick but his words still clear to everyone sitting at the table. 'The shame of you, Robert MacKenzie, breaking bread at this table when you know this place is rightfully mine.'

'Ach now, Dougie, not this nonsense again,' Robert said, clearly trying to keep the tone light and jovial. 'Why don't you come and eat with us, man? You've been invited.'

Douglas McKean shot Anna a look that was pure dislike.

'As if I'd sit at this thieving harlot's table. How can you sit here when I've been robbed—'

Robert was out of his seat so quickly that the old man actually took a step back. 'Enough,' he said, his voice darkly threatening in a way Anna had not yet heard from him. 'That is *enough*, Douglas McKean. You will never speak of Anna or to her again. Never, from this day. Anna owns this place fair and square, as Bren did before her, and unless you begin to show some respect you've had the last help you'll ever get from me, do you understand? Remember whose house it is you live in.'

The old man's eyes widened and his gaze shot from Robert to Anna. A look of shock bloomed on his face, followed quickly by something that might have been confusion. He shrunk into himself. His face crumbled. Then he turned his back and stumbled away.

Robert turned back to the table. 'I'm sorry,' he said, to everyone, before looking at Anna.

Anna turned back to the table, smiling and hoping that it seemed genuine. Even the children had fallen quiet, aware of the strange, unintelligible adult storm that had broken over their heads. Her heart sank when she saw that the only two actual guests at her table were looking on with faint horror, their desserts abandoned.

'I'm so sorry,' she said. 'Please, do carry on. Can I get you some coffee? Boys, would you like another drink? I've got fizzy orange, or cola.'

It was Fraser who got the conversation going again, looking up at her with a warm smile. 'Coffee would be fantastic. And I bet Jamie would love some fizzy orange, wouldn't you? Saturday treat. Don't tell Ma.'

The murmur of chatter slowly began to rise again around the table. Anna left it and went inside, the hot shame of mortification still burning in her chest.

The diners didn't linger long over their coffee. Anna wasn't surprised when Nathan and Kate made their excuses to leave. Kate shook her hand with a warm enough smile, however, and pressed a sheaf of notes into Anna's hand.

'Oh no,' Anna told her, 'please – I can't take anything, not after that!'

'Don't be ridiculous,' Kate smiled. 'The food was more than worth it. As for the old man . . . that wasn't your fault. Please, take it. And good luck – I hope you do more of these, I think it's a wonderful idea.'

Fraser was the next to stand up, taking out another couple of notes and slipping them beneath one of the glasses still standing on the bench.

'Really,' Anna began. 'Please don't—'

'Ahh,' Fraser said, holding up a finger to stop her. 'Your poster says I should pay what I think is appropriate, and I think this is what's appropriate. It's probably worth a darn sight more, to be honest. Look forward to eating here again – my wife Emma would love it. Wouldn't your mum love it, Jamie?'

'Yeah,' said his son. 'She would! Can we come again next week?'

Fraser raised an eyebrow in question but Anna shook her head with a weary half-laugh. 'Oh, I don't think I'll be doing this again.'

'Why not?' Fraser protested. 'Ach, because of one grumpy old man? He'll not be trying that again, that's for sure.'

Anna smiled, but said no more. She knew, though, how very important word of mouth was to a venture such as this one. However understanding and friendly Kate and Nathan had been, it was inevitable that if they spoke about eating at the Fishergirl's Luck, what had happened would come up. To them, who did not know the history that had led to Old Robbie's words, it would seem as if a frail old man with a stick had been bullied right there in front of them. Besides, someone had already tried to prevent her from opening the lunch club at all. Together the two incidents would doubtless sour things far beyond her current embarrassment. Not to mention that, were Anna to attempt it again, she would now

always be reminded of that sharp look of shock and humiliation on an old man's face as he'd turned away.

Fraser rounded up the two boys and the three of them
headed for the harbour, where the *Cassie's Joy* was waiting.
Robert MacKenzie hung back, helping her clear the last bits
from the table.

'I'm sorry,' he said, once they stood in the kitchen.

Anna kept her back to him, adding her load to the sink of
dishes. She leaned against the rim briefly, looking out of her
little window onto the sea. 'You knew that he was planning
to make trouble,' she said. 'Didn't you?'

There was a second of silence from behind her. 'I heard
something in the pub last night. That he'd seen the poster
was up again and had been on the phone to a few people
about it, wanting to shut you down.'

She nodded and turned around. 'So that's why you came?'

He looked away. 'I thought . . . that if I was here, he might
think twice. But I'm sorry. I should have gone to his door
sooner, or taken him away from the table.'

'I'm an adult. I don't need anyone to fight my battles for
me. You should have told me and let me deal with it.'

He looked at her, his eyes dark. 'You're right. I'm sorry.'

She nodded. 'What was all that about his house?'

'After the landslide, he refused to move – he was born
there, it's all he's ever known. But the place needed a lot of
work that he couldn't afford. He'd never had a mortgage, but
he had to take one out. Then he couldn't keep up with the
payments. So I took it on.'

Anna watched him. 'That was good of you.'

He shook his head. 'I do what I can. It's what Cassie would have wanted. We're all related around here, us locals, in one way or another.'

She turned to look at the pile of washing in her sink. 'You'd better go,' she said. 'They'll be waiting for you and I should get on with this lot.'

There was a moment of silence. She didn't turn around.

'Thank you for lunch,' he said.

Then he was gone.

Selkie lass,

I've done something daft. I thought I was helping, but I only made things worse. You would have told me it was a bad idea before I'd even done it. You're good at that, seeing what should be done and the right way to do it.

I don't know why it bothers me so much. I don't even know her, really.

If you were here, you could tell me how to fix it. If you were here, you would have done the right thing in the first place.

Why aren't you here?

Eighteen

Heavy fatigue crept into Anna's bones. She couldn't shake the melancholy that settled on her after Robert MacKenzie had departed. She cleaned down in silence and declined Pat's offer of a drink, unable to bear the thought of having to detail the humiliation of her latest run-in with Douglas McKean, assuming that Pat hadn't seen it all from her window anyway. Anna racked her brains, trying to work out what she could have done differently, but drew a blank.

'This isn't on you,' Cathy told her, once the kitchen was spotless and Anna was curled on the sofa with the phone to her ear. 'Some people are simply like that. I'm glad this MacKenzie bloke put him in his place.'

'You didn't see his face, though,' Anna said. 'He looked as if his whole world had ended.'

'Don't feel sorry for him. He doesn't deserve it.'

'I don't. Not really. But it made me realize ... there are so many things here that I don't know. Whole histories that I'll never understand, connections that I'll never be able to make. I thought I was settling in but ... I don't know how I'll ever really be a part of this place.'

'Don't think like that,' Cathy told her. 'You've only been there a couple of months. Think of all the positives – all the friends you've made.'

Anna thought about Robert's face as he'd left. She'd been annoyed by his interference, by the unspoken suggestion that she couldn't look after herself. But he'd only been trying to help. Had she even accepted his apology? She couldn't remember.

'I'm not sure I've done a great job of that, either,' she sighed. 'Look, I'm going to go. I'm so tired. I need to sleep.'

'That doesn't sound like you,' said her friend. 'It's still early. You're not sickening for something, are you?'

'Just want this day to be over as soon as possible, that's all.'

Cathy hummed in sympathy. 'Tomorrow will be better. Call me?'

On Sunday morning Anna woke before the sun had faded up the ocean waves from black to green and felt so nauseous that even sitting up was an effort. She cursed herself – it was a stress reaction she'd battled when she was first at catering college, and then every new job she had taken afterwards, and she had no intention of having to conquer it again. Anna forced herself to get up, made tea and then sat cross-legged in front of the window of her bedroom with the muslin drawn back and her duvet around her shoulders. She watched the improbable colours of dawn change as the light swelled over the horizon, hyper-real stripes of colour that looked more like the glaze on one of Rhona's plates than the reality of a northern sky. To her right the cliff and the houses of Crovie looked one and the same in the early morning glare: part and parcel of each other, never to be separated, much like its people. *We're all related around here, us locals, in one way or another.*

She left that thought where it was and went downstairs to shower.

Shortly after 9 a.m. there was a knock at the door. Anna assumed it was David and Glynn stopping by as usual with Bill and readied an excuse – the very thought of walking the clifftops was exhausting – but instead she opened the door to two small, familiar boys.

'Anna! Today we're going to follow the dolphins as far as they go to see exactly how many of them there are because Jamie and me still can't decide and that meant we had to come right past Crovie because it looks as if they're on their way out to Fraserburgh and so I said to Dad could we please stop and ask if you wanted to come with us. He said no because you'd already seen the dolphins now and would probably rather have a nice Sunday lie-in, but I said I don't think you have seen them, not really properly, and anyway Uncle Fraser and Auntie Emma thought it was a good idea. So here we are and do you want to come with us? But you have to be quick because otherwise we might lose them.'

Young Robbie MacKenzie finally paused to draw breath and push his glasses up his nose. Anna opened her mouth, first in surprise and then in an attempt to give the boy an answer, but instead what came out was a question. 'Auntie Emma?'

'That's my ma,' Jamie supplied. 'So you won't be the only lady.'

'Oh, right. I see.'

'Come on!' Robbie urged her. 'I told you, we've got to be quick!'

'Boys,' said a woman's voice, floating along the path mid-laugh, 'we told you to ask Anna *politely*.'

'We *are* being polite!' Robbie said fervently, as the owner of the mystery voice came into view. 'But we want her to hurry up, too!'

'Ssh,' said the woman, as she rested one hand on the boy's head. 'Hello, Anna – I'm Emma, Jamie's mum. I'm sorry to disturb you on a Sunday morning.'

'You're not,' Anna said, holding out a hand with a smile. Emma shook it in a warm, strong grip. 'It's nice to meet you. Thank you for stopping by and the offer. But I'm not feeling one hundred per cent this morning, so I think it might be better if I stayed here today.'

'No!' Robbie moaned. 'But you'll miss them all! Pleeeeeeease come!'

Emma smiled and glanced along the path towards the far end of the village. 'Sure you don't want to blow away a few cobwebs?'

Anna was about to say yes, she was sure, but then she remembered the mantra she'd adopted when she moved in. *Say yes. Say yes to as many things as you can.* Besides, now that she'd been standing in the fresh air for a few minutes, she was feeling better.

'Well,' she said, wavering, 'I suppose it *is* a beautiful morning . . .'

'Yes!' crowed the boys in triumphant unison, followed by Young Robbie's, 'Hurry up!'

'Can you give me five minutes?' Anna asked Emma.

'Of course we can – it'll take me at least that to herd these two terrors back to the boat,' Emma laughed. 'We'll see you at the pier – whenever you're ready.'

Anna left the door open, hearing the shout and chatter of the boys as they headed down the sea wall. She grabbed an extra layer and her coat before pulling on her walking boots and following. The hubbub from the waiting boat floated towards her, but to her surprise it wasn't the outline of the *Cassie's Joy* that she saw. Instead a larger pleasure craft with a sleek, shining white hull and chrome rails crouched beside Crovie's pier. Fraser was at the helm, a ridiculously small skipper's hat perched precariously on his head: Anna had a hunch it belonged to his son. Emma was towards the rear of the boat, busily wrestling the two boys into life jackets that they were vocally protesting as being 'for silly bairns!' A new uneasiness rattled in Anna's gut as she realized this wasn't Robert's boat.

'Ahoy there, landlubber!' Fraser shouted, catching sight of her. 'Ready for an adventure on the high seas?'

'If you've got room for one more,' Anna said, as she finally saw Robert MacKenzie. He was crouched on the deck beside Fraser, his back to her, tying down a folded tarp. He didn't even turn his head at the sound of her voice, which only caused the growing doubt to sink even deeper into her bones. The substance of his son's excited words as he'd stood on the doorstep of the Fishergirl's Luck came back to her, their meaning finally and far too late marked out in the flow.

Dad said no.

Robert hadn't wanted her to join them – why would he, after their awkward parting the day before? But it wasn't his boat and he'd been overruled by Fraser and Emma. Anna wished she'd stuck to her original conviction that staying at home would be a better idea.

'Of course there's room,' Fraser said. 'Come on, get yourself aboard.'

Old Robbie finally got up, turning around as Anna stepped onto the boat. He gave her a smile that was slightly reserved and came closer as Fraser began to pull out into open water.

'Morning,' he said quietly, beneath the roar of the boat's engine.

'Hi.'

'How are you?'

'Fine, thanks.'

There was a slight commotion from the other end of the boat. Anna looked past Robert to see Emma wrestling with Young Robbie, as if trying to stop him from coming towards them.

'Robbie said you didn't want me to come.'

'I didn't want you to feel put on the spot after I offended you so badly yesterday.'

Anna sighed. 'You didn't offend me. It was only ... I've had quite a few years of not being able to do things the way I would choose to for myself.'

He nodded. 'I get that, and I'm sorry.'

'And I probably owe you an apology for yesterday,' Anna added. 'I know you were trying to help.'

'There's nothing to apologize for,' he told her. 'Unless, that is, you let what happened with Dougie stop you from trying again. That really would be something to be sorry for.'

Anna looked away, out towards the open ocean before them. The boat picked up speed as they cleared the bay and the coast stretched out before them, cliff and shore and wave undulating together in perfect curves of earth and water.

'Dolphins ahoy!' Fraser shouted from the shelter of the boat's protected helm. 'We've found them, boys! We've found them!'

The two children whooped and ran forward, leaning over the rail.

'I'll think about it,' she told him. 'Let's concentrate on the dolphins for a while.'

Nineteen

The pod hopped and skipped ahead of the boat, sleek shapes leaping out of the ocean so cleanly that they barely even seemed to trail water while airborne. Anna and Emma leaned against the rail beside the two boys, who were trying to number the pod. It was a difficult proposition with the creatures' exuberant, here-one-second-gone-the-next movements. Jamie and Robbie pointed and shouted, ducked and whooped, shimmering with excitement and purpose.

Anna caught Emma's eye and smiled. 'Do you think they know we're here?'

'The boys, or the dolphins?' Emma asked dryly. The two children did seem to be growing more excited by the second.

Anna laughed, pointing at a singing curve as it leapt through a wave and splashed smoothly down again, disappearing from view. 'That's so amazing to see. Why do they even do that?'

Emma shook her head. 'For my money they do it because they can. Wouldn't you, if you could?'

'I absolutely would.'

The two women talked as the day wore on, exchanging

histories and becoming acquainted. Emma, as Fraser had already said, commuted to Inverness each day, where she managed a branch of one of the major banks.

'It's maybe not what I planned to be doing all my life,' she confessed, 'but it's made us financially stable, and that's nothing to be sniffed at these days. It's why I admire you so much, Anna, giving everything up to change your life completely to start over.'

'Well, it was a bit different for me. I don't have a family to support.'

'True,' Emma agreed, 'but it's still such a big thing to do. How are you finding it so far?' she asked, and then laughed at Anna's immediate grimace. 'That good, eh?'

'Oh, parts of it have been wonderful,' Anna told her. 'Meeting people like you and Fraser and Robert and the boys. Spending time in such a beautiful place. But I assume you heard about the run-in with Douglas McKean yesterday?'

'Give it time, is my advice,' Emma said. 'These things don't happen overnight, and we Scots can find it hard to let anyone in. Especially,' she said, with a twinkling laugh, 'an English newcomer.'

As they laughed together the boat's engine cut out. They both turned towards the wheelhouse, registering a renewed tumult of noise from the two children.

'Look,' Fraser said, pointing towards the dolphins. 'Didn't you two hear the boys shouting?'

Out in the water the pod had circled on itself and was now leaping towards the boat, dodging waves and the white water broken by the wind. In a moment the animals were along-side, sinuous bodies curling beneath the surface, breaking it, calling with their unmistakable high-pitched whistle. The two boys rushed past them to the other end of the boat. Anna followed, leaning over as the pod billowed past, almost seem-ing to look up at the humans as much as the humans were looking down at them. The boys stretched out their arms, palms down. A second later Jamie shouted in astonishment as one of the dolphins dove upwards, slapping its nose against his fingers with a wet thwack.

'See?' Young Robbie shouted, pointing to the periphery. 'I told you there was a baby! I told you!'

There, hovering beside its mother, was a little calf, paler than its elders, with inquisitive eyes that followed its inquisitive nose, watching them with eyes far shrewder than one would expect.

They stayed out on the boat late into the afternoon, until the summer sun finally began to dip lower in the sky. By the time they got back to Crovie, Anna was tired again, but smil-ing as she climbed back down to the harbour. It was strange to be on solid ground after so many hours of the boat's chop.

'Thank you for taking me with you,' she said, to all of them. 'It's been a lovely day – and I'm so glad we got to see the dolphin calf!'

'You should come out with us again,' Young Robbie called. 'We'll be going out to check on it every day until it's fully grown.'

'Oh, will we now?' asked his father. 'That's the first I've heard of it.'

'We have to make sure he or she is safe, Dad,' his son said, with a distinct air of pressed childlike patience. 'It's our *responsibility*.'

'Right, I see.' Robert turned back to Anna with a grimace and his hands on his hips. 'Nothing like making a rod for your own back, is there?'

Anna laughed. 'Well, I'm always here if you want some company on patrol.'

He smiled, a wide, relaxed expression that made his face younger and happier than she'd yet seen it. 'Sounds good to me. Thanks for coming, Anna.'

'Thanks for asking! I had a good time.'

The boat pulled out of the harbour as he hooked an arm around his son's shoulders. He raised his voice and shouted over the waves, over the engine.

'Do another lunch at the Fishergirl's Luck.'

'Maybe,' she shouted back.

'Promise me!'

She laughed. 'I don't make promises I might not be able to keep.'

He threw up his arms in mock exasperation, but he was still smiling. In another moment the boat had disappeared around the promontory, heading for Gamrie.

Twenty

'Well,' said Cathy, who had called not long after Anna had arrived back from her unexpected expedition. 'That sounds like a pretty full weekend to me. What are you going to do now?'

Anna glanced at the clock. It was barely eight o'clock, but she was struggling to keep her eyes open. 'Well, right now I think I'm probably going to crash into bed and go out like a light.'

'What, again? That's really not like you,' said Cathy.

'I know,' Anna laughed. 'Being here is making me soft. I think it's all the sea air I've had today – I'm exhausted. Or maybe it's my age. It usually is if you're a woman, isn't it, one way or another?'

'As long as it's not depression,' Cathy said seriously. 'I know you say you're fine about the fling with the hot Kiwi ending, but—'

'It's not depression,' Anna assured her. 'I promise.'

'All right, then. And actually, I was talking about life in general. The pop-up, for example. Doing another few of those would keep you busy, wouldn't it?'

Anna sighed. 'Robert MacKenzie was trying to talk me into doing another lunch, too.'

'Smart man. I knew there was a reason I liked him.'

'You've never even met him.'

'Don't need to. He's clearly got my girl's back, and that's enough for me. Besides, as if there's any chance of me not liking someone you described as "a young Robert Redford".'

Anna leaned back against the sofa, shaking her head. 'I'm still not sure about doing another lunch.'

'But it went so well!'

'Aside from the humiliating addition of Douglas McKean, you mean?'

'You can't let one cantankerous old bastard ruin it for you.'

'Robert said that too. Or words to that effect.'

'I told you – smart man. Besides, think of everything you got together for that first lunch – the dishes, for example. You can't not use those again.'

'I know, I know. It's not only one old man though, is it? It wasn't him that called the health and safety people. There's someone else out there who doesn't like me.'

Cathy made a dismissive sound in her throat. 'What do you care? There are clearly more people who support you than who don't. Do another one, pronto. I'll get a poster done. Hey, you know what would be a good idea? You should set up a TripAdvisor entry for the Fishergirl's Luck.'

'Oh, I don't think so,' said Anna, over the sound of Cathy moving around on the other end of the line. 'It's only going to be for this summer.'

'Why should that matter?' Cathy asked, over the sound of her tapping keys. 'It'll be great publicity. I bet it's really easy to do. Hold on, I'm just looking now ...'

There was a couple of seconds of silence. Then:

'Bloody hell.'

'What?' Anna asked.

'There's already an entry here. It's got a five-star review.'

Anna sat up. 'What?'

'Someone's already set up a page for the Fishergirl's Luck. There's a photo of the bench and everything. "A unique dining experience, as close to the sea as it's possible to get,"' Cathy read aloud, as Anna scrabbled for her iPad and flipped it open. '"Food so fresh the fish was practically still flapping ... We've rarely eaten so well outside a five-star restaurant ... Local colour—"' Cathy laughed. '"Local colour"! That's one way to put it! "Local colour and company combined to make an unforgettable lunch. We wish the Fishergirl's Luck well and hope to be able to eat there again soon in its very bright future."'

Anna stared at the review on her screen.

'Have you found it?' Cathy asked.

'Yes,' Anna said faintly.

'It was posted by Nathan and Kate Archer yesterday.'

'They're the couple who were guests along with Robert and Fraser.'

'They must have set up the page themselves,' Cathy said. 'Wow, what a first review to get!'

Anna said nothing, still staring at the page.

'Anna? Are you all right?'

'Yes,' she said. 'Taking it in, that's all.'

'You know what?' Cathy said. 'Now you really *do* have to do some more lunches at the Fishergirl's Luck.'

Rhona was of the same mind. She came over the following evening and the two women shared a glass of wine and a lemon and pea risotto.

'Ach, you must do more,' Rhona said, as they relaxed after dinner, her tall frame folded easily into one of the armchairs. 'It would be such a pity if you didn't. And one thing's for sure – if you waste your time trying to understand the inside workings of an old man's head, you'll drive yourself mad. So don't, is my advice. This place is yours now, Anna, well and truly. Stop acting as if you need permission to be here, because you don't. Plus, the good weather won't last forever. We get caught by a lot of summer storms here,' Rhona told her. 'So I'd make the most of it while you can if I were you.'

'All right, all right,' Anna said, with a laugh. 'You've convinced me. Lunch at the Fishergirl's Luck will return.'

'Excellent,' Rhona said. 'When?'

Anna grimaced. 'You're a hard taskmaster. Later this week, if I can get myself together. Friday, let's say.'

Her friend lifted her glass in a silent toast. 'I'll drink to that.'

The two women smiled at each other and clinked glasses, and Anna thought it would have been a perfect evening if only she hadn't been quite so tired again. The next time she went into town, she really must remember to get some multivitamins.

The next morning, Anna woke so nauseous that she barely made it to the bathroom before she threw up. Afterwards she felt better, and could not work out where an illness would have come from. She wondered briefly if it could have been her own cooking from the night before, but no, surely not – she could cook a risotto perfectly even in her sleep. It was worrying because she could not reopen lunch club if she had any form of stomach flu. She didn't feel as if she had a fever, but unless she had forty-eight hours free with no sickness, she couldn't serve food to guests. She began to feel better later in the day, though, which was a relief. Whatever it was seemed to be passing.

It was only when Anna was sick for the third morning running that the shadow that had been lurking at the back of her mind began to coalesce into a full-on phantom. She stared at the calendar hanging on the wall beside the door of the Fishergirl's Luck, counting days, but that made things worse, not better. Her periods had always been erratic, arriving early, or late, or sometimes not at all. It had caused her endless mental agonies as a teenager. The gap her mother's death had made in her life had always been present, but that was the point that it became impossible to ignore. Her dad had tried, bless him, but the idea of talking to him about such things had filled Anna with complete dismay. At sixteen, she still hadn't bled, and secretly thought that there was something terribly wrong with her. Then, one day, there it was, following the faintest of pangs – a pale stain when she got up in the morning that worsened only slightly throughout the day. The next day it had gone again. She'd religiously written down the date and then looked out for it the next month, but there was nothing. It took another three months for her to bleed again, and even then it was the same why-bother event.

It was only when she'd been hustled to the doctor by one of her mother's old friends that her mind was finally set at rest. She'd started seeing a boy called Nick who was in the sixth form at school, which had sent her dad into such paroxysms of panic that he'd drafted in 'Aunt Violet' to talk to Anna about it. Violet had given her three pieces of advice.

'Always, *always* use a condom; never, *ever* let him talk you into doing anything you're not sure you want to do; and go on the pill.'

That had led her to a consultation with her doctor in which the full extent of Anna's worries had come tumbling out. Doctor Jeffries, who had been a constant all her life, had listened carefully, nodding her neatly coiffed grey head every now and then.

'You've been worried about this for a long time, haven't you?' she'd asked, once Anna had finished. 'Your mother had the same issue, you know. In fact, her cycle was so uneven that she was two months pregnant before she even realized you were on the way.'

Anna hadn't thought of that conversation for years. She wasn't on the pill – she had been all the time that she'd been with Geoff because he'd insisted on it, even though Anna had always been told that the likelihood of her falling pregnant by accident with a cycle so uneven was so low. Not that Geoff had believed that, or ever had any intention of considering the fact that the contraceptive's hormones had made her skin break out and her moods uneven. *Condoms aren't 100 per cent. Accidents happen. I don't want that worry. All you have to do is take a pill. What's the problem?*

Taking the pill was one of the first things she'd ditched after their break-up, because apart from anything else she hadn't expected to find herself in another relationship so soon.

But Liam and I did use condoms, she thought. *Every time. Always. Didn't we? Except . . . Was there one time early on, when we'd both drunk a little too much, and maybe . . . maybe . . . ?*

Anna's heart did an uneven jig in her chest. Oh, God. She couldn't be, could she? She couldn't be pregnant. *I was on the pill for so long. Everyone says it takes forever to leave your system. And my cycle is so irregular anyway, and then there's my age. And it was only once, only that one time . . .*

She sat down on the sofa, things suddenly falling into place. The inexplicable and abject exhaustion, the nausea, the sickness in the mornings . . .

Oh God. Oh, *God.*

Anna tried to breathe evenly. Either way, she had to know for sure, and the sooner the better. There wasn't any sense in putting it off. There could only be one of two outcomes: either it would be negative and she could laugh at the whole thing, or it would be positive and she'd have to work out how to deal with it. Steeling herself, Anna got up, picked up her coat and keys, and headed out.

Within an hour Anna was back, leaning against the tiny

sink in the bathroom of the Fishergirl's Luck. The nausea of early that morning had transformed into a knot of anxiety edged with something else – a form of anticipation that kept kicking at her heart and shivering in her gut.

A career of gauging time had made her good at estimating the passage of minutes. Anna forced herself to leave four before she looked down at the small white tube. She didn't even have to pick it up to know the truth.

Two strong blue lines. Two.

Anna's legs turned to water and she sank to the floor, slumping back against the wall between the sink and the door. For a moment her mind was completely blank. She put one hand on her stomach and then felt foolish – as if there would be anything to feel. It couldn't be more than six weeks old, this bundle of furtive nerves with the power to turn her life upside down.

The cold of the flags beneath her forced Anna to her feet. She got up and went out into the living room still dazed. She sat down on the sofa, rested her elbows on her knees, and put her hands over her face.

Pregnant.

Selkie lass,

We're going to have to keep a really close watch on the wee lad. I caught him trying to go off to the dinghy on his own today. I got a call out right as we were about to go on dolphin patrol and told him to stay put until Barbara could get here and that patrol would have to wait, but then as I turned the car around I saw him sneaking out with his backpack. He said he couldn't not check on the dolphin calf. I had to walk him right to Barbara's door, just to make sure.

We've raised a kid too conscientious for his own good, that's the trouble.

Keep an eye on him, won't you? I'm not doing a good enough job on my own.

Twenty-One

'Where are you? Hope you're not avoiding me. Can't imagine why you would be.'

Sunday morning, Cathy's voice on her landline messages.

'I haven't spoken to you for what feels like ages,' Cathy went on. 'It's all emails and texts. Come on, woman, give me a call. I want to know how the lunches went.'

Anna waited for the beep and then deleted the message before heading blearily for the kitchen. No sickness this morning, she noticed, just an underlying but bearable feeling of nausea. She stared through the little picture window over her sink as she filled the kettle. The sea was rougher today, streaks of azure and turquoise quilting together in a surf rolling endlessly towards her beneath the wind. She stood staring out at the shapes the waves made, curved and angular all at once, soothing to a mind exhausted by circular thinking and physical fatigue.

The answer to Cathy's question was, very well. Her table had been full on both Friday and Saturday, and this time there had been no embarrassing interruptions from Douglas McKean. For Anna, lunch had passed in a pleasant bubble of activity and chat. She had floated through it all, confident in the bustle of kitchen work, enjoying the cushion that physical labour provided between theory and thought.

Now it was Sunday and she had nothing for which to prepare – nothing to stop her thoughts churning over and over like the waves outside her tiny home. She made herself tea and sat on the sofa, listening to the wail of the wind as it tore around the corners of the Fishergirl's Luck. She imagined Bren and wondered if she'd ever sat in the same place, nursing a quandary, trying to see her way through the murk of uncertainty towards a difficult decision. Anna doubted it, somehow. When she thought of Bren MacKenzie what came to mind was a capable, collected woman who had always known her own mind, a woman who had travelled through life on a simple yet direct and determined trajectory of her own choosing. Who else could have seen this old stone shack and realized it could be lived in, and then proceeded to turn it into such a haven? At the time Bren had decided to do so, too, when women, especially here on the ragged edge of a harsh shore, would have been expected to take a far different route than the one she had chosen. Part of Anna wished Bren were here now. She could imagine her as a good listener, who would sit opposite with her own steaming cup of tea and a patient look on her face as Anna spilled her troubles out over the small coffee table. What would Bren's advice be? She'd never married, never had children. Was that a choice, Anna wondered now, or simply that the opportunity had never afforded itself?

Bren wasn't there and could help her with none of these questions, especially not the most difficult one that Anna had to answer for herself. She lifted her mug to her lips, realized she'd drunk her tea already, got up to put the kettle on again and glanced at the clock. It was almost 10 a.m. This would usually be the time that Glynn and David might knock on the door, but they were away in Portugal for a week, soaking up some more certain sun. Anna waited until her second tea of the day was ready, her heart thumping a little quicker as she stirred milk into her mug. Then she went to the phone and dialled Cathy's number.

This is it, she thought, as the phone rang out. *Once I say it out loud to someone else, it'll be real and I'll have to deal with it.*

'There you are!' Cathy exclaimed, once Anna had said hello. 'I was beginning to think the hot Kiwi had come back on his hands and knees and whisked you off to New Zealand.'

Anna couldn't raise a laugh. 'No, nothing like that.'

'What's wrong?' her friend asked, immediately. 'The old man didn't cause trouble again?'

'No, no. The lunches went well. Really well, actually.'

'Right. Well, that's great, but what's going on?'

Anna swallowed hard, but the words still stuck in her throat.

'Anna?'

'I'm pregnant,' she said. 'I found out on Wednesday.'

There was a brief silence, and then, 'Ahh.'

'You sound oddly relieved.'

'I am. For a moment there I thought you were going to

drop some horrible bombshell about all that extreme tiredness being caused by something else. Something much worse.'

'Well, it's not,' Anna said, tracing her fingers over her stomach, looking down at a non-existent bump. 'It's a baby. Or what could be a baby.'

'Okay then,' her friend said, carefully. 'Are you all right?'

'I don't know. I mean – physically I'm fine. Everything else . . .'

'Yeah. I bet.'

Anna shut her eyes. 'I don't know what to do.'

'That's okay. You've got a bit of time to decide. Not much, but you can't be that far gone. And I'm here to listen.'

'I'm such an idiot.'

'Accidents happen. Anyway, there's no point dwelling on that now, is there?' Cathy said gently. 'It's what you do next that's important. I'm going to ask you something. There's no wrong answer to it and you can tell me or not, it's up to you, but it's something you need to think about. All right?'

Anna's heart turned over. 'All right.'

'At some point since you found out, you had a gut reaction. Maybe more than one. What did it tell you?'

'That morning sickness is the pits?' Anna joked feebly.

'It's been there,' Cathy probed. 'Hasn't it?'

Anna thought about the shadow that had been lurking at the back of her mind for the past few days.

'I think I want to keep it,' she said, and once she'd started the words didn't seem to want to stop. 'I think that's what my gut reaction is. I'll be forty next year. I'm not in a relationship. There's no one on the horizon. Maybe this is my one chance to have a child and if I don't have one now I think I'd regret it. But the father is going back home to the other side of the world, I don't have a job and I'm living in a shed that could be washed off the sea wall in the next big storm.'

Cathy let out a breath tinged with a wisp of laughter. 'Okay.'

Anna took a breath, frowning to herself. 'I don't – I don't know where all that came from. I can't keep it. It's a ridiculous idea. There are so many reasons why—'

'Hey,' her friend interrupted. 'If everyone thought about the decision to have children logically, there would be barely any babies born at all and they'd all come out with silver spoons in their mouths. Having a child is always difficult, and if you didn't want it, that would be fine too. But if you want it, then everything else is a problem that can be solved.'

'That easy?'

'I never said it would be easy. In fact, I think you can probably bet it'll be anything but that. But women in worse positions than you have had babies and the world hasn't ended.'

Anna leaned forward and put her head to her knees. 'Oh, God. This is insane. What was I thinking?'

'I'm guessing that in the moment there wasn't really that much thinking involved . . .'

'If I keep it, I'm going to have to tell Liam. How on earth do I do that? "Hi, I know we said that the thing between us was casual, nothing more than a bit of fun, and we've both already moved on and I also know you're about to go home and this is going to be a massive bombshell, but just so you know, you're going to be a father." Oh, *God*. It's going to be awful.'

'Well,' Cathy said, 'playing devil's advocate here: he'll be gone very soon. You probably won't even be showing much by then, and if he's never coming back . . .'

'That would be a terrible thing to do.'

'Probably. On the other hand, he might think ignorance is bliss. This needs to be your decision, Anna. If you went to him and told him you wanted it and he said he didn't – or vice versa, for that matter – I know you, you'd put what he wants first because Geoff has spent decades convincing you that's how a relationship works. And it can't, not in this. You'll be the one living with the results of the decision. Either way, he'll be on the other side of the planet doing exactly what he always planned to do.'

Anna groaned. 'I need to think. I need to live with the idea of actually having a baby for a day or two. See how that changes things.'

'All right, you do that. Call me any time you want to talk, all right? And remember, there is no wrong decision unless it goes against what you want. Steve and I will be here to support you whatever you decide. Okay?'

Anna let out a long breath. 'Thanks.'

'Chin up, chick,' Cathy said, putting on an absurd Northern accent. 'You'll be reet.'

Anna laughed. 'I miss you.'

'I miss you, too. Thanks for telling me. And

listen – whatever happens, everything's going to be all right. Okay?'

They talked for a while longer, Anna detailing the events of both lunch clubs, but it was clear that the subject looming largest between them needed some air to breathe. As, Anna decided, did she.

'The wind's really up here today,' she told Cathy. 'I think I'll go out for a walk. Blow out the cobwebs, let in some air.'

They said their goodbyes and Anna suited up for a chilly walk on the cliff, adding a waterproof jacket over her fleece and jeans. She was locking the door of the Fishergirl's Luck when a voice soared to her over the wind whipping along the sea wall.

'Looks as if we're in the nick of time!'

She turned to see the two Roberts MacKenzie coming towards her from the pier, grins on their faces, hair blown into an unruly muss by the wind. Both were in their yellow jackets.

'We're going on dolphin patrol!' Young Robbie yelled. 'You'll come too, won't you?'

For a moment Anna forgot the secret she carried, forgot how it would change everything and everyone around her once it was known. The sight of them: their simple enthusiasm, the way the wind had rubbed their cheeks red – made her smile and laugh as if this was any other Sunday afternoon.

'It's only us today,' Old Robbie added as he came to a standstill in front of her, eyes crinkling in a smile that rarely seemed to go away. 'Fraser and Jamie have taken Emma out for afternoon tea in Inverness. It's her birthday.'

'Oh! I wish I'd known, I'd have got her something,' Anna said. 'I'll have to make a note for next year so I don't forget.'

Robert MacKenzie's smile became deeper, warmer. 'Well, that's a relief,' he said.

'What is?'

'That you're planning to be here next year.'

Anna blinked. She hadn't even noticed her slip.

'It wasn't so many weeks ago that you said you weren't sure you'd stay, or even come back.' Robert nudged his son's arm and Anna realized that Young Robbie had grown even in the short time that she'd known him. 'We must be doing something right, lad.'

Young Robbie beamed a smile and pushed his glasses up his nose. 'You should learn to sail,' he said, 'and get a boat! Then you can be a proper part of dolphin patrol.'

'Ach, she's a proper part anyway,' Robert mock-scolded. 'She's coming out with us in this bluster instead of tucking herself away for a Sunday on the sofa, isn't she?'

Anna watched them both and felt a strange pang, a vague longing that knew no place to settle except on her heart. Something must have shown on her face because when Robert looked at her his smile faded.

'Hey – it's fine if you don't want to come,' he said.

'No,' Anna said quickly, 'it's not that. I'd love to come. Let's go, before it decides to rain.'

He still looked doubtful as they followed the boy towards the boat bobbing on the waves in Crovie's tiny harbour.

'Sorry,' he said quietly. 'Robbie can be a tad overwhelming, I know, and I don't do anything to discourage him. Maybe I should.'

'Don't be daft,' Anna said. 'He's a wonderful boy. You're a wonderful father. I don't know how you do it. I don't know that I could.'

'You could,' he told her, his voice still quiet. 'I have a feeling you could do anything you set your mind to. And you'd be a great mum. Look how the boy loves you already.'

Anna said nothing as he helped her down onto the boat. She pretended that it was the wind bringing tears to her eyes as they cleared Crovie and cut out through the North Sea waves.

Twenty-Two

'We've got you to thank for a booking, you know,' Pat said, as she put a mug of tea down in front of Anna a couple of days later.

Anna looked up at her. 'What do you mean?'

'A woman called and asked how close we were to the Fishergirl's Luck, as she and her partner had read that it was the best new place to eat on the coast and they wanted to have a good chance of getting a seat.'

'Really?'

'Really!' Pat joined her at the kitchen table with a plate of biscuits. 'She didn't sound local, either.'

'Neither do we . . .'

Pat laughed. 'True. Still, that's good, eh? You've caught the attention of the foodies.'

'But how? I haven't even done ten lunches.'

'Hmm. Never underestimate the power of the Internet,' Pat said. 'Have you looked to see if you've had more reviews? I bet there are some after the last two you did. And it wouldn't take much to make you stand out in this area — there's not a lot of choice, is there?'

Anna stared into her tea. 'I suppose that means I'd better carry on then. For a while, at least.'

'Are you all right, love?' Pat asked, watching her carefully. 'You've seemed a bit preoccupied lately. We've hardly seen you. I know the thing with Liam is off – has that dragged you down a bit?'

Anna smiled. 'Maybe a little. I'm fine, though, really. I'm sorry I've not been around. Tell you what, why don't we get the Usual Suspects together at the weekend? Have a good catch-up.'

'Sounds like a fine idea.' Pat looked at Anna over her mug as she took a mouthful of tea, and then said, 'I saw you heading out with the MacKenzie boys on Sunday.'

Anna laughed. 'Oh yes. It seems I've become an unwitting honorary member of dolphin patrol. Young Robbie is so enthusiastic, it's hard not to get carried away too. And Robert's easy company.'

Pat smiled. 'It's nice to see you getting along. All of you.'

'Ahh, Pat,' Anna warned. 'Don't.'

Her friend held up a hand. 'I'm not stirring. Really I'm not. But honestly, you looked so good, the three of you, laughing and chatting as you went along. It's been a long time since I've seen Old Robbie smile so much. The two of you obviously get on. And now Liam's no longer on the scene . . . it seems to me . . .'

Anna reached out and put a hand over Pat's. 'I know you mean well. But please, stop. Nothing's going to happen between Robert MacKenzie and me. We're friends, that's all.

Neither of us is looking for anything else, and it'd be great if you could let anyone you hear talking about it know that. You wouldn't want what we do have spoiled by gossip, would you?'

Pat sighed. 'Of course not. It seems a pity, that's all.'

Anna ignored the very tiny pang in her heart that agreed. It was still a ridiculous notion for all the reasons she had put to Rhona weeks ago, not to mention the even bigger new reason that she'd spent most – all – of her time thinking about since she'd first spoken to Cathy. They'd been on and off the phone frequently since.

Anna thought that really, she had probably already decided before she'd even told Cathy. She was going to have a baby. A *baby*. It was absurd, surreal, terrifying and wonderful. The fact that she found herself thinking the latter more than the former had convinced Anna that not keeping it wasn't an option she'd be able to live with. So there it was. However difficult it was, she was going to have a baby. A *child*, that would eventually turn into a delicious, exhausting, noisy whirlwind of activity like Young Robbie MacKenzie. Right now she didn't even know where she'd be living when the baby arrived, but it was decided: Anna Campbell was going to bring a new person into the world. Absurd. Surreal. Terrifying. Wonderful.

How long should I carry on with the lunches? she wondered. *If I serve shellfish, I'll have to get someone else to taste it. Besides, I need somewhere proper to live, and I'm not made of money. I'm going to need an actual job that can support me and a child. Maybe it'd be better to stop now, put all my energy into that. Except that then I'd be disappointing this crazy woman who's coming from God knows where to eat at Liam's bench and paying Pat and Frank so she can . . .*

'Penny for them?' Pat asked, pushing the plate of biscuits across the table.

'Oh,' Anna said, taking one. 'Just wondering about menus for next week.'

Pat beamed. 'That's my girl. This guest of ours won't be the last, I bet. The Fishergirl's Luck is going to put Crovie on the foodie map, I know it.'

Anna laughed. 'I doubt that very much. Not with twelve covers at most a week and no guarantee of getting a table.'

'Ahh, but people love that, don't they?' Pat said. 'Exclusivity, that kind of thing.'

The next big conundrum that Anna had to solve was when and how to tell Liam. A big part of her felt as if she wanted to live with the idea on her own for a while longer, to keep the secret just hers. Cathy knew, of course, but she'd tell no one, and besides, she was so far away from the bubble of life inside the bay that it didn't even seem to count.

The problem was that keeping any secret in Crovie was almost impossible, and Anna was worried that someone would work out the truth. If that happened, it'd be everywhere before she'd even had time to take a breath, and the thought of Liam finding out he was to be a father from someone else was awful. She did her best to keep everything entirely normal, but then came a sunny Tuesday afternoon and a call from Rhona.

'I'm coming over with gin, all right?' Rhona declared. 'I've had a hell of a day. Be there in twenty.'

'I'll get the glasses out,' Anna said, and her friend had rung off before it had occurred to her that she couldn't drink, and that there was no bigger giveaway. She phoned Cathy in a panic.

'Antibiotics,' Cathy told her. 'You can't drink if you're taking them. Invent something invisible and innocuous. Ear infection, that always works.'

'You're good at this,' Anna observed.

'Blame a lifetime of avoiding getting utterly hammered at corporate events with creepy old white men with a black girl fantasy,' Cathy said. 'By the way, I've done a new poster for the Fishergirl's Luck. It reflects the one hundred per cent five-star ratings you've got on TripAdvisor, you clever thing. I'll send it over.'

Cathy's subterfuge worked. Rhona betrayed only momentary disappointment at Anna's enforced sobriety, and absolutely no suspicion.

'All the more for me,' she quipped, as Anna nursed a lime cordial while Rhona splashed an overly generous measure of Hendricks into her tall glass.

It was not long after five o'clock and the sun was still high, a light breeze curling through the village as it so often did at this time of day. Rhona had arrived looking harried.

'What's happened?' Anna asked, as they sat at the bench, a bowl of crisps and some artichoke dip between them. 'You look done in.'

Rhona took a large gulp of her drink, holding up one

finger in a 'bear-with' gesture. Then she put down her glass and blew out a breath.

'Bloody bank,' she growled. 'Bloody economy, bloody men, bloody *money*. When I started up I took out a loan for the kiln and I'm struggling to keep up with the payments. When I agreed the terms, I thought I'd be fine. Stuart and I – my ex – had this house in Aberdeen that we'd bought as a development property. After the divorce we agreed that he'd go ahead and do the renovations as planned and then sell it, after which we'd split the proceeds because although it'd be him doing all the work, the initial investment was all mine. But he's only now finished the renovations – it's taken him years – and he's arguing that because he paid for all of them, and because the housing market has dropped off and it'll be hard to sell, I'm not due anything from the sale.'

'What?' said Anna. 'But surely he doesn't have a leg to stand on.'

Rhona finished her drink and immediately poured another. 'Probably not, but I don't have money for a lawyer. It seems that he – or his new wife, more likely – does.' She groaned. 'I think I'm going to have to cut my losses. But business hasn't been great. I've been scraping by, and with the loan to pay every month . . .' Rhona shook her head. 'I'm worried I'm going to lose it all. I can't do that, Anna, I can't. I've already started over from nothing once, I'm too old to do it again.'

Anna put her hand over Rhona's and squeezed her fingers. 'It won't come to that. I won't let it. Your pieces are so beautiful, Rhona, all they need is to find their place and they'll take off, I know it.'

Rhona gave her a watery smile. 'Aye, hen. Take over the pub, use all my crockery, get famous and start a chain,' she said. 'That'll solve all my problems!'

Anna looked out over the bay, thinking. 'Top-flight restaurants aren't a bad idea for a market, you know. Maybe I can help there.'

Rhona looked hopeful. 'You think Geoff Rowcliffe might be interested?'

Something in Anna shuddered at the idea of having to be in touch with her ex, especially at the moment. How he'd crow if he knew. She could imagine exactly how he'd react: she'd run off to the back of beyond and got knocked up straight away like the stupid woman she had always been.

'Let me see what I can do,' she said. 'It's worth a phone call or two, at least, isn't it?'

Rhona gripped her hand hard. 'Thank you. Thank you so much. We're so lucky to have you here, Anna.'

Anna looked down at her drink. 'People keep saying that.'

'That's because it's true! Look at what you've achieved already!'

Anna laughed. 'You mean successfully serving lunch to a handful of people a couple of times a week?'

Rhona shook her head. 'I think you're going to find yourself in demand for far more than a couple of times a week from now on, hen.'

'What do you mean?'

Rhona pulled a piece of paper from her pocket. She handed it to Anna, who unfolded it to find a clipping from the *Banffshire Journal*. THE HOTTEST NEW EATERY ON THE COAST, screamed the headline. 'Michelin-starred chef launches lunch club venture in Crovie,' it went on, followed by a couple of paragraphs of almost-accurate information and a stock photograph of the village, with the Fishergirl's Luck, as always, in the foreground.

Anna felt suddenly faint. 'Oh God.'

'Are you all right?' Rhona said.

Anna put one hand over her eyes. 'Yes ... a bit over-whelmed, that's all.'

'Oh, bless you,' said her friend, squeezing her shoulder. 'You should be proud of yourself. The village is certainly proud of you – Gamrie is, too. It's not often we've got something to crow about that the bigger places haven't. You can bet that this clipping will be in every holiday home welcome pack for fifty miles! Which is why I think you're going to find yourself pretty busy. I don't think you'd find it difficult to fill the bench every day of the week from now on, if you wanted to.'

'But I don't take bookings, and to get to us people have to walk down the cliff,' Anna pointed out. 'Who's going to risk coming along on the off chance when there are only six seats?'

Rhona tapped the side of her nose and raised her eye-brows. 'Maybe this will put Crovie and Gardenstown on the map again, how about that? And hey – maybe *that*'s how you're going to save me and my workshop.'

212

Oh my selkie lass,

Robbie was late home because of bloody dolphin patrol but I was out on a call so I didn't know. Barbara didn't want me to worry when she knew I couldn't get back. Anything could have happened. Anything. Can you imagine? Of course you can't.

Why isn't it getting easier? Everyone says it will. It doesn't. It just gets further away.

Love you. Like a stuck record, skipping, skipping.

PS: Beetroot. I'm sorry there hasn't been any lately. I don't know why.

Twenty-Three

'Shipping is really bad news for cetaceans in the North Sea,' Young Robbie said, with great authority. 'We don't know how many dolphins and whales we lose to ship-strike every year, because if they get hit by one of those massive container carriers, the ship doesn't even notice, and then the body floats away to the bottom of the sea.'

'That's horrible,' Anna said, watching as he rolled the pastry with endearing diligence. 'Those poor creatures.'

'Yeah,' Robbie agreed. 'Then there's all the invasive species that come in with the ballast water. Container ships have these compartments in their hulls that scoop up water to balance their weight. They hold thousands of gallons. If they suck up a load of seawater near Japan, say, and then they come all the way over here to the Northern Hemisphere and unload, they have to dump all of that water – and whatever's in it – here. And with climate change our water is warmer, and species that wouldn't have been able to survive here before can now, and they're breeding, which is bad for the local ecosystem as it disrupts the food chain. That's how we've ended up with colonies of Japanese skeleton shrimp and the leathery sea squirt.'

'The what?' Anna laughed.

'The leathery sea squirt.'

'You made that name up!'

'I didn't!' Robbie said, laughing too. 'It's a real thing! It comes from Asia, and now it's here. Look it up.'

'I will,' she assured him, handing him the pastry cutter. He bent over the table, frowning as he concentrated on pressing out the fluted circles. *He's only ten*, she thought. *Eleven years ago he didn't exist, and yet here he is now, helping me with pastry and telling me things I didn't know.*

'Fishing can cause problems too,' the boy said. 'If a net gets lost, it stays around for years. Fish can get stuck in it, and then dolphins are attracted to the food source and can get stuck too. Then they suffocate, it's horrible.' He stopped what he was doing and looked at her with serious eyes. 'That's why you should only ever serve sustainably caught fish on your bench. There are labels you can look for.'

'Noted,' Anna said. 'You said something about nets the first time I met you. Remember, when you I gave you the sea purslane to try?'

'Oh yeah,' said the boy. 'Ghost nets get caught there all the time, especially after a storm.' He pushed the cutter into the last patch of pastry and leaned back. 'Is that all right?'

'Perfect. Okay, now to put them in the cases.' She handed him the tart tray.

Robbie nodded, his face a mask of utter concentration, and Anna was filled with a rush of affection for this little boy. She was glad she'd said yes to this evening, in fact, because

215

when Robert had called and asked her if she could watch Robbie at his place, Anna had almost said no.

'Me?'

'I know it's an imposition,' said Robert. 'I wouldn't usually ask, but I've had a call out on the lifeboat and Barbara's away in Inverness for the night. I wasn't supposed to be on the roster, but Mikey's gone down sick with some stomach bug and Robbie's begged me to ask you. He says there's a bake sale for charity at the school tomorrow and he wants you to help him make something for it. Don't worry if you'd rather not – I can ask someone else. He'll be all right for an hour or so until I can round someone up. I just don't want to leave him all evening.'

'No,' Anna said. 'It's fine, of course it is. I'll be there in half an hour.'

'Thank you, Anna,' he said, and she could hear the relief in his voice. 'Make yourself at home. I'll be back as soon as I can.'

So it was that Anna found herself in the MacKenzie family home, a stone-built two-storey house tucked away right at the top of Gamrie's tangle of sloping streets. Robert had gone by the time she'd arrived. Young Robbie had opened the door with a beaming smile on his face, and the frank happiness of the greeting settled the uncomfortable niggle in Anna's stomach. The boy offered her tea and biscuits in a large kitchen made comfortable by clutter, and by the time she held the mug in her hand, any trace of awkwardness Anna felt had melted away, perhaps because the place was so comfortably a home. Photographs and notes peppered the fridge door, a cobweb lurked in the corner of one window, a stack of correspondence was piled untidily on the kitchen table beside some half-done homework. Anna couldn't remember the last time she'd been in a place that felt so clearly shaped by the natural forces of family life.

'So, what are we going to put in the pastry?' the boy asked, as he neatly smoothed the last fluted circle into the tart tin.

'Have you got some jam?' she asked, crossing to the oven and flicking it on. 'You can't go wrong with a jam tart.'

Young Robbie wrinkled his nose. 'Can we make something a bit fancier? Otherwise Queen Victoria will win again and nobody wants that.'

'Queen Victoria?'

'A girl in my class. She's good at *everything*. Likes everyone to know it, too. I'd like to beat her at something for once.'

'It's not a competition though, is it?'

Robbie pushed his glasses up his nose. '*Everything*'s a competition where she's concerned.'

Anna laughed. 'All right. Let's see what else we can do, then. Put them in the fridge to chill for a minute. Your dad won't mind if I look in your cupboards for suggestions, will he? If not, I'll pop down the road and get something; the shop will still be open.'

'He won't mind. Food cupboards are those ones up there.' Robbie nodded at the four cabinets above the work surface as he carried the tray to the fridge.

Anna opened the first to find tins and packets of savoury

staples banked in semi-neat rows and quickly moved on to the second. She'd thought she'd found the same again and was about to shut the cupboard when a realization brought her to a standstill. The whole cabinet was full of jars of pickled beetroot, stacks and stacks of it. There must have been fifty unopened containers jammed into the space.

'Ahh,' Young Robbie's voice said, behind her. 'Yeah, not that cupboard.'

'You're beetroot fans in this house then, eh?'

'No,' the boy sighed. 'Dad can't stand it. Calls it the Devil's vegetable. Hates the smell. He won't even open a jar.' Anna looked at him over her shoulder and he shrugged. 'I've had it a couple of times. It's okay.'

'Then why—'

'My mum loved it. My grandma says that she ate so much of it when she was expecting me, they used to joke I was going to come out purple. And Dad ... he's got this thing where he always buys a jar every time he goes shopping. He says he doesn't even realize he's done it until he gets home and there it is in the bag. But then he can't throw it out. So it stays. You should see the cupboard under the stairs. It's so full I have to keep my skateboard in my room.'

Anna looked back at the jars of pickle. Her mouth had run dry.

'He's not weird,' Robbie said. 'He's not, I promise.'

She swallowed and turned around with a watery smile. 'I don't think he's weird.'

He tapped his fingers on the table, chewing his lower

lip, looking so much like a miniature version of his father. 'Grandma says he's still grieving, that's all.'

'I know. He loved your mum very much.'

Robbie nodded, distracted. 'Have you seen a picture? Of my mum?'

'No, never. I'd like to, though.'

The boy went to the fridge door and pulled a photograph from the papery melee. He looked at it for a second and then brought it over to her, holding it out with a solemn face. Anna took the photograph and looked at it. In it the *Cassie's Joy* floated at anchor in Gamrie's harbour, Crovie's line of houses barely visible in the distance across the water. A small woman with short dark hair stood on the deck, holding a toddler against her hip. Beside her stood Robert MacKenzie, both arms around the two of them, his face half-hidden against her hair as he kissed her head. Cassie and little Robbie were both laughing at the camera, her one free hand clutching at her husband's arm where it crossed over her chest. Anna was reminded, sharply, of that laughing picture of herself and her parents, the one that was beside her hearth in the Fishergirl's Luck. She took a breath and felt the heavy, painful thump of her heart, and tried to hold at bay the gathering tears.

'It's my favourite picture,' Robbie said quietly. 'Even if I don't remember it happening.'

Anna smiled. 'It's perfect.'

They were silent for a few more minutes, and the boy then took the photo and pinned it back on the fridge.

'He didn't buy any this time,' Robbie said, with his back still to her. 'He came home with the shopping but there wasn't any beetroot. I think—'

He stopped, and Anna hurriedly wiped the tears from her eyes before he turned around again.

'You think – what?' she asked, to cover the motion.

He gave a half-shrug. 'Doesn't matter.'

She wanted to pull him into a hug, but couldn't. Anna turned to the next cupboard instead, pulled it open and spied a jar of jam and a packet of ground almonds.

'Raspberry frangipane tarts,' she said. 'That should give Queen Victoria a run for her money, don't you think?'

Two hours later, the tarts were cooling on a rack and Anna sat beside Robbie at the table, helping him to finish his homework. The front door opened, the sound of the wind gusting through it, and then Robert MacKenzie appeared in the doorway, wet with rain. He looked tired, but smiled at the sight of them at the table.

'Hey,' he said. 'Looks as if you two have been busy.'

'You've got a budding baker here,' Anna said as she stood, not quite looking at him. 'Robbie did most of the work himself. I should be going.' She laid a hand on Young Robbie's shoulder, squeezing gently. 'Let me know how the bake sale goes tomorrow, eh?'

'You won't stay for a drink?' Robert asked, as he shrugged off his wet coat and hung it on a peg, scrubbing a hand through his hair.

'Thanks, but I'd best get going.'

'Where's your car? I didn't see it outside.'

'I didn't bring it. I walked.'

He dropped his hand. 'Then I'll take you home. You can't walk back – the storm's rolling onto shore.'

'I'll be fine. Really, I'd rather walk.' She couldn't bear the idea of being in the confined space of a car with him, trying to make small talk. Five years, and he was still buying his wife pickles he couldn't bring himself to throw out. The tragedy of it was too awful. 'Besides, you've got to get Robbie to bed.'

He looked at her, trying to fathom her out, a spark of concern deep in his eyes. Robert glanced over at his son, still at the table, and then back to her.

'I can look after myself,' she reminded him.

'Well, if you get down to the harbour and change your mind, you call me. And let me know when you get home. I'll not sleep otherwise.'

Anna gave a faint smile. 'All right.'

He frowned. 'Robbie, say thank you and goodbye.'

The boy shocked her by jumping up from the table and throwing his arms around her waist, holding on to her tightly. 'Thank you,' he said.

She wrapped her arms around him for a moment, hugging him against her belly, against the hidden bundle of nerves within. For a moment she felt tears pressing behind her lashes again. *Bloody hormones*, she thought, desperate that neither of them should see.

Robert followed her into the hallway to the door, watching silently as she pulled on her coat.

221

'Anna,' he said, when her hand was on the latch. 'Are you all right?'

'A bit tired, that's all,' she said, turning and flashing a quick smile. 'I'll see you sometime soon, I'm sure.'

There was a slight pause. 'Yeah,' he said quietly. 'Thank you. Really, you were a lifesaver. And don't worry. I promise I won't ask again.'

Nothing she could have said then would have been right. She nodded and pulled open the door. 'Night, Robert.'

'Night.'

Outside, a strong wind was whipping the first drops of cold rain into flurries that stung her cheeks. Anna turned down towards the ocean and then stopped for a moment, breathing in the coming storm. By the time she reached the harbour it was raining hard, but she had no intention of going back to the MacKenzie house. In Gamrie's harbour she saw the trawler Liam crewed on moored securely against the bobbing water, in port because of the storm that had seen the lifeboat called out. She stared at it, rain peppering her face, wind tearing at her hair. Across the bay flickered the faint lights of Crovie, the cliff a sheer block of darkness between.

Anna pulled out her phone.

'Liam,' she said, through lips growing numb, when he answered. 'Are you in Gamrie? I need to talk to you.'

'Well,' Cathy said. 'Look at it this way. At least now you've told him.'

Outside, the north wind was doing its best to blow the

Fishergirl's Luck into the sea. Inside, Anna lay curled in her bed with the phone to her ear as the rain lashed so hard against the window she could barely hear her friend speak.

'Yes,' she said. 'There is that.'

She'd stood in Liam's small room in the house near the harbour where he was lodging, the storm outside gathering more strength by the minute, and talked as simply as she could about something that was not simple at all. Liam had listened, head bowed in concentration, not looking at her.

'I know this isn't ideal, but I'm going to keep it,' she'd told him.

He'd looked at her then, his usual twinkle dimmed by a frown that creased his forehead. 'But I've got to go back to New Zealand. I'm going home really soon.'

'I know.'

He'd shaken his head, as if in denial that these two factors could ever be compatible.

'Maybe I shouldn't have told you,' Anna had ventured. 'Maybe it would have been better for you never to know.'

The look he'd given her had been a dark one. 'Maybe.'

'I'm going to go now,' she'd told him then. 'If you want to talk to me again, you know where I am.'

She was at the bottom of the stairs when he appeared at the top of them. 'You can't walk in this,' he said. 'I'll drive you.'

'It's fine, I'll—'

He was already on his way down. 'I'll drive you.'

Back at home in the Fishergirl's Luck, she'd stared at that photograph of her and her parents from so many years ago

and tried not to think about the cupboard full of more pickled beetroot than any one family could reasonably eat. What
would it be, to be loved like that? She saw Young Robbie's
solemn face in her mind. She'd picked up her phone and sent
Cathy a text that read *Are you awake?*

Now here she was, numb and empty apart from that tiny
part of herself that would one day, sooner than she could
currently comprehend, be another person.

'What are you going to do now?' Cathy asked.

'I told him it's up to him if he wants to talk to me again.
In the meantime . . .'

'In the meantime?'

Anna rolled over and stared at her ceiling, wondering how
many tiles the Fishergirl's Luck would have lost by morning.
'I'll work.'

Despite the elements beating against the walls, Anna
slept heavily through the night. By the time she'd woken
the next morning the worst of the storm had huffed itself
out, leaving behind it a scattering of debris and a stiff
breeze. Anna opened her front door to see Pat sweeping
the path in front of the Weaver's Nook, the sky overhead
leaden and grey.

Pat looked up as Anna stepped out of the Fishergirl's Luck.
Anna was struck by how tired her friend looked.

'Morning,' she said. 'That was a rough one.'

'Wasn't it just,' Pat said, wearily. 'Did you get any
sleep at all?'

'I slept really well, actually,' Anna said. 'I always feel safe

in the Fishergirl's Luck, no matter what's going on outside.'
Or even inside, she thought.

Pat smiled, but there was a shadow in her eyes that Anna hadn't seen before. 'Long may it last.'

'Pat? Are you all right?'

'There was another slip above the rental. Not a big one, there's not much damage, but it's a reminder of what could happen that we could do without. Not to mention it's another excuse for Frank to conveniently forget he's not the young man he used to be. He's up there now, scrambling about as if he's half the age he actually is, despite everything the doctor said.'

'I'll come and help,' Anna said immediately, and then realized something and had to think fast. 'Although – I've twanged something in my back. I'm not sure how much heavy lifting I'll be good for.'

'Don't you worry, love. Glynn and David are here if we need them. We'll manage.'

Anna looked out over the sea. The water was choppy, its depths stirred by the storm into shades of blue and green she'd not yet seen.

'I didn't expect summer storms when I moved here,' she said. 'I assumed that winters would be hard to deal with, but beyond that I hadn't thought. Will we get more?'

'Probably,' Pat told her. 'They've been getting worse every year, although this is the worst season we've had that I can remember. Let's hope that's it for a while, though. It wouldn't do for you not to be able to run lunches when we've had more people asking about you.'

Anna turned back. 'Really?'

'Oh, yes. Out of the five bookings we've got this week – including for the other house – four of them asked about the Fishergirl's Luck.'

'Wow. Guess I'd better be prepared then.'

Pat finished sweeping, and Anna could see how weary she was. It worried her, a nebulous fear. She was suddenly acutely aware how important the people she knew here had become to her.

But you're not staying, said a voice in her head. *Especially not now. Not with the baby on the way. How would that work, in the Fishergirl's Luck?*

'Why don't you and Frank come to me for dinner later?' she said. 'It'll save you having to think about it if you spend all day sorting out the rental.'

Later, Anna used the antibiotics excuse as a reason for not taking a glass of red with their spaghetti bolognese, glad and guilty in equal measure that neither of her friends questioned it any more than they had her excuse of having a bad back. She didn't like lying to Pat and Frank any more than she had liked lying to Rhona, and wondered how long she could hold out before telling her friends the true reason for her abstinence.

For the next two weeks she saw neither Liam Harper nor either of the MacKenzies, partly by design and partly because she was so genuinely busy. Anna happily sunk herself into work. The demand for lunch at the Fishergirl's Luck was so great that for the first week she ended up opening the bench on Thursday as well as Friday and Saturday, and on the second she added Wednesday as well.

'I've honestly never seen the village so busy, love,' Frank told her. 'It's obviously not a coincidence. You'd think we were Pennan, the number of people wandering about and taking photographs!'

By the time the second week came around, queues for the bench were already forming by 11.30 a.m., and by 11.50 the space Anna had available was full.

'You should add another bench,' said one frustrated customer. 'This is the third day we've tried to get a seat.'

'There's still the Inn, you know,' Phil reminded her, as he was passing and saw her in action as she was serving the mains on Saturday afternoon. 'I think it's clear now that you'd be more than capable of taking on the challenge and making it work.'

The thought was a pleasant one, and Anna realized that cooking at the Fishergirl's Luck had given her a new level of confidence in her own abilities. It made her wonder what she could have achieved in her life already if she hadn't been under Geoff's thumb for so long.

'Do you know who owns the Inn?' she asked Frank a few days later. 'Is there someone I could talk to about it, do you think?'

Frank's face, which had seemed to Anna to have taken on a greyish pall since the last storm, brightened. 'That sounds as if you're thinking of ways to stay here permanently!'

'Not seriously,' she said, keen to nip any gossip in the bud. 'Don't mention it to anyone, please.'

But when Frank tracked down a name and number for the owner, the conversation wasn't encouraging. They wanted to sell, not to rent, and the figure quoted to Anna, though modest by most standards, was far beyond what she could afford.

When she wasn't working, Anna slept like the dead. She'd clean down and all but crawl up the stairs to her bedroom, asleep before her head even touched the pillow. The nausea of her earliest weeks of pregnancy had eased off, much to her relief, but the exhaustion seemed permanent. She couldn't imagine pulling a full shift in a busy kitchen in this state.

The TripAdvisor reviews, meanwhile, racked up and up, never less than four stars and more usually five. They often mentioned more than the Fishergirl's Luck too, talking favourably about the places nearby that there were to stay, and other eateries along the coast.

'You should be so proud of yourself,' Cathy said, over the phone. 'I'm almost tempted to print all of these out and post them to Geoff. Imagine the look on his smug face!'

'Oh God, please don't even joke about that,' Anna shuddered. She could imagine the look all too well, and the fury that would replace it soon enough. 'He'd do something to sabotage me, I know he would.'

'You're a tiny place at the other end of the country,' Cathy said. 'Surely he can't be so insecure that he'd begrudge you your small measure of success?' There was a pause, and then her friend answered her own question. 'Actually, don't bother to answer that. God, that man is a dick. Still, at least we have the consolation that ratings are down for this new show of his.'

'Really?' Anna was genuinely surprised.

'Yup. Maybe the public is finally getting wise to Geoff Rowcliffe's brand of smug arrogance and seeing that it's neither an act, nor warranted.'

Anna sucked air over her bottom lip. 'Well then, I really do hope he never finds out about this place,' she said. 'He'd be sure to take it out on me if he did.'

Twenty-Four

July rolled on, and so did the storms. It seemed to Anna that not a week went by without at least one night where she was woken by the wind raging like an old drunk outside her window. It was after another rocky night of wind and rain that Douglas McKean resurfaced in Anna's life. Opening her door on Saturday morning to see how the flower tubs had fared overnight, she saw Frank leaving the Weaver's Nook with a plate sealed over with tinfoil.

'Frank?' she said. 'Where are you going?'

He turned to look at her, and she was struck by how old he looked. Perhaps he'd been kept awake by the storm and hadn't slept, she thought. He and Pat had been busy with the B&B at full capacity for weeks now, and the pace was obviously taking its toll.

'Morning, love. I'm running breakfast around for Dougie. His kitchen — well, what he calls a kitchen — is still out of commission.'

'When did that happen?'

'That slip a few weeks back,' said her neighbour. 'He won't let anyone but Old Robbie in to fix it, and the poor lad has got enough on his plate as it is. Pat and I said we'd make sure he's fed until it's sorted.'

Anna frowned. 'Oh, Frank – you and Pat have got enough of your own to do.'

Frank lifted one shoulder in a shrug and smiled. 'It's what neighbours do, love. Otherwise it'd be Old Robbie having to run over here umpteen times a week. Can't let the old man starve now, can we?'

Anna let him go but the conversation lingered as she prepped for lunchtime service. She served black cod on sticky rice with samphire and a sauce influenced by Japanese flavours, followed by a sorbet shot through with sea purslane and apple alongside a twist of caramel brittle and a shortbread crumble. It was an idea that had lingered in her mind since the night she'd looked after Young Robbie, and she tried not to think of him or his father as she made it.

'This is truly inspired,' said one of her guests, whose face was vaguely familiar though Anna couldn't quite place it. 'I've loved this. A lot of chefs talk about taking food to another level but I think this is the first time I've actually thought a chef has achieved it. Ironic, since I've not heard you say such a thing at all.'

Anna thanked the woman as she took her empty dessert plate. 'I'm using what I have, that's all,' she said. 'My dishes are pretty simple, really. It's a lot about the setting, I think.'

'As all the best chefs do,' the woman replied. 'As all the best meals are.'

Her takings, which were always fair, seemed to be far higher than usual that day.

Later, as Anna cleaned down, she looked at the ingredients she hadn't used and realized that there was enough for another small meal. She went over and knocked on Pat's door, following her friend into the kitchen when she answered.

'I can do Douglas McKean's dinner tonight,' Anna said. 'In fact, why don't we say I'll do it every night that I'm running lunches. Take some of the pressure off you.'

Pat looked surprised. 'Oh, you don't have to do that.'

'I know I don't, but I want to. I'm doing it for you and Frank, mind, not for that old troublemaker. And someone else will have to take it down there, I don't think I could bear to.'

Pat smiled, but it was a tired expression. 'Frank can do that. Thank you. If you're really sure, that would be a great help.'

Anna leaned forward and gave the older woman a hug. 'Of course I'm sure. Can't guarantee he won't find something to complain about in my food, though. Probably best not to tell him who cooked it.'

Later that evening her phone rang. Anna answered it expecting it to be Cathy, but it wasn't.

'It's Robert. Robert MacKenzie. Hi.'

'Hi.' For some reason her throat constricted. 'I— hi. How are you?'

'I'm fine. I've spoken to Frank and he's told me what you're doing for Dougie. I wanted to thank you, Anna. It's a very kind thing, especially considering how he's treated you.'

Anna found herself scrubbing her thumbnail against a non-existent mark on her worktop. 'It's nothing.'

'It's not nothing,' he said softly.

Anna cleared her throat, wishing she didn't like the sound of his voice quite so much. 'How's Robbie? I didn't hear how the bake sale went.'

'That was my fault, sorry. That you didn't hear, I mean.'

'Oh?'

There was a pause. 'He wanted to come and see you the next day to tell you all about it, but I got the impression that I'd overstepped the mark that night, by asking you to look after him. I thought it'd be better to take a step back.'

'No,' Anna said, 'No, I—' She stopped, unsure what to say. 'It wasn't that.'

'It was the beetroot, wasn't it?' Robert went on, in the same tone of voice. 'He told me you'd found it.'

'No – yes.' She sighed. 'I mean – it wasn't only the beetroot. It was – it was all a bit overwhelming, that's all. And I know that sounds weird, when all I was doing was baking in your kitchen with your son, but I've got stuff going on myself at the moment and it . . .' she trailed off, wondering why she couldn't be more articulate, wondering why it had all become such a big deal.

'No, I get it,' Robert said. 'I do. And I'm sorry, I really am.'

'You don't need to be sorry,' she said. 'It's nothing to do with you. It's me.'

'It's really not,' he said. 'I told you before, didn't I? Other people's grief is hard to deal with.'

'It wasn't—' Anna stopped herself. *It wasn't the grief,* she thought. *It was the love.*

'I've stopped buying it,' he said. 'The beetroot, I mean.'

'Yes,' she said. 'Yes, Robbie told me that, too.'

There was another silence. 'Well, I'd better go,' he said. 'Thanks again. I'll see you around?'

'Yeah,' Anna said. 'I'm sure.'

She held the phone in her hand for a long time after he'd hung up. Outside, the wind had dropped to barely a whisper.

Anna had been true to her word to Rhona, and had been trying to interest her friends in the industry in her pottery. It was a tricky proposition: chef-patrons were notoriously picky about what they chose to serve their food on, especially when setting up a new venture. In Anna's experience the process was a long one and required extensive testing, usually at the premises involved and alongside other pieces for comparative purposes. Rhona's style would also only fit a particular type of establishment. Still, Anna had faith in her friend's work and knew several chefs who were in various stages of opening or refurbishing eateries, so it couldn't hurt to encourage them to include Rhona's work in the mix.

Late on the Sunday morning following Anna's decision to help keep Douglas McKean fed, she was sitting on the sofa with a cup of tea and a bacon sandwich, wondering whether Glynn and David were going to come by, when the phone rang. She assumed it would be Cathy – they usually chatted at some point on a Sunday – and was surprised to hear a voice she recognized only vaguely.

'Anna?'

'Yes?'

'It's Brigitte March. You emailed me a few weeks ago about your friend's handmade flatware?'

Anna sat up straighter, putting her bacon sandwich down on the table and licking grease from her fingers. She'd met Brigitte at the filming of 'A Chef's Table' for *MasterChef* a few years before – Geoff had been one of the chefs, of course, and Anna had been invited along because the producers wanted more women's faces in the room. She and March – an up-and-coming head chef at that time – had been seated next to each other and the two women had chatted easily. When Anna had been contacting chefs on Rhona's behalf, Brigitte had been one of the first on Anna's list. When they had met Brigitte didn't have her own restaurant, but Anna had seen that it was surely only a matter of time.

'Brigitte! I'm so sorry, I didn't recognize your voice.'

Brigitte laughed. 'There's no reason you should. Look, I don't want to bother you for long – and I must apologize that it's taken so long for me to answer. The thing is that when I saw the review this morning – congratulations, by the way – it all came rushing back. And seeing Rhona's plates in action in the photograph made me realize that they're exactly what I've been trying to find for my new place.'

'Review?' Anna said. 'Do you mean on TripAdvisor? Did someone post a photo?'

There was a pause. 'You mean you haven't seen it? The Fishergirl's Luck has got a splash review in the *Observer* today. It's a great one, Anna – five stars and a wonderful write-up.'

Anna's mind went blank. Then something clicked into place. 'Adrienne Gail.'

'Yeah, she's the critic. Absolutely *loves* you.' Brigitte laughed again. 'If she raves about my place the way she did about yours when we finally open, I'll be on cloud nine.'

Anna remembered the woman at the bench the day before and kicked herself for not recognizing one of the UK's foremost food critics.

'I didn't recognize her,' Anna said. 'I've never met her in person myself, she always dealt with Geoff. I've only seen her in photos and on screen. Oh, *God*.'

'I wouldn't worry about that – she probably prefers it when restaurateurs are clueless about who she is,' Brigitte said.

'But it's only a bench in my garden! I'm not a real restaurant. I'm not even planning to run beyond the summer!'

'Well, whatever you're doing, you're doing it right. Good for you. I'd love to come and visit myself, but it's going to be months until I have time. But listen – could you put me in touch with this potter friend of yours? I'd really like to talk to her about custom flatware for this place.'

She and Brigitte talked for another few minutes before hanging up, but Anna was no longer really concentrating on the conversation. A review in the *Observer* – she had to know what it said. The minute she'd put the phone down she was opening her iPad to find the article online.

THE FISHERGIRL'S LUCK, ran the header, in huge bold type. Below it the standfirst read: 'A Tiny Hidden Jewel on the Wild Scottish Coast.'

It was, as Brigitte had said, a rave review. Adrienne Gail had apparently loved everything about her experience of eating at the Fishergirl's Luck, from the unconventional entrance into the village itself, which for her apparently constituted a perfect transition into the experience – 'I have never in my life before had to hike down a cliff to get to an eatery, and it is only now I see what a tragedy that is' – to having to queue with her five fellow guests. The food she called, among other rapturous descriptions, 'an inspired fusion of idea with practicality, skill with passion' that 'sat perfectly in its lonely, ocean-front setting'.

Anna read the whole thing twice and still struggled to take it in. There were far more experienced chefs than she who had never had a review like this from such a respected critic. An entire career could turn on this kind of attention. People with influence kept an eye on reviews like this, and new establishments deemed worthy of the column inches inevitably became talking points between other chefs, not to mention destinations for minted foodies who prided themselves on not being outdone by others of like mind. She wondered quite how this was going to affect her. After all, it had only taken a small write-up in a local freesheet to fill her table every time she opened it. Now Adrienne Gail had sent her national.

The review and all its implications were still rattling around Anna's head when a knock sounded at her door. Anna opened it to find Liam Harper hunched over against the brisk wind, his eyes dark beneath his thick wool hat.

'Hi,' he said. 'I probably should have called first. Sorry.'

'Come in,' Anna said, holding the door open wider for him. 'I'll make us some tea.'

Liam was quiet as she boiled the kettle, sitting on the sofa and contemplating something in the middle distance. Anna glanced at him from the kitchen, remembering the first night he had spent here, which seemed both years ago and yesterday. If she'd known then what she knew now, would she have let him stay that night, or any other? Anna didn't know.

'Here,' she said, once she'd poured the tea, holding out the mug. Liam took it with a faint smile. Anna sat opposite and sipped at her drink, waiting him out.

'I'm sorry I've not been in touch,' he said. 'I'm sorry that I haven't checked on you since that night that you came to tell me. It ... it was a lot to take in.'

'I know. It's all right.'

Liam gave a half-shrug. 'It's not all right. You're the one with the hard bit to do. I'm nothing but a bystander at this point.'

Anna raised a smile at that.

'Are you all right?' he said. 'I mean, you and ...' he nodded at her, eyes on her stomach.

'Far as I know,' she said. 'I feel fine. Scan's not for another three weeks.'

He looked bereft. 'That's not long before I'm booked to go home.'

'I know,' she said softly.

'That's what I wanted to talk to you about.'

'The scan?'

'No,' he shifted uncomfortably. 'Going home.'

'Okay,' Anna said. 'What about it?'

'I want you to come with me.'

Out of everything he could have said at that moment, those words were the last that she had been expecting. Anna almost dropped her mug in surprise. '*What?*'

Liam leaned forward. 'I want you to come with me to New Zealand. No – listen,' he said, as she opened her mouth to speak. 'Please, hear me out. Please?'

Anna nodded, and he took a breath and began to speak.

'I know this isn't what either of us planned. But I wasn't raised to abandon my responsibilities. If I was the kind of man to do that I wouldn't be going back to take over the farm in the first place. I'm not going to leave you to do this alone. But I have to go back. I have to. So . . . I want you to think about coming with me. There's plenty of room on the farm – there's an empty cottage I was planning to do up in any case, for me. We can have it for our own.'

'Whoa—' Anna said, putting her mug down on the floor and holding up both hands. 'Liam, stop. We're not even a couple! If I hadn't told you I was pregnant, you'd have never thought about me again. Now you want to set up home together, on the other side of the world?'

'It's not the other side of the world for me,' Liam said. 'It's home.'

'But—'

Liam put down his own mug, grasped her hands. 'We had fun, didn't we? We enjoyed each other's company. Why can't that carry on? It's worth a try, isn't it?'

'I can't just up sticks and move across the planet!'

'Why not?' he asked. 'I did. And you're not planning to stay here anyway, are you? So why *not* come to New Zealand? This place is no more home for you than it is for me. You don't have any family here. You don't have any ties. In New Zealand you'd have a family. You'd have me, you'd have my mum and dad, and so would our *baby*, Anna.'

'But I don't love you, Liam, not in the way that would make a move like that make sense. And you don't love me, either. You *know* you don't.'

'Maybe we'd fall in love,' he said stubbornly. 'We like each other. We find each other attractive. I've known relationships grow out of less than that, haven't you? Surely it's worth a try?'

Anna pulled her hands out of his and stood. She turned away from him, putting her hands over her face for a moment before dropping them to her sides. 'It won't work. We'd barely been seeing each other two months before your eye was caught by someone else. And that's fine. But to expect me to give up my entire life, to move to a country I don't know, with people I don't know . . .'

'You made friends here, you can make friends there. Even

if we don't end up a couple, it'd be a fresh start. You could make something fantastic out of that. You could start your own restaurant there, and you'd be a big fish in a small pond.'

'I'd have a *child*. How much time and energy do you think I'd really have to start a new business in an entirely new country? And what about money?'

'You'd have me and my parents to help you out,' he pointed out. 'And our baby would have a dad. Isn't that worth thinking about?'

'That's not fair.'

'No, it's not,' he said, eyes flashing. 'But then I don't really see that there's much about this situation that's fair to me, either.'

'Liam—'

He stood. 'All I'm asking is that you think about it. Please? Tell me you'll think about it.'

Anna raised her hands, a gesture of helplessness. 'Okay. I will. I'll think about it.'

'Ah,' said Cathy. 'Have to say, I did not see that coming.'

Anna rubbed a hand over her eyes. 'This is all such a mess. I can't go. I can't. It's ridiculous of him to even suggest it. So why do I feel as if I'm being an arse for dismissing it out of hand?'

'That's the patriarchy talking,' Cathy said. 'That bit of every woman ingrained to believe they can't make it without a man around.'

'But what if I can't?'

'Pish,' said her friend. 'Besides, you will have men around, just not this one. If he's so bent on taking responsibilities for his actions, if he wants to be an active part of his kid's life, then he's the one who's going to have to make the tough decision, not you. You aren't responsible for his parents, Anna, he is, and if it's a choice between staying here and being a good father and going home and being a good son, that's his problem, not yours.'

'That's harsh.'

'It is. Also not your problem. Don't let him make you think it is. If he was that bothered about it, he should have been more careful to be certain his wild oats were going to stay in his own field, shouldn't he?'

'I should never have come here,' Anna muttered. 'I should have done what you said and gone to Spain for a month.'

'Well,' said Cathy, 'say it quietly, but I think I was wrong about that.' Anna heard the rustle of paper and knew it was the copy of the *Observer* that her friend had on her lap. 'Anna, this review is huge. It's going to send you stratospheric. I can't wait to see what happens next.'

Anna sighed. 'What happens next is probably a nap, to be honest. Doesn't take much to wear me out, these days. This is far too much excitement for one day.'

Her nap was not to be, however, because no sooner had Anna said goodbye to Cathy and hung up than there was a loud knock at the door. It was Rhona, flush-cheeked and out of breath, as if she'd run all the way from Gamrie.

'You,' Rhona cried, flinging an arm around Anna as

soon as she opened the door, 'are the stuff dreams are made of, hen!'

Anna laughed and hugged her friend back. 'Why, what's happened?'

Rhona pulled back, a broad grin on her face. 'Brigitte bloody March, that's what's happened!'

Anna had forgotten her phone call amid the tumult of the review and Liam's visit. 'Ah! Did she call you?'

'She did indeed,' said Rhona, as Anna ushered her in and shut the door behind them. 'I said you and your restaurant were going to save me, didn't I? I said! Here, get this open, quick!' She held up a bottle. 'It's prosecco, not champers, but all in good time, eh?'

Anna took the bottle with a grin and went to get glasses. 'Well then, tell me what she said. It must have been good!'

'Good doesn't even cover it, my lass. She said she'd seen the review and the pictures – congratulations, by the way – and that she's been searching for the right flatware for her new place, and she thinks my work will be perfect. Wants me to kit out the whole bloody shebang!'

Anna returned with two full glasses of bubbles and held one out to Rhona. They chinked rims and sipped.

'Congratulations,' Anna said, genuinely delighted for her friend. 'I'm so happy for you, Rhona.'

'Aye well, I've no one but you to thank for it,' Rhona said, drinking deeply. 'You and that wee bench out there. You're a wonder.'

Anna was tempted to have more of her drink to celebrate

with her friend, but decided not to risk it. On her first visit to the doctor, a slightly patrician man who reminded Anna of her first headmaster, he'd pointed out rather bluntly that she wasn't as young as most of the women who came to him with their first pregnancy. She hoped that Rhona was too excited to notice that Anna wasn't drinking, but she should have known better.

'Eh, you can't still be on the pills, can you?' Rhona asked. 'Besides, there's hardly anything in this stuff. It's Sunday, you can sleep it off! Drink up, we're celebrating!'

Anna smiled. 'I'd best not.'

There was a moment where Anna could almost see the cogs turning in her friend's head. Then Rhona's eyes suddenly widened. 'Oh my God.'

'What?'

Her friend leaned forward. 'Are you ... *pregnant?*'

Anna felt the heat rush to her cheeks and cursed herself for it. 'What?'

'I saw Frank and Pat the other day. I asked after you and they said you were completely exhausted from all the catering, so much so that they thought you were conking out every moment you could get. It seemed strange to me – you're so fit, clambering over the cliffs like you do, not to mention that you said in London you used to work split-shifts. Then they said you'd cried off helping with the slip clear-up, which isn't like you at all ...'

'I've got a bad back,' Anna said weakly.

'What, as well as the ear infection? Really?'

'No, I—'

Anna glanced up at her friend and knew her face was red. Rhona's eyebrows were near her hairline.

'You are,' Rhona whispered. 'Aren't you? You're *pregnant*.'

With a burst of relief that brushed very close to euphoria, Anna gave in and nodded. 'Yes,' she said. 'I am. And I'm sorry I haven't told you before, that I lied, but my first scan isn't for another three weeks and—'

Rhona put down her glass, took Anna's from her and pulled her into a fierce hug. 'Are you happy about it?' she asked, her chin on Anna's shoulder.

Anna took a shuddering breath. 'Yes,' she said. 'It was such a huge shock at first, but ... yes. I am happy. Really happy, despite everything.'

Rhona pulled back, and Anna was touched to see that her friend's eyes were glistening. 'Then I'm happy for you, hen, and I'm here if you need anything. Anything at all. All right?'

Anna laughed, another explosion of relief, and pulled Rhona against her again. She'd only known this woman for a few months, but was suddenly so grateful for her that she could barely breathe. 'Thank you. Thank you so much.'

Twenty-Five

The fallout from the *Observer* review meant that Anna's email went into overdrive. Some messages were from surprised old acquaintances, well-wishes from people she had left behind following her split from Geoff. Others were from newspapers and magazines wanting to know the story behind what the Internet was dubbing 'The smallest restaurant in the UK', although how they'd got her email in the first place was anyone's guess. Anna was intensely glad that she'd made her landline number ex-directory, and that her mobile number wasn't public. That didn't stop the call she got a few days later, though. Anna looked at her screen and saw a name she hadn't thought about in years.

'Hello, Anna,' said the voice, when she answered the phone. 'This is Melissa Stark here. You probably won't remember me, but—'

'Melissa, hi,' said Anna. 'Of course I remember you. The editor of Geoff's cookbooks, right? How are you? It's been a while.'

Melissa laughed. 'I should have known better than to think you'd forget,' she said. 'You always were so attentive to detail. I'm fine, thank you. Actually, I'm publishing director now.

I would ask how you are, but I'm not sure I need to – I read Adrienne Gail's review of your place. It sounds so amazing.'

'Oh,' Anna said, faintly embarrassed. This woman regularly worked on the cookbooks of hugely popular celebrity chefs. 'Well, thank you, that's kind of you to say.'

'Actually, it's why I'm calling,' Melissa went on. 'Look, I'm going to be honest. I've kept your number all this time because I always had a feeling you were one to watch. We both know you were the one who did the heavy lifting on Geoff's first book. Even then I could see that you had an instinct for how a recipe should be presented. We've been on the lookout for new voices in the cookery genre here, and Anna – I think you're exactly what we need on our list.'

Anna found herself staring out of the window at the quilted seascape beyond the Fishergirl's Luck. 'Sorry,' she said, at a loss. 'I don't think I know what you mean.'

'I'd like to produce a cookbook with you,' the woman said. '"*Lunch at the Fishergirl's Luck*: *recipes from the house beneath the cliffs*." It's early days and that's only a tentative title, of course, and open for discussion, but I can see the cover now. The press release would almost write itself.'

'I—' Anna tried to find something to say, but found she couldn't.

'Sorry,' Melissa laughed again. 'I know this is out of the blue. You were probably right in the middle of something. I can call back, if you like, at a more convenient time?'

'No, it's fine,' Anna said. 'You caught me a bit by surprise, that's all. Thank you for being interested. I have actually always wanted to produce a cookbook. I've been writing up the recipes I've cooked here as I've gone along.'

'See, I knew you'd be a dream to work with,' Melissa said. 'Maybe we can schedule a Zoom chat for sometime next week?'

Not all the publicity was as positive as that, however. Anna was upset to read a letter in the same local newspaper that had first told the area of the lunch club's existence, written by someone who was clearly unimpressed by her little venture. It was by a woman called Jean Padgett, who lived in Macduff and described herself as 'worried for the traditional and intrinsic fabric of these villages', and accused Anna of eroding the very nature of what made Crovie so special for the 'genuine residents'.

'I don't know what she means,' Anna said to Frank, as they discussed it. 'How am I doing damage? Is it because so many more people are visiting and staying? That's a good thing, isn't it? Without people renting these places, how would their owners pay for the upkeep?'

'Ignore it, love,' Frank advised her. 'Padgett is one of those people who's always angry about something, usually some terrible injustice that she feels has been inflicted on her. She and Dougie go way back.'

'Oh, I see,' Anna said. She'd thought she'd finally escaped McKean's ire. He'd been mercifully quiet for weeks. She wondered whether there was any mention of Jean Padgett in Bren's cookbook.

'Don't let it bother you,' Pat advised her. 'What right does she have to complain on our behalf? Frank and I will write a letter of our own, saying how much we love what you're doing. We'll ask the rest of the Usual Suspects to do the same. That'll put her in her place.'

'Oh no, please don't,' Anna said.

'Looks like the mystery of who called the council on you has been solved, at least,' Frank pointed out. 'She also takes the health and safety division to task for not doing their job properly and shutting you down. She all but accuses them of corruption for giving you your five-star rating!'

Anna resolved to do what Frank said and put the letter behind her, but that proved impossible when the BBC's area office sent a film crew to do a piece for the local news. She tried to be accommodating, even letting them film as she prepped for the Friday service, answering questions as she worked. When she mentioned how supportive the local community had been, though, the reporter interjected.

'Not everyone's happy about "Lunch at the Fishergirl's Luck" though, are they?' he said. 'We spoke to a woman called Jean Padgett, who was unhappy enough to write to the local paper about what you're doing here.'

'I'm sorry that Ms Padgett's unhappy,' Anna said carefully. 'But she doesn't live here, or know me or the locals who *are* in favour of the lunch club. Perhaps if she did, she'd see that so far it's been nothing but positive for the village.'

'I know your friends are supportive, but that doesn't tell the whole story, does it?' the reporter pressed.

'What do you mean?' Anna asked, although she had a horrible feeling she already knew.

'Well, Mrs Padgett put us in touch with an old acquaintance of hers who *does* live here. His name is Douglas McKean. We went to see Mr McKean before we came here. Are you aware how unhappy he is with the situation?'

Anna took a breath. 'Yes, I am. I've tried to talk to him, and I've even invited him to eat here, but he's ignored my attempts to be friendly.'

'Mr McKean is the last original resident of Crovie, isn't he? Do you feel that newcomers have a responsibility to be respectful of such residents?'

'Of course I do,' Anna said. 'But I don't believe I'm doing anything disrespectful, either to Crovie or to Mr McKean. I've made every attempt to be as respectful as I can. I'm not sure he can claim the same. And in fact, I can tell you exactly where Mr McKean's dislike of the Fishergirl's Luck comes from,' she said. 'For years he has been telling everyone who will listen that he is the real owner of this building.'

'He told us the same thing,' said the reporter. 'It sounds as if the previous owner might have benefitted unfairly from a badly written legal transfer of property. We were planning to do some investigating into the matter.'

Anna took a deep breath. She'd been hoping the subject wouldn't come up, but had thought it best to be prepared anyway. She turned to pick up a folder that had arrived from her solicitor in the post a few days before. Sliding the contents out, she spread the documents on the table.

'These are the original deeds to the property,' Anna said, pointing to the date. 'Brenda MacKenzie purchased this shed – as it was then – in 1938, from her father, who owned it. If you check the records, you will see that the MacKenzie family home, land and the boat that was their business was transferred in totality to the family of Douglas McKean in 1943, years after Bren had become the owner. Perhaps Mr McKean wasn't aware of the formal agreement that Bren had made to become the owner of this property, but as you can see, the legal standing is clear. This place has never belonged to any McKean, least of all to Douglas.'

The interview was wrapped up shortly afterwards, and the reporter seemed warm enough as he was leaving, but Anna spent the rest of the day worrying about how the piece would make her look. She had to watch the report, though, Anna knew that – if there was a wider group of locals unhappy about the lunch club she needed to know.

It quickly became apparent that Anna needn't have worried. Out of Jean Padgett, Douglas McKean and herself, even Anna could tell that she was the only one who sounded even vaguely reasonable. Anna looked closely at the woman accusing her of being insensitive, but didn't recognize her. To her relief, Anna realized that the journalist had also spoken to other people Anna didn't know but who all seemed enthusiastic about the idea of a restaurant, however small, in Crovie.

'We could do with more places opening along this coast,' said one man. 'Too many closing every year. It's a good thing, what she's about. Cannae see why anyone would ha' a problem wi' it.'

Douglas McKean himself was as angry as Anna had ever seen him. 'Taking our property,' he spat. 'Should be ashamed to show her face.' The report finished with the revelation that Anna – and Bren before her – had most definitely acquired the bothy legally, and owed nothing to the furious old man.

'You came across really well, hen,' Rhona told her, when she called later that evening, something she'd done every day since she'd learned of the pregnancy, which touched Anna more than she could say. 'You don't need to worry.'

'I'm not anymore,' Anna said. 'It was nice to hear a few locals I don't know speaking in my favour. Made me think there might be more out there.'

'There are,' Rhona assured her. 'So stick to listening to those voices, not the negative ones.'

'Did you hear Douglas McKean?' Anna asked.

'Ach, that old fool doesn't know how to talk sense, never has,' Rhona said. 'You've got better things to think about. Don't give him the time of day. By the way, I bumped into Phil and Marie in the Co-Op a few days ago. Phil's still banging on about you taking the Inn.'

'He says the same to me every time I see him,' Anna said. 'He might change his tune if he knew the chef was going to be out of action for a few months with a new baby.'

'Nah, of course he wouldn't,' Rhona said. 'That place would need a ton of doing up before you could open. Bairn could be crawling by the time it was ready.'

Anna leaned over the kitchen sink to look out of the window. There was a dark smudge on the horizon, pressing down over the unsettled sea. Another storm spinning towards the coast.

'I'd still have to raise the money,' she pointed out. 'My savings are going to be eaten up pretty quickly in the next few months.'

'Have you started buying baby stuff yet?'

'No, I don't want to until after the scan next week. Besides, I haven't had time, to be honest.' She didn't add that surely there was no point until she had somewhere permanent to live. Someplace that might actually be practical to raise a child in. Someplace that wasn't Crovie. Anna had the feeling that would upset Rhona, who, along with everyone else, seemed to have forgotten that Anna intended to leave, and soon. 'On top of that, I hate the thought of Pat and Frank seeing something that lets on before I've told them.'

'Ach, they'd understand. Do you want me to come with you for the scan?' Rhona asked. 'I'm happy to.'

Anna turned away from the window. 'That's really sweet of you, but Liam's going to come. He called the other day and said he wanted to.' That had been a taut conversation, but Anna hadn't felt as if she could refuse. Whatever happened, wherever she and Liam ended up, he was still the baby's father. They had to find some way to make it work.

'Fair enough,' said Rhona. 'Right then, I'd best be off. Got to set another firing off yet tonight. It's all go!'

Anna went outside to drag her tubs of flowers closer to the house, the better to survive the wind, which was already getting up.

The storm made landfall overnight, rattling the windows of the Fishergirl's Luck hard enough to wake her. She lay

253

with one hand on her stomach, listening to the whistle and scream of the wind against the window until she drifted off again, her dreams full of indistinct shapes transcribed from nebulous fears. She had an unspoken terror that there was a second shoe about to drop, and could only hope it wasn't a premonition about the scan.

The next morning the wind was high and it was still raining hard. Anna realized there was no way she could go ahead with lunch club. She had set up a Facebook page specifically so that she could alert would-be visitors any time she would have to cancel for any reason, and by ten o'clock she had posted to explain that the weather had forced her to cancel for the day. She immediately received a few replies, some expressing their support, others their disappointment. More than one person, presumably those who had never visited Crovie and so had no real idea of what the village or the Fishergirl's Luck was truly like, suggested that at times like these she move lunch club indoors.

Anna closed her iPad and listened to the whistle of the wind outside, wondering what to do with her day now that she didn't have six three-course meals to prepare. These days, her week revolved around these lunchtime services – what she would cook for them, what produce she could find from local sources, what inspiration she could take from Bren's notebook, from her own grandmother's. Sometimes she didn't recognize the person she had become in the short months since she had arrived in Crovie. When she'd got here,

Anna had been considering giving up cooking for good. She couldn't begin to imagine, now, how that thought had ever crossed her mind.

Resolved to spend a lazy morning on the sofa under a blanket, Anna made herself a mug of tea and settled down with Bren's recipe book. Even if she couldn't cook today, she could look at recipes for future lunch services. She flicked gently through the book, searching out more of her predecessor's neat little annotations. It was almost like time-travel, the way they flitted back and forth through the years with their sometimes cryptic memories of times past. Beside a recipe for hot ginger pudding, for example, Bren had scribbled a mention that in December 1996 she'd had to make it with ground ginger instead of stem ginger from a jar, which was fine but in future if she did so she would add a teaspoon of mixed spice to lift the flavour. In January 1979, Bren wrote an entirely new recipe, a lemon sponge cake with home-made raspberry jam stirred in alongside nibs of marzipan, and noted that this had evolved out of necessity because a snowstorm had left the village cut off for a week and she'd been using up what she had left in the cupboards.

Took a piece to each house, the note added. *Even DM, though he would not accept it. Cut his nose off to spite his face, that fool would.*

Anna shook her head at Douglas McKean's stubborn determination. Then she wondered if Bren had mentioned adverse weather anywhere, particularly the event in 1953 that had changed the place forever. She kept reading through notes, all too fascinating to pass over, until she came to one that spoke of the great storm. It was jotted beside a recipe for Dundee cake. Bren's penmanship had taken on a spiky quality, less neat than usual, and Anna could almost feel the shock, echoing down through the years.

Terrible night, terrible day. I baked in the stove, cake after cake, all through the night, just to drown out the rage of the sea. I heard the crash of the boats being torn from the shore. One hit the side of the bothy before it rolled out to its end beneath the waves. I thought I would be next, that I and this place would be swallowed up whole by the storm. But this morning, here we still are, while so much else has gone from the village. All of Douglas McKean's boats, including my father's, gone, gone without a trace. He can't ever hope to replace them. He's done for. Yet here, in this place, I was fairly untouched. A tile or two from the roof will need replacing, that's all. In this place I made my luck, and it has always been lucky for me. In fact I think I should rename her. She's more than a shed. She is the Fishergirl's Luck.

Anna sat back, looking at the stove, trying to imagine Bren moving around this small space as that immense storm had ripped and battered its cruel way around her. How terrifying it must have been, and yet how safe these walls had proven to be. Immovable, like the house's first owner. Anna was delighted, too, to have the knowledge of how the bothy had come by its unusual name, straight from the words of the woman who had named it.

I must tell Robert, she thought, and before Anna had registered what she was doing, she had picked up the phone and dialled his number.

The call was answered on the first ring and a harried voice on the other end barked, 'Yes?'

Anna was taken aback, both at the tone and the timbre. It was a woman's voice, not either of the MacKenzie boys. 'I – I'm sorry, perhaps I've dialled the wrong number? I was trying to reach the MacKenzie house.'

'You have. This is Barbara,' said the voice, still fractious. 'Is this about Young Robbie? If not, I have to keep the line clear.'

Anna's heart froze. 'What? What's happened?'

'Who is this?' Barbara asked.

'I – sorry,' Anna said. 'I'm a friend. My name's Anna Campbell, I bought the Fishergirl's Luck from Robert, and—'

'Oh,' said the woman on the other end of the line. 'Yes. Young Robbie was so pleased with the baking the two of you did together.'

'Is he all right?' Anna asked. 'Has something happened?'

'He hasn't come back from dolphin patrol,' Barbara said, her voice laced with tears. 'I stayed here last night because Old Robbie was with the lifeboat. When I got up this morning he'd snuck out, left a note telling me not to worry. But the dinghy's gone! I've got the lads out looking for him, but – look, I've got to go. In case he calls – or they do.'

'Of course,' Anna said, her heart beating to a sick rhythm. 'Call me if there's anything I can do.'

257

Anna sat staring at the phone once they had hung up. The thought that Young Robbie MacKenzie had been out amid the storm tide was horrifying. Even if the worst of the weather had passed, the chop was still bad even now. How could a boy of ten navigate a wooden dinghy through such a swell? The cold Anna felt gave way to sweat. She sat on the sofa and put both hands over her face. Did Robert know that his son was missing? She hadn't thought to ask Barbara. He wasn't home, so probably not. Unless he knew but couldn't come back for some reason. If he was stuck out somewhere on a call with the lifeboat, for example. Anna couldn't bear to think of how awful that would be for him – not knowing where Robbie was, unable to search for the boy himself. Look at how broken he had been by his wife's death. If his son were to—

'Oh, Robbie,' Anna whispered, close to tears.

She thought of the last time she'd seen the boy. It was a few weeks past now. She'd been up on the cliffs walk, headed towards Troup Head, searching to see if any of the wild gooseberries that Bren had mentioned in one of her notes were still growing where she had described. Anna had passed the cove where she'd picked the sea purslane on the day she'd first met both of the MacKenzies together. Young Robbie had been too far away to see her, but the bright flash of his yellow windcheater had stood out so vividly against the grey-green sea, like a pennant calling for her attention. He'd been bringing the dinghy into shore. That was obviously a favourite spot of his, she thought, although that wasn't surprising, given what he'd told her on that first day, when he and his father had rescued her from the cliff and brought her back to Crovie. What was it Robbie said? That the cove was on the dolphins' route. Anna had assumed that's why he'd gone back there again, because it'd give him a good chance to see the pod.

Anna sat up straighter, her heart thumping. What had the boy been doing down there? She recalled him now, leaning over the side of the tiny boat, pulling at something.

A net. He'd been dragging a net out of the water.

Anna grabbed at Bren's notebook, frantically paging through it until she found the note that had led her to look for the gooseberries in the first place. Bren had made a gooseberry fool with the small, tart fruits, but Anna had in mind to use the recipe as a base for a gooseberry and amaretto semifreddo that she thought would be a perfect way to follow a rich Cullen Skink. But there had been something else mentioned in Bren's note, too.

Bushes laden this day, the note read. *Looked down upon the shore and saw a dolphin belly-up on the beach, poor wee beastie. Rolled in a net, t'was, and drowned. August 1976.*

Anna pressed the fingers of one hand to her lips, her heart racing. What else had Robbie told her, the night she'd ended up baking with him? He'd talked about how lost fishing nets were terrible for dolphins and how they were always washing up in that cove, especially after a storm.

With a cry Anna was off the sofa and out of the door, pausing only to push her feet into her walking boots and grab her coat. Outside, she crossed to the Weaver's Nook amid a squall of wind and rain and banged rapidly on the door.

'Anna! Whatever's the matter?' Frank Thorpe asked, as he opened the tradesman's entrance.

Selkie lass,

    I'm sorry, I'm so sorry. If you're out there, keep him safe.
I'll find him. I promise I'll never leave him alone again.
    Bring him back to me.
    Please. Please.
    I can't lose him too.
    I can't—

Twenty-Six

Frank insisted on coming with her, despite the wind and rain.

'I don't even know if I'm right,' Anna told him, shouting into the wind as they climbed the village steps towards the cliff track.

'Better safe than sorry, love. We've got to check,' Frank shouted back, hefting the rope she'd asked for with him. He'd insisted on carrying it. Pat had tried to suggest that Anna went to David and Glynn instead, and as soon as she'd said it, Anna wished she'd thought of that herself in the first place. Once he'd heard what was going on, though, Frank was adamant. He was going with her, he was carrying the rope, and that was that.

They didn't talk much as they rushed along the route, concentrating instead on keeping their footing on the wet ground. The rain blatted at their faces as Anna looked for the place where she'd left the path the first time she'd been up here on her own. They reached the gorse bush that blocked the way.

'Be careful,' she warned Frank. 'It looks as if there's been more slippage.'

'Probably last night,' he told her. 'There's been another

over the village. Poured yet more earth on the rental's roof. On Dougie's place, too. It's a mess.'

The sea was still washing rough waves against the shore, scattering tattered, breaking curls of ashy blue-green. The rain had lessened but Anna had to shield her eyes and squint to make out the lower cliff.

'I can't see anything,' she called. 'I don't think he's—'

Her words died in her throat as she saw something in the tide. It caught her eye, turned over by a wave, disappeared, rose again.

'Oh God! Is that – is that the dinghy?'

Turquoise blue and gleaming white, the splintered remains of the *Silver Darling* were rolling in the waves, almost too small to see amid the turbulent expanse of the Moray Firth.

Frank's face told of Anna's own horror. 'No,' he muttered, ghostly white, 'Oh, no, no.'

Anna stumbled forward, trying to see the stretch of shore she knew was beneath them. Loose stones and earth moved beneath her feet. Below, more of the wrecked dinghy revealed itself, Bren's faithful little boat washed up in pieces no more substantial than kindling. It must have been smashed against the rocks by the waves.

No one could survive that, Anna thought, numb, frozen to the bone. Yet she kept edging down, losing her footing on the wet earth with each step, grasping clumps of foliage as she went.

'Anna,' Frank shouted. 'It's not safe. Come back! Here—'

She glanced back up at him to see that he was winding

the rope around the gorse bush. Frank tied it off, then threw the coil down to her.

'Come back up, love,' he urged her. 'There's nowt we can do now.'

Anna took hold of the rope. Her feet were slipping constantly. Frank was right, there was nothing they could do. Robert MacKenzie's face appeared in her mind, the depth of that flash of pain she'd seen cross his face on the first night they'd met, and the breath left her lungs as if someone had crushed her chest. How could he survive this? How could anyone?

'Anna,' Frank shouted, again.

As she turned back to the cliff, something caught her eye. A flash, below her, barely there. Anna turned back again but it had gone.

'Anna,' Frank urged. 'I'm worried this bush isn't going to hold. You've got to come back.'

'Wait,' she said, as much to herself as to him. 'I need – give me a minute.'

Holding on to the rope she edged lower, leaning out as far as she dared, praying that the bush would hold her weight. There it was again, so close to the cliff that the overhang on which she stood had almost hidden it from her.

A flash of yellow.

Anna screamed. No words, just an explosion of sound.

'What?' Frank shouted, as she started scrambling down the cliff.

'He's here!' Anna yelled back. 'He's here, Robbie's here!'

'Anna, wait!'

She looked back up at Frank. 'I can't leave him there on his own! I can't see how badly he's hurt! Call the lifeguard! Call *someone*! I'm going down.'

'Anna!'

She didn't hear anything else Frank said. Anna inched her way down the cliff, more of the shoreline appearing as she did so. Robbie was a tiny figure wrapped up in his yellow waterproof, backed against the cliff.

'Robbie,' she shouted. 'ROBBIE!'

The boy looked up, pushing back his hood. Anna almost sobbed with relief as he got to his feet. *He can move*, she told herself, the relief acute. She couldn't even see any scrapes on his face.

'Anna!'

She reached out an arm and he stretched out his, but there was still too much distance between them. The rope didn't quite reach. The ground beneath her feet began to give way and she scrabbled to find her footing.

'Stay back!' Anna shouted down to the boy.

She made it to the ground and Robbie threw himself against her. Anna hugged him tightly and they held on to each other, crying.

'I thought the waves would be okay but they weren't and I couldn't turn around to get back home,' Robbie sobbed. 'I brought the *Silver Darling* in here and anchored her but then a wave smashed her on the rocks and I was trapped. I dropped my phone! Dad always makes sure there's a flare in the dinghy but it got washed away and every time I tried to climb the cliff it kept slipping and I was scared. I thought no one would ever find me. I didn't – I didn't – I didn't know what to do.'

'It's all right,' Anna said, still holding him close. 'Frank will call someone. They'll come and get us. It's all right. Are you hurt? Did you bang your head?'

'No,' Robbie cried. 'But I'm so cold!'

Anna looked around and saw that Robbie had been sitting in what was probably the most sheltered part of the cove. 'Come on,' she said.

Anna took off her coat and then sat down with her body between a large boulder and the cliff. She pulled the boy onto her lap. Robbie curled against her, his head beneath her chin, the wet hood of his jacket pressing into her throat. Anna tucked her coat under her feet, then pulled it over Robbie up to his chin. She wrapped her arms around him and felt him shivering against her.

'It's all right,' she said. 'Someone will be here soon. We're going to be all right.'

Her back and legs were cold, but gradually the boy stopped shivering. Anna didn't want him to sleep and so tried to keep him talking.

'Tell me about the bake sale,' she said. 'I haven't seen you since we made the tarts.'

'I sold them all!' Robbie said, the pride clear in his voice, despite the tremor. 'Every single one! They made £9.50!'

'That's amazing!' Anna said. 'Well done. I'm not surprised, though, they were delicious.'

'You know the best bit, though?' Robbie said, in a

conspiratorial tone. 'Queen Victoria had two of her buns left at the end of the day, even though they had icing on!'

'Well,' said Anna, smiling despite her discomfort. 'That sounds to me as if she definitely didn't win for once.'

'No, she did not,' the boy said emphatically. 'And she was *not* happy. She'll try even harder for the next one now. You'll have to help me again.'

'I'm always happy to help you,' Anna said, and hugged him tighter, aware of how very true the words were.

After that, Anna tried to ask him as many questions about dolphins as she could come up with. It was as much to distract herself as it was to keep Robbie awake. She couldn't have left him on his own down here and there was no way Anna would have sent Frank down the cliff himself, but now her thoughts rotated around an unquenchable fear. *What about the baby? Is it all right? What have I done?*

Even with her chef's internal clock, Anna had no idea how long they sat there. The wind dropped but the rain persisted, even as the clouds began to break overhead. It was the horn they heard first, a low bellow that echoed against the rock over their heads. Robbie moved against Anna, pushing himself up.

'That's the lifeboat!' the boy shouted, as the sound came again. 'That's my dad!'

The lifeboat ploughed into view, pushing through the wash as it turned towards the cove, Robert MacKenzie standing at its prow. As soon as it got close enough he was over the side and into the water, splashing towards them as if he were racing the waves to the shore. Robbie scrambled up and ran towards his dad. When Robert reached his son he collapsed to his knees in the wet sand, crushing the boy to him.

'I'm sorry, Dad,' Anna could hear Young Robbie saying against his dad's shoulder. 'I only wanted to make sure the dolphins were safe. I'm sorry.'

'It's all right,' Robert told him, his cheek against his son's hair, his face wet with rain and tears. 'But what would I do without you? What would I *do*?'

More of the lifeboat crew were on land now. One wrapped a blanket around Robbie's shoulders, another held one out to Anna. As she reached the MacKenzies, Robert grabbed her hand and pulled her down to him, wrapping an arm around her so that he held her as tightly as he held his son. After a second he pulled back to frame Anna's face with one hand.

'Are you all right?' he asked. 'Tell me you're not hurt.'

Anna smiled through tears. 'I'm okay,' she said. 'I'm okay.'

Robert studied her face before brushing his thumb against her bottom lip. Then he pulled her against him again, his face in her damp hair. Anna felt Young Robbie snake one arm around her waist, the three of them holding each other on that wet, cold shore.

'Thank you,' said Robert MacKenzie, into her ear. 'Thank you.'

At the hospital, they had to explain that no, Anna wasn't

Robbie's mother; no, she wasn't his stepmother, either. Perhaps that was when she should have told Robert about the baby, but he was so relieved to have Robbie back unharmed that she couldn't bear to put her worries on his shoulders.

'I'm pregnant,' she told the doctor who came to the small, sterile cubicle to check her over. 'I'm due to have my first scan this week. I'm afraid that—' Anna couldn't say the words, couldn't vocalize her fear.

The doctor nodded her understanding with a brief, efficient smile. 'Okay, well, let's do the scan now, shall we? Is there anyone you want to call?'

For a split second, Anna found herself thinking of Robert MacKenzie. She could still feel his thumb brushing over her lip.

'Yes,' she said. 'I need to call the father.'

Anna asked one of the nurses to tell the MacKenzies that she had gone home. She waited for Liam in the maternity wing, listening to the cry of new lives not long into the world. How strange it was, she thought, that she could want something so badly that three months ago had not even occurred to her could exist.

'The baby seems fine,' said the sonographer, as she and Liam stared at the pulsing black-and-white image on the screen. 'Good heart rate, no sign that there's anything to be worried about. Would you like a picture?'

'Yes,' Anna tried to say, and realized that her voice was hoarse from the lump that had formed in her throat. Looking at an image of the tiny form on the screen was humbling in a way she had never before experienced. *Hi, baby,* she thought, light-headed with relief. *Hi there. I'm your mum. We're going to have so much fun together, you and I. And I promise never to put you in danger like that again.*

Liam took her hand and Anna looked up at him.

'I'm going to be a dad,' Liam said, his voice cracking. 'Just look at that little thing!'

Anna laughed and squeezed his hand, glad that he was there.

Afterwards, they found a café for some lunch, quietly absorbing the morning's events. Outside, the sun had broken through the clouds and shone on puddles left by the rain.

'Are you going to tell your folks now?' Anna asked.

Liam shrugged. 'I'm not sure whether to do that straight away or when I get home,' he said. 'It's not long until I go now.'

Anna nodded, sipping her tea and wondering if he would bring up the idea of her going with him again. From his face it looked as if he wanted to, but was reluctant.

'Are *you* planning to start telling people?' he asked, instead.

'A couple of people already know,' Anna said. 'I can wait until you've gone to tell everyone else though, if you like.'

He looked out of the window. The sky was darkening again, a brusque wind buffeting the street. 'I wouldn't ask you to do that. They're going to think what they think, whenever you tell them.' Liam looked at her and smiled slightly. 'Although if any of them can change your mind about coming with me ...'

Anna shifted uncomfortably. 'Liam ...'

'I know, I know.' He tilted his head to one side. 'It's amazing, what's been happening with the lunch club. Everyone's talking about it. It seems to me that you could really be going places – but how's that going to fit in with raising a baby on your own?'

Anna shrugged. 'Women have done it before. I'll work it out.'

He took a mouthful of his coffee. 'Maybe I should come back and visit.'

She laid a hand on his arm. 'Of course you should.'

'I can tell you now that my mum's going to want to come.'

Anna smiled. 'That's okay.'

'And when the baby's old enough, you can come and visit New Zealand, too.'

'And in between, there's the Internet. Right?'

Liam nodded.

'I'm not going to pretend you're not part of our baby's life, Liam,' Anna said. 'We have to find a way to make it work for us, that's all. The three of us.'

'I wish I was going to be here longer, if only to make sure you look after yourself,' Liam said. 'What with all this restaurant stuff, I was already worried you were working too hard. And now – Anna, climbing down a cliff?'

She sipped her tea. 'I couldn't leave Robbie there on his own. I couldn't. And everything's fine, isn't it? I'll never do anything like that again. One daring rescue in a lifetime is enough. Don't worry, Liam. Besides, once I tell Pat and Frank I suspect I'll have two pairs of eyes watching out for me very closely.'

Liam drove her back to Crovie and lit her a fire before

leaving her curled up on the sofa beneath a blanket. Anna lay in the warm, one hand against her belly, thinking over everything that had happened. Most of all, she found herself thinking of Robert MacKenzie. After the night that she'd looked after Young Robbie, she'd pulled back, and Robert had done the same. There had been no more invitations to join dolphin patrol. She wondered whether this was because they hadn't been out as much because of the storms, or if it had more to do with a deliberate withdrawal on the part of the elder MacKenzie in the wake of her obvious discomfort that night. He must have known how busy she was – Anna was sure there was no one on this coast who didn't know about the flurry of activity that had overtaken sleepy Crovie thanks to her. But he hadn't called, except for that one time to thank her for making meals for Douglas McKean. She hadn't called him, either, of course. Why would she?

Anna wondered what he would think when he found out about the baby. Something in her became unsettled as she thought of how that conversation would go. Would he be awkward? Would she? She thought back to that afternoon of harvesting razor clams together, back to that carefree day they'd had on Fraser and Emma's boat. She realized, not for the first time, but with a sense that the knowledge meant more than she had previously thought, that she missed him. She missed *them*.

There was a knock at the door.

'Come in,' Anna called, unearthing herself from the blankets. She expected it to be Pat or Frank checking on her, but as she stood up she found herself looking at Robert MacKenzie, and had to take a sudden breath around the skipped beat of her heart.

In his hands he was carrying the plates she'd used for Douglas McKean's dinner the day before. It seemed months ago now, not twenty-four hours. Robert smiled as he saw her.

'Hey,' he said softly. 'Long time no see.'

'How's Robbie?'

'He's fine,' he said. 'Thanks to you. I left him with Barbara. I don't think she'll ever let him out of her sight again. I didn't want to let him out of mine, either, but I had to come over to check on Douglas and see the new damage to the house. Last night's storm caused another slip.' Robert shook his head. 'Anna, seeing it like that and knowing what you did – for Robbie, for me ... What you risked in going down that cliff. I can't—'

'Please. It was nothing,' she said, cutting him off. 'Anyone would have done the same. I'm just glad he's safe.'

There was a pause, in which they did no more than look at each other, and Anna felt the enormity of something looming on the periphery, like a cliff towering behind her.

'There's something I should—'

'I was thinking that maybe—'

They both stopped, Anna with a slightly nervous laugh and Robert with a smile. 'Sorry,' he said. 'Go on.'

Anna shook her head. The momentary impulse to tell him about the baby had gone. 'No. Really, you go. What were you going to say?'

'I was thinking that I should go out there and get some more razor clams for you,' he said. 'Rhona's still raving about that meal you made for her with the last lot. And it's free food, isn't it? What with the lunch club taking off the way it has – you've got to make a bit of profit some-where, eh?'

She smiled. 'That would be really kind of you, but you don't have to do that. I won't have time to come with you, and—'

'Consider it a very minor repayment,' he said, cutting her off. 'For me dragging you into the middle of my crazy little family.'

I like being in the middle of your crazy little family.

She only just stopped the thought becoming words. Anna realized he was still holding the dishes and reached for them to cover her internal confusion. Their fingers tangled together as they juggled the plates and Anna found herself thinking that she liked the feel of them: the coarse skin of his fingertips, roughened by work.

'Hope Douglas liked his dinner,' she said, looking any-where but his face.

'He did. Although I can't help but think he must know where the food's coming from. I wouldn't shut up about you today. I made him listen to how you saved my son.' He gave her a serious look. 'How you saved *me.*'

They parted on Robert's promise to bring her a bucket of clams. Anna stood on the step of the Fishergirl's Luck, watching him go, wondering if she could blame hormones for her current emotional tumult. When she turned back to the door, a figure at the end of the village caught her eye. He was swathed in the shadows from the cliff, watching.

Douglas McKean.

Anna's heart sank. *Not now,* she thought. *Please, not right now.*

The old man stared at her for a few more seconds. Then, very slowly, he lifted his cane and tapped it against his forehead in some kind of ungainly salute.

A moment later he had shuffled away.

'Well, well, well,' said Pat. 'That's a turn up for the books.'

'Aye,' said Frank. 'Douglas McKean saying thank you? It'll be cats and dogs living together next.'

'I'm still not taking him his dinner myself,' Anna warned them.

Frank patted her hand. 'Understood.'

It was evening, and the day's light had been swallowed by the cliff. They were all sitting at the kitchen table in the Weaver's Nook – it had been a while since they'd had time to do that, and Anna missed it. Pat had insisted that Frank go for his own check-up after his escapade on the cliff, and as a result declared that he was now under official orders to take it easy.

'How are you two doing?' Anna asked.

'Well, we could do with these storms taking a hike. We've never known a season like this, have we, Frank?'

Frank shook his head.

'Are your bookings down because of it?'

They both laughed. 'You must be joking!' Pat said. 'We could have filled this place three times over this week! Anna, you could open the Inn tomorrow and book the restaurant out for the next six months before you'd even tried.'

'Then I'm sorry I'm giving you so much extra work.'

'Don't be daft, love,' Frank said. 'It's the best summer we've had in years, workwise. Not your fault we're getting on. Can't fix that as easily as you have our business worries.'

'To tell you the truth,' Anna confessed, 'I'm not sure what to do. I'm operating over capacity as it is, and people are becoming irate that there's only six seats, but I can't see how I can expand. The Inn is the only place in Crovie that would make that a possibility and unless I win the lottery, that's not going to happen. And . . .' She took a breath. 'There's another, bigger reason to be considering the future of the lunch club.'

Pat eyed her. 'Oh? This doesn't have anything to do with Liam Harper, does it?'

'What? How do you know that?'

'Susan said she saw you having lunch with the lad in Fraserburgh earlier and figured you'd called him to pick you up from the hospital. We thought maybe that meant you two were back together again, and what with him about to head back home . . . Well.' Pat sighed, unhappily. 'You do keep saying you're going to move on.'

Anna bit her lip. Now that the moment had come, her stomach lurched with nerves.

'That's not why he came to get me from the hospital.' She

slipped her hand into her pocket and pulled out the envelope that contained the scan, pushing it across the table towards her friends. 'This is why.'

Pat gave her a quizzical look before picking up the envelope. When she saw what was inside, her eyes widened. She and Frank both stared at Anna in astonishment.

'It was an accident,' Anna told them. 'But I've decided it's a happy one. The baby's due in January. And before you ask, everything's fine. *We're* fine.'

'Oh!' Pat leapt out of her chair and enveloped Anna in a hug. Anna laughed as Frank joined them, and for a second the three of them held on to each other. Anna found her face wet with tears. She was relieved beyond belief, both that they finally knew and that they had reacted so happily.

Eventually Pat pulled back. 'So . . .' she said, as Frank sat down beside Anna. 'Liam's staying here, then? In the UK, with you?'

'No. He's still going home. He asked me to go with him, but I don't want to.'

Pat shook her head, taking Anna's hand and squeezing it. 'Brave,' she said, her voice a little thick.

'No, just determined,' Anna said. 'And a bit daft. Maybe more than a bit.'

'But you're still planning to move on?' Pat asked. 'You won't stay here?'

Anna shook her head. 'Honestly? The sensible thing to do is move before the baby gets here, try to get settled somewhere else. But . . .'

'But?' There was a hopeful look on Pat's face.

Anna raised her hands, palm up, a 'What can I do?' gesture. 'A big part of me wants to have the baby here. I honestly don't know how to make that work, but this place . . . everyone here . . .'

Pat smiled beatifically. 'We've got under your skin, eh?'

Anna laughed, though there were tears threatening, too. 'I suppose you have. You told me you would, didn't you?'

'A crib,' Frank announced arbitrarily. 'That's what the Fishergirl's Luck needs. A custom-built crib that'll be a perfect fit. I can do that. Will you let me?'

The tears kept coming. 'Of course I will,' Anna said. 'I'm so glad you're both happy about it. I think I'm going to need you. I'm going to need you both.'

Pat hugged her again. 'We'll be here, love.'

'You know what they say,' Frank said with a grin. 'It takes a village to raise a child.'

Anna laughed through her tears. 'Yes! And do you know what? This is home now. I don't really know when it happened, but I can't imagine living anywhere else. I don't want to, either. I miss the Usual Suspects. It's been too long since we had a get-together, and it's my fault because I've been so busy.'

'Don't you worry about that, love,' Frank said. 'None of us are going anywhere, either.'

My own selkie lass,

If I bought you flowers, yellow ones, every single one I could find between Inverness and Cromarty, if I filled the house with them, all for you, would I feel better?

I bought beetroot. It was deliberate. It was a penance, and it isn't enough.

I love you. I love the memory of you, so much that I wish it were more than a memory. But it isn't.

I never expected her. I never did.

Twenty-Seven

Anna had thought her escapade with Young Robbie beneath the cliff had been the second shoe she'd been waiting to drop, but she was wrong. That came a few days later on Thursday, when Anna was about to begin service at the Fishergirl's Luck. Seeing her baby and then being able to talk to Pat and Frank about it had lifted a weight from Anna's shoulders that she hadn't known she'd been carrying. As a result she floated through the week, still tired but with a new happiness that made her buoyant.

'Enjoy it,' Cathy told her. 'I'm so glad you're surrounded by good people, Anna. I hate that I'm not closer.'

'I know,' Anna said. 'Me too. But I know you'll visit when you can. It would be so good to see you.'

The frequency of her phone calls to Cathy had lessened, and Anna realized that this was an indication of how close her newer friendships were becoming. *Roots*, she thought to herself, as she shaped gnocchi with a swift, practised twist of her thumb. *I've put them down here. They're taking, despite the rock.*

She prepared for service with a sense of confidence that

had only developed since she'd been in Crovie. This was *her* place. Maybe she didn't know it as well as someone like Douglas McKean or Robert MacKenzie, but she had the rest of her life to learn it, and she had decided that was exactly what she wanted to do.

The six successful guests had been seated – there were always still a lot of people who hung around, as if she might miraculously be able to produce another table for them to eat at – and she was inside organizing drinks when Anna heard a commotion outside. It began as a loud murmur followed by a storm of clapping, over which she could hear a voice speaking. She went to see what was happening and stopped dead on the step.

'Well, well, well, here she is,' said Geoff Rowcliffe, his television smile firmly in place. 'Anna Campbell, the girl of the moment.'

Anna could feel the blood draining from her face. 'What are you doing here?'

Geoff turned to the gathered crowd, spreading his arms and widening his smile. There was a smattering of laughter. 'I wanted to see first-hand how my protégé was getting on, of course!' he said.

Anna could feel her throat seizing up. She felt cold. 'Your protégé?'

The celebrity chef turned back to her. His smile was still in place, but she knew him well enough to read the knife-edge in his eyes. 'Twenty years in my kitchens has obviously stood you well, hasn't it? Thought I'd come and show my support.'

She swallowed. 'I'm afraid the table's full for today,' Anna said. 'There's no more room.'

'Oh no – please join us,' said one of the women that Anna had seated at the bench. She was leaning out over the fence, her face bursting with excitement. 'We can all squeeze up!'

Anna shook her head. 'No, I really don't think—'

'We don't mind,' the woman insisted, turning to gather support from her fellow diners. 'Do we?'

Geoff looked pointedly at Anna. She briefly considered lying and saying that she only had enough ingredients for six meals, but knew he'd never believe that. She gave in. 'I'll bring an extra chair.'

He smiled, showing her all his teeth. 'Great. I can't wait to taste this food of yours. The reviews make it sound as if you should already have a Michelin star.'

At that he turned his back on her and went towards the woman, who was chattering excitedly about what an honour it was to share a table with such a renowned chef. Anna went back inside and grabbed an extra chair. When she took it out, Geoff was standing at the end of the table with his arms crossed. He barely even looked at her as he took the chair and positioned it right at the head of the bench.

Anna went back into the Fishergirl's Luck again and pushed the door shut. She was shaking and her fingers felt numb. All of her confidence had vanished and now she was reduced once more to that minion in Geoff's kitchen, waiting for him to criticize her food. She felt sick.

She grabbed the phone and dialled Cathy's number. Her friend answered on the first ring.

'Hello – what are you doing? Shouldn't you be in service? Is everything all right?'

'He's here. Geoff's here.'

'*What?*'

'He turned up out of the blue. The guests – they've made room for him. He's sitting at the bench, waiting to eat. I'm not going to be able to plate, my hands are shaking too much.'

'Hey,' Cathy said, her voice snapping over from shocked to strong. 'You listen to me. You can do this. I know you can. *You* know you can. You are not in his kitchen anymore. This is your table, your food. Take a moment. Drink a glass of water. Breathe. Then do what you were born to do. He can't take this away from you, because he did not give it to you in the first place. Got it?'

Anna shut her eyes and sucked in a breath. 'Yes. I can do this. I can.'

'Damn straight, sister. I love you. Now go and do your job. Call me later.'

Anna hung up the phone and went into the kitchen. She poured a pint of water and drank it down in one go, staring at the sea beyond her window. Then she put the glass down and took a series of deep breaths. As she did so she realized that her panic was being subsumed by rage.

Protégé? As if they hadn't trained in the same place, at the same time! As if she was only able to cook because of Geoff bloody Rowcliffe!

Anna blew out one last breath. She'd make this the best service she'd ever delivered. She was a better cook than Geoff had ever been. She knew it, and so did he, because why else would he be here? Why else would he care? Why else would he have spent twenty years making sure she'd never thought enough of herself to realize it?

Well, he was on her turf now.

Screw you, Geoff Rowcliffe, she thought. *Screw you and the spatula you strode in with.*

Then she squared her shoulders and went into battle.

'I have to admit, it wasn't bad. Maybe not as refined as I'd expected, given the reviews, but a good show of potential nonetheless.'

Anna was collecting the last items from the bench. Her other diners had finally left, though only because the wind was beginning to get up again. Otherwise they probably would have sat there for another three hours, listening to Geoff giving them the benefit of his wisdom. As it was, only Anna was left to hear her ex downplay the success of the meal as he watched her clear.

'How generous of you to say so,' Anna said, as she walked past him to the door of the Fishergirl's Luck.

'No need to be snippy. I'm offering a few thoughts, that's all. We all need them if we're going to improve, don't we?'

She didn't invite him in, but that didn't stop him following her. Anna went to the sink and stacked the cups for washing. She knew the meal had been outstanding, which was why he had tried to find fault with her 'refinement' instead. He couldn't be negative about the food itself, because it had been perfect, and he knew it. So did she. She didn't need him to say so, which was fortunate, because she knew he never would. Anna turned to face him.

'What do you want, Geoff?' she asked. 'Why are you here?'

He didn't answer her immediately, pausing instead to look around her home with a barely disguised expression of disdain.

'I'm here to offer you a shot at the big time. A proper shot. A chance to turn your dabble here into something with an actual future.'

The rage Anna had felt earlier began to bubble in her veins again. She crossed her arms. 'Oh yes? And what chance would that be?'

'I've got a new restaurant opening in Manchester next year. I want you to be the executive chef. I'm offering you your own kitchen, Anna – a *real* kitchen.'

Anna stared at him. 'You ... *What?*'

Geoff smiled, sliding his hands into his pockets. 'That's right. I'm willing to give you a kitchen. And with it a glittering future.'

She was so stunned she could barely speak. 'Why?'

He shrugged. 'I need someone who will shape up. It's going to have the Rowcliffe name over the door, it's my rep on the line.'

'And you think you can "shape me up", do you?'

He took one hand out of his pocket and pointed a finger

at her. 'Don't get cocky, Anna. Don't believe your own hype. Look at where you are, for God's sake. You think serving six covers a couple of days a week out of the arse end of civilization makes you a real chef? It's ridiculous. Look at yourself. No one else in their right mind would offer you this.'

Anna turned away. He was right. No one walked straight into their own commercial kitchen, especially not one that was guaranteed to be on the Michelin radar before it even opened.

'When are you planning to open?'

'Next December. I don't want to rush it. I'm determined that this will be a success, and so are my investors. We're more than a year out – I'm keen for you to be in right at the beginning of the planning. The kitchen and dining room would be built to your specs – with me overseeing, obviously. We'd develop the menu together.'

December, Anna thought. She'd imagined he would want to open in summer, but by December the baby would be eleven months old. Even if she had six months of maternity leave after the birth, that would still leave five months before opening where she would be fully involved.

'Anna?' Geoff asked, into her silence. 'How are you not biting my hand off to take this offer?'

Anna swallowed, hard, and turned to face him. 'Because by then, I'll have a child to think about. I'm pregnant.'

The shocked look on his face might have been comical if it hadn't quickly transformed into a smirking leer. 'Wow. You didn't hang around. I know that once women get to a certain age they can't hear anything but their body clock, but even so—'

'I'm due in January,' Anna said, to shut him up.

He narrowed his eyes. 'Well then. The messy stuff will all be out of the way in plenty of time, won't it?' Geoff looked around the Fishergirl's Luck again. 'What are you planning to do? Keep the baby in a box under the table? This place is small enough to be a garden playhouse. Who's the father?'

'None of that is any of your business.'

He turned back to her with another smirk. 'Knocked you up and did a runner then, did he? Smart man.'

Anna bit her lip and tried to tamp down on her anger. 'It's time you were going,' she told him. 'I've got to clean down.'

'We need to start discussing arrangements,' Geoff said. 'I'll need you to sign a contract and an NDA. There'll be a non-compete clause, so you'll have to stop serving out there, and—'

'I won't be doing any of that,' Anna said.

Geoff crossed his arms. 'You'll have to, or no deal.'

'No problem. No deal. Goodbye, Geoff.'

He stared at her. 'What?'

'I'm saying no to your offer,' Anna said. 'You can go now.'

'You can't be serious,' Geoff said. 'Not even you could be that—'

There was a sudden sound at the door. Geoff had left it open, only bothering to partially close the inner vestibule door as he'd come in. It opened now and Robert MacKenzie backed through it, carrying two buckets that looked heavy and sloshed with water.

'Sorry to burst in,' he said, 'but—' He looked up and saw Geoff. 'Damn, sorry. I only wanted to drop the razor clams off for tomorrow.'

Anna went to Robert and took one of the buckets, which was full of both razor clams and seawater. 'Thank you,' she said, 'that's really good of you.'

Geoff crossed his arms, watching. 'Delivery straight to the door, eh? That's service indeed.'

Robert gave him an easy smile as he straightened up. 'Oh, Anna deserves the best for her kitchen. Have you tried her food? Hands down the best I've ever had.'

'Hmm,' Geoff said. 'We've been discussing it, actually.' He seemed to decide something and stuck out a hand for Robert to shake. 'Geoff Rowcliffe.'

'Robert MacKenzie,' Robert glanced at Anna with a smile. 'You're one of Anna's friends from down south? It's nice to meet you.'

Anna's heart sank. Robert clearly didn't know who Geoff was, and from experience she knew there was no surer way to insult her ex than be ignorant of his stardom. Geoff smiled tightly.

'And I'm guessing you must be the father,' he said smoothly. 'Congratulations. Due in January, I believe?'

The smile dropped from Robert's face.

'Oh, sorry, did I say something out of turn?' Geoff asked, with a studied innocence that Anna knew far better than to believe.

'It's fine,' Anna said, refusing to let him see how he'd

riled her. 'No, Robert is not the father of my baby. He's just a very good friend. He's the person I bought this place from.'

Geoff nodded, losing interest. 'Well, I've got to go.' He gave Anna a pointed look. 'My number hasn't changed. I'll be waiting to hear from you.'

Anna ignored that. 'Goodbye, Geoff.'

Geoff flicked a glance at Robert. 'Nice to meet you.'

Robert stepped aside to let him out. 'And you.'

Anna closed the door behind Geoff and turned back to Robert. They were silent for a moment.

'I'm sorry I hadn't told you yet,' Anna said.

He held up a hand. 'No need, it's not . . .' He shook his head slightly as he trailed off. 'You're okay? The baby's okay? After everything—'

'Yes. We're both fine. Thank you.'

'Good. And you're happy?'

Anna smiled. 'Yes. A bit scared, maybe. But very happy.'

He smiled back. 'Then so am I.'

They lapsed into silence again. 'I'd better go,' Robert said, after a moment. 'Fraser and Emma are dropping the wee boy off soon.'

'Okay. Thanks again for the clams.'

'You're welcome,' he said. And then, 'If you need any-thing, you let me know. Anything. Any time. Okay?'

Anna smiled again as something in her chest swelled and then contracted, leaving an ache she couldn't quite explain. 'Thank you. That means a lot.'

Robert MacKenzie nodded again, frowned a little, smiled a little. Then he was gone, into the twilight wind.

'That bastard,' Cathy said immediately, when Anna told her of Geoff's offer. 'He's looking for a way to be able to say that your success is down to him. He wants you somewhere he can control you, Anna. You'd develop the menu together, sure – but we both know what that means. You'll come up with it, and he'd be the one who cooks it on TV. His name will be three times bigger than yours whenever they appear together, and that will only be when he can't ditch your name completely.'

Anna fiddled absently with the hem of her shirt. It felt tighter than usual. 'I know. I *know*. And that's why I told him to get lost.'

'Good,' Cathy said, the relief clear in her voice. 'I hate the way that sorry excuse for a man can get into your head.'

'I won't ever let that happen again,' Anna assured her. 'But I can't help but think . . .' She sighed. 'Cathy, with the baby I'm going to need work sooner rather than later now. And I'm never going to get another offer like that one.'

'You don't know that,' her friend insisted. 'Look what you've achieved in just a few months!'

'What I've achieved?' Anna repeated, with a slight laugh. 'Come on – he's not exactly wrong about that, either, is he? All I've actually managed to do is serve six covers three days a week and get myself knocked up.'

'This is him talking,' Cathy said, irritated. 'He *has* got inside your head!'

'He hasn't,' Anna assured her. 'Not really. I know my worth now. I know I could run my own kitchen. If I could do it at the Inn here, I would. But I can't.'

'I can't believe Geoff Rowcliffe is the only person who would offer you a job if you went looking for one,' Cathy said. 'You've got a reputation now. A body of work that has nothing to do with him. That has to count for something. Doesn't it?'

'I'd hope so, yeah. It's worth asking the question. There could be somewhere not too far away from here looking for a chef.'

'Right,' said Cathy. 'If you could stay local and that would make it easier to keep living in the Fishergirl's Luck, wouldn't it?'

Anna lay back amid the cushions, staring up at her quirky bookshelves overhead, full of her own collection of colourful cookbooks. 'It would.'

'So promise me you'll forget about Geoff's offer.'

'It's already forgotten. I promise.'

'All right,' Cathy sighed, and then changed the subject. 'Now tell me about Robert MacKenzie. How did he take the news?'

'He was absolutely fine. To be honest, it's kind of a relief that it came out the way it did. I . . . didn't really know how to tell him myself.'

'Oh? Why not?'

Anna shrugged. 'I don't know. It felt – awkward, somehow.'

'Are you falling for him?'

Her heart leapt into her throat. Anna swallowed, hard. 'No! Of course I'm not. He's a friend, that's all. A good friend.'

'Would you miss him?' her friend asked. 'If you had to leave Crovie now?'

'I'd miss everyone here,' Anna told her, thinking of Robert standing on her doorstep in the wind. 'Everyone.'

Selkie lass,

Sometimes I wonder if you're still here. Whether all you did was go back to where you always belonged, back to the sea, but no further than that. Do you watch us from the waves, me and the wee lad? Was it you who took her up there on that cliff, got her to risk herself to climb down it to our boy? Or is that just who she is?

Do you laugh at the tangles we tie ourselves into?

The tangle I've tied myself into.

The wee lad seems fine. He's still as much into dolphins as he ever was. There's no dampening that spirit, thank the fishes. It's me that feels . . . I don't know.

I don't know what I feel.

Twenty-Eight

The rest of July passed peacefully for Anna. The lunch club continued to be fully booked out every day she opened her kitchen. As the month turned over into August, though, the weather closed in. It began to rain, lashing against the Fishergirl's Luck in harsh torrents that sounded more like rocks being thrown at the walls than water falling from the sky. The waves churned, the sea's swirling colours melding into a blanket of dull grey that fused with the indistinguishable horizon. The forecast was not promising – this was not going to blow out soon – and so Anna used the social media accounts she had set up for the Fishergirl's Luck to cancel lunch club for the week. She was glad of her decision when, three days later, the rain was still falling and the road down into the village had turned into a river.

Anna cooked evening meals for those of Pat and Frank's guests who did not want to brave the road, and for a few other holiday makers stuck in the village. She dashed back and forth to the Fishergirl's Luck for equipment and ingredients and was drenched every time she set foot outside the door. By Friday though, when the forecast showed the rain was going to continue for longer yet, the last of the village's guests decided to cut short their stay and leave.

'This is ridiculous,' Pat said, as the three of them sat at the kitchen table in the Weaver's Nook, listening to the rain. It was already dark, though it was barely touching three o'clock. 'I've never known it like this.'

'I'm worried,' Frank muttered over his mug. 'The cliff can't take much more of this.'

'Don't say that,' Pat shivered.

'I'm serious. I even asked Douglas to come and stay here, to be out of the way if it does come down.'

'What did he say?' Anna asked.

Frank snorted. 'What do you think? Daft old sod.'

On Sunday Anna was sitting at her breakfast bench working on the cookbook project for Melissa Stark when Robert MacKenzie appeared at her door, the yellow of his fisherman's waterproof glistening with rain. Anna brought him into the warmth of the bothy.

'I wanted to check on you,' he said, as she made tea. 'Robbie wanted to come too but I wasn't going to bring him out in this if I could help it.'

'You didn't come out in the boat?' Anna asked, the thought of him navigating the raging waves between Gamrie and Crovie sending a visceral shiver down her spine.

'No, I'd never risk it in the *Cassie's Joy*,' he said. 'I came by road. How are you? Is there anything you need?'

'Running low on milk but I'm otherwise fine.'

'Give me a list,' he said, as he took the mug. 'I'm going to do a supply run for anyone who doesn't want to brave that road if it's still raining. I'll aim to come down tomorrow.'

'You don't have to do that,' Anna told him. 'You must have more than enough to worry about.'

'I've got to come over for Dougie anyway. It's no trouble.'

Anna thought that couldn't possibly be true, but she wrote a list nonetheless. As she did they talked, the constant roar of rain a backdrop to their conversation.

'Look,' he said, as Anna passed him the piece of paper she'd scrawled on. 'There's always room at ours if you want to get out of Crovie for a while. Or I'm sure Rhona will offer you a bed at hers. I can take you back with me now.'

Anna looked at him over the rim of her mug. 'Do you think it's that bad?'

Robert shrugged. 'I've never seen it like this before, and the forecast's showing another storm blowing in behind this one.'

'The council must have plans to evacuate if it gets really risky. Won't they let us know if they think it's time to go?'

'Probably.' He smiled, despite the trace of worry in his eyes. 'You really don't want to leave, do you?'

Anna smiled too, looking around her home. 'I feel safe here. I think the Fishergirl's Luck could withstand anything.'

'Aye, well. Bren was the same.' He took another mouthful of tea and once he'd swallowed it, said, 'I'm glad to hear you say it. I wondered whether this would be the last straw and you'd leave us after all.'

'What do you mean?'

He hitched one shoulder. 'Liam's made it known that he asked you to go home with him.'

'Oh, he has, has he?'

'I think he wanted to make it clear he wasn't abandoning you in your time of need.'

Anna snorted. 'My time of need?'

'You know what I mean.'

'I'm not going to New Zealand,' Anna told him. 'And I want to stay in Crovie if I can. But I have to get some kind of job. Especially now.'

'Because of the weather?'

Anna laughed. 'No! Because my savings will run out quickly now there's a baby to provide for. What I'm hoping is that I can find something in the area, or close enough to it that will make it possible to commute. But if I can't . . .'

He nodded silently as she left that thought to finish itself.

'What I need is to win the lottery,' she quipped. 'Or for a fairy godmother to turn up with a pot of gold so I can buy the Crovie Inn.'

Robert clasped his hands together between his knees, smiling at the floor. 'I'd give you the money if I had it,' he said quietly. 'You've changed this place by being here. Just by doing what you do. It'd miss you if you go.' There was a pause, and then he said, very deliberately, as if forcing it out despite some instinct that told him not to, '*I'd* miss you.'

Anna's heart pulsed a strange beat. She put down her mug, not knowing what to say. She watched his downturned head, and for a moment it seemed that Robert didn't want to look up at her again. When he did, he gave a lopsided smile as their eyes met.

'I'd miss you too,' Anna said quietly. 'You're one of the reasons I came here in the first place. You, Bren and the Fishergirl's Luck. Without you, I might have visited, but I wouldn't have had a reason to stay.'

Robert said nothing, but the way he looked at her made Anna feel as if there was no air in the room. Then he blinked and stood.

'Robbie, I—' he said, his voice hoarse for a moment, until he'd cleared it. 'I have to make sure he's home. He promised, but—'

Anna swallowed her heart, dislodging it from where it seemed to have beat its way up into her throat. 'Dolphins?'

'Aye. Dolphins.'

Robert went to the door, where he hesitated for a second, half turning back to her. 'This old place,' he said. 'I hope it stands forever.'

They said goodbye, though there was a moment when what Anna wanted most was to ask him to stay. If he hadn't mentioned Young Robbie, perhaps she would have. Instead Anna shut the door and imagined him battling his way out of the village through a storm that seemed to have grown exponentially worse since he arrived, the memory of that look in his eye making her heart expand and contract so quickly that she had to take a breath.

The village locals clubbed together with what they had for a joint supper at the Weaver's Nook. David had driven over to check on their place, leaving Glynn and Bill in Inverness. Terry and Susan were there too. Rhona was absent, and no one would wish her there given what she'd have had to come through to join them. The wind raged outside, the rain hammering the village hard.

'Perhaps we should have gone, as Old Robbie said,' Pat fretted, reaching over to grasp Anna's hand. 'Or you should have, at least. He'll be worrying about you.'

Anna squeezed Pat's hand. 'He'll be worrying about all of us.'

'Yes, but it's different with you, love, isn't it? You know that.'

'Pat,' Frank warned, gently.

'What? With Liam going—'

'*Pat*,' Frank said, again.

'It's all right,' Anna said, covering his hand with hers. 'Pat, Robert and I are friends. That's all. You *know* that.'

Pat looked downcast. 'But I've seen the way he looks at you, love.' She glanced around the table. 'We all have.'

Anna laughed, as much to cover the echoing pulse of her heart than anything else. 'I'm carrying another man's *baby*.'

There was a brief, uncomfortable silence.

'It's not blood that matters,' Pat said quietly into it. 'That's why I think of you as our family, Anna. Mine and Frank's. And I don't think I'm wrong when I say you've become part of Robert MacKenzie's, too.'

When she stepped outside the Weaver's Nook to go home, the rain lashed Anna's face hard enough to drown her tears.

The inside of the Fishergirl's Luck was warm and snug, the stove still alight. The walls were so thick that the ferocity of the storm outside seemed so much less. It was there, though, throwing its rage at Anna's home, making sure that she couldn't forget what was lurking outside. Inside the Fishergirl's Luck the rest of the world seemed far away, but Anna knew it was waiting there, pressing close, trying to get in.

She flopped down on the sofa and reached for the phone, wanting to call Cathy, but the line was dead. A few moments later her lamp flickered off. Anna looked out of the door into pitch-black darkness. The electricity to the whole of the village was out.

It must have been around 3 a.m. when she was woken by a sound so loud and so deep that Anna thought it felt like movement. She sat up in bed and reached for the light switch, but the power was still off. She wrapped herself in a blanket, so used to the howl of the wind now that she barely heard it as she made her way downstairs. Anna opened the front door of the bothy a crack, but the sound had ceased, or at least lessened enough that the rage of the storm had swallowed it completely. There was no light anywhere, no sign of activity in any of the houses. Thinking she must have dreamed it, Anna went back to bed.

The next morning, though, Frank rapped on her front door, his face pale beneath his drenched hair. The sun had failed to rise at all, the clouded sky squatting heavily over the village, dark as bruises. The rain was still pelting everything in its way.

'Frank? What is it?' Anna asked, alarmed by the grim look on his face as he stepped inside out of the storm. 'What's happened?'

'It's the cliff. It's bad. The worst slip we've had so far.'

'Oh no – the rental?'

'I think the roof's gone, maybe the whole of the back wall, too. Can't see how it'll be saved, to be honest.'

Anna grabbed her coat from the peg. 'What can I do?'

'Nothing, love. There's no point worrying about that old place now. I think we all need to leave. Pat's packing a bag – you should too. When Old Robbie gets here, you should be ready to go with him.'

'What?' Anna said, shocked. 'But – the Weaver's Nook isn't in danger, is it? Or David's place, or the others?'

Frank's face was grey with worry and fatigue. 'I don't want to think so, but there's another storm coming in, and with no power we can't call for help. If there's another slide, and heaven forbid if it's worse than the one last night, we could be in real trouble.'

'What about Douglas McKean? Is he all right?'

'I couldn't rouse him. I came back to get a crowbar and David – he's going to help me knock the door in if there's still no answer when we go back. But I wanted to let you know what's going on first. It's not safe to stay, love. Not anymore.'

Anna nodded. 'I'll pack now.'

'Good lass.' Frank reached for the latch. 'I'll knock again in a bit, or you can head over to Pat when you're ready to go.'

He stepped out into the storm again, and Anna followed

him to the door. 'Are you well enough to be doing this?' she asked. 'I can go with David.'

Frank squared his shoulders beneath the rain and grinned. 'I'm fit as a fiddle,' he said. 'You don't want to listen to everything Pat says. She's a born worrier. Wants to wrap a man in cotton wool.'

Anna shook her head. 'She loves you, that's all.' She had to yell the words into the wind and rain.

Frank smiled again as he headed into the rain, shouting back at her through the storm. 'Get back in the warm. Pack that bag!'

Anna shut the door and went into the living room. For a moment she looked around. She'd only lived here for six months but the idea that she had to leave, and like this, when the Fishergirl's Luck might not be here to come back to, felt like the worst kind of abandonment. Bren would never have left, she knew. She'd have stayed here no matter how bad the storm. She'd have felt safe inside the four walls of the Fishergirl's Luck.

'I'm sorry,' Anna whispered, wondering if anything of Bren was still left here, whether any wisp of her existence had imprinted itself on these stone walls. 'I don't want to go. I don't.' If it had only been her, maybe she'd have stayed and waited out the storm. Maybe she'd have trusted that this place would stay standing, no matter what the elements threw at it, as Bren had in 1953, when it must have seemed as if the world outside was ending. But Anna's life wasn't just hers anymore. She had the baby to think of.

'I'll come back,' she said. 'As soon as it's safe. As soon as I can.'

Anna went upstairs and quickly packed her overnight bag. The last things she put into it were her precious family photograph and three notebooks – Bren's, her grandmother's, and the one in which she had been writing down her own recipes. Then she went out into the hallway and pulled on her coat, checking that her utility torch was in her pocket. As she was opening the door there came another almighty sound. It sounded like one mountain shearing against another. She looked up at the cliff behind the houses, but she could see nothing. The wind was stronger than she'd ever felt it, and seemed to be blasting harder by the second. The rain was blinding, sharp, cold slashes through a gloom dark enough to be night.

Anna flicked on her flashlight and hesitated on the door-step in its blue-white glare, her heart pounding. If the cliff was coming down right now—

'*Anna!* AN—!'

The swallowed yell came from the sea path. Anna saw a figure ducking through the slashing waves, almost knocked off its feet by the force of the water. At first she thought it was Robert MacKenzie. She dropped her bag in the doorway and ran out into the storm, grabbing one outstretched arm and pulling whoever it was into the lee of the bothy. Water sloshed around their ankles – the path was flooding anew with each new wave that broke against the wall.

'Anna,' the person gasped, and she realized that it was

David. She glanced into the darkness over his shoulder, looking for Frank, but there was no sign of him. The rumble came again and Anna looked up, half expecting to see an avalanche of rock and earth rolling towards them.

'It's not the cliff,' David shouted through lips blue with cold. 'It's the road. The road's gone. We can't get out, not even on foot. And no one can get in to help us.'

Another sound came, another rumble, louder even than before and right over their heads.

'Oh, God,' David shouted, horror on his face. '*That*'s the cliff!'

The noise of this latest landslide was deafening, terrifying, amplified by the blind confusion of light lack and storm. The door to the Weaver's Nook opened and Pat appeared, her face a mask of terror as she ran out into the rain, trying to see what was happening.

'The Fishergirl's Luck,' Anna bellowed, right into David's ear. 'If the landslide really hits the houses, it's the only place that might stay safe. Get everyone here. Quickly!'

Twenty-Nine

Pat wanted to go after Frank, but Anna stopped her.

'David will get him,' she promised. 'He's going to get everyone. Please, Pat. I need your help. We need to get as many supplies as we can carry into the Fishergirl's Luck. Food, blankets, fuel, matches. Whatever you've got that might be useful.'

They started ferrying goods from the B&B to the bothy, drenched every time they stepped outside. The worst of the roar from the cliff had lessened, but it was clear it hadn't yet stopped falling. Terry and Susan appeared, both distressed, but ready to pitch in. As they stacked the floor of the Fishergirl's Luck with supplies, Anna began to fill containers with water in case the pipes gave out. Then she ran upstairs to dig out what blankets she had to add to the pile. By the time she came back down again, David and Frank were dripping water on her floor.

'Where's Dougie?' she asked, grabbing them both towels and helping Frank out of his coat.

'He's alive,' Frank said, darkly, 'but goodness knows for how long.'

'He won't leave the house,' David explained, catching his breath. 'Says the place has been standing since Crovie was built and it'll still be standing when the rest of us have gone. He doesn't seem to understand how serious this is.'

'Short of knocking him out and dragging him down here, there's nothing more we can do,' Frank said, looking around with a frown. 'Where's Pat?'

'Getting the last supplies she can from your place. Terry and Susan are with her.'

'I'll go and help,' Frank said, standing up again.

'I'll go,' David said. 'You stay here and get warm. We'll be back before you know it.'

'But—'

'Frank,' David said, already half out of the door and holding up a hand, 'Seriously. Be sensible. You look done in.'

'I need your help, anyway,' Anna said, to distract him. 'You ever boiled water on a stove before? Everyone's going to need some hot tea once they get back.'

Frank cast a glance at her tiny wood burner and snorted. 'We'd best get on with it then, lass,' he said. 'Else they'll still be waiting at Christmas.'

Twenty minutes later, the small living area of the Fishergirl's Luck was crammed with people. David dragged the coffee table out of the way and Terry pushed the armchairs back, leaving enough space on the floor for those without seats to sit. Anna tried to organize the supplies. There were multiple loaves of bread and bags of muesli from Pat's B&B stores, packs of ham, cheese and butter, punnets of tomatoes, cans and cans of soup. Pat and Susan had also thought to bring as many toilet rolls as they could, as well as warm wool blankets and candles.

'What will happen?' Anna asked, as they all sat drinking tea and listening to the intermittent rumble of the cliff. They had made a pact not to look outside. After all, there was nowhere else they could go, no matter what they saw. 'I mean – how long do you think it'll take for anyone to realize we're trapped?'

'I think it'll be down to Old Robbie,' Terry said. 'He's the only person we know is going to try to get down that road any time soon. He'll see that it's out and raise the alarm.'

'But then what?' Pat asked. 'I don't see how they can get us out, even if they know what's happened.'

'The coastguard will find a way,' Frank said. 'We're lucky there's not more of us, truth be told.'

'What about Douglas?' Anna asked again, still thinking about that stubborn old man sitting in his house as it crumbled on top of him.

Frank rubbed a thumb across his eyebrow. 'Aye. I don't know, lass, is the answer. He knows where we are. If he has any sense he'll knock on that door in the next half an hour, begging you to take pity on him.'

The hours passed in the semi-darkness of flickering candle and fire light. Douglas McKean did not appear. The storm seemed to grow worse with every minute, the slow rumbling of the crumbling cliff swelling and shrinking beneath the roar of the wind. They kept the wood burner stoked so that the room was warm, but no one could sleep. Time seemed to have entered a fugue state – Anna had long ago lost track of the hour when a clattering, tearing sound came from the kitchen. They all turned to look, but nothing had fallen from the shelves. It was Anna who realized that the wind had finally found its way beneath the edges of the shutters over her tiny window and ripped them away. She got up, a blanket around her shoulders, and went to look out. Aside from the rain beating frantically at the thick glass, she could see nothing but pitch-black. Yet the last time she'd looked at the clock it had surely been morning?

'This is horrible,' Susan said. She was sharing one of the armchairs with Terry, sitting across his knee with them both swaddled in Anna's quilt. 'Like waiting for the end.' Terry held her closer.

'We'll be all right,' Anna said, sounding calmer than she felt. Why hadn't she taken up Robert's offer of a lift out of here yesterday? Why hadn't she made Frank and Pat come with her, Terry and Susan too? 'The Fishergirl's Luck survived in 1953. In fact, that's when Bren came up with the name.'

'What do you mean?' Pat asked.

'Bren wrote about it in her recipe book. Here, I'll read you what she said.' Anna found her overnight bag amid the tumult and pulled out the old notebook. The others listened as she read out Bren's account of baking all night in the stove that was now keeping them in fresh tea.

'Well, I'll be damned,' said Frank.

'That storm is what the Fishergirl's Luck was born out of,' Anna said. 'And if it survived then, it can survive this, too.'

'But the cliff didn't come down in 1953,' Susan said, her voice shaky. 'Bren wasn't facing being pushed off the sea wall by a landslide as well as the storm coming in from the sea. I don't think—'

Her words were interrupted by a frantic hammering at the door. Anna leapt up and ran to it, expecting to see a bedraggled Douglas McKean shivering on her doorstep. She threw back the bolts they'd set against the wind and yanked it open.

'Robert!'

'Anna!' He barrelled inside, his wet face furrowed with worry, grasping her arms with gloved hands. 'Are you all right?'

The others appeared around them, all asking questions at once.

'There's no time,' Robert said, still catching his breath from his battle with the wind. 'We have to go, now. Is everyone here?'

'All but Dougie McKean,' Terry supplied. 'Can't get him to leave his nest.'

Robert glowered at that, then pulled Anna's coat from the peg beside him and thrust it at her. 'Everyone get down to the harbour. The lifeboat's waiting but it won't be able to hold at anchor for long. You have to go. I'll get Dougie.'

'No!' Anna exclaimed. 'You can't—'

He grabbed her hand and held it. 'I can't leave him, Anna.'

'I'll come with you,' Frank said, as the wind rattled the door. 'Might take two to drag him out of there.'

'No,' Robbie said firmly, before Pat had a chance to. 'And there's no time to argue. You're going.' The second he began to open the door the wind found the gap and threw it wide to crash against the wall.

The blast of wet air took Anna's breath away as she followed Robbie out into the darkness, clutching her coat around her. He turned to her again and pulled her close. She held on to him, her face against his shoulder, hands clutching at his jacket as the wind threatened to blow them off their feet and the waves tugged at their ankles.

'The lights,' he yelled, his lips against her ear. 'Make for the lights.'

Then he was gone. Anna didn't know what he meant, and without his bulk surrounding her she felt as if she'd been cast into the maelstrom. The second Robert moved away he was lost to the stormy darkness. Anna felt a hand on her back – David, holding on to her. None of them could hear each other speak over the wind. They moved like a flock of sheep down the sea wall, staying as far from the edge as they could, holding each other upright as waves crashed around their feet. Then, up ahead, something shone through the roiling black. It looked like a festival of lights, huge blue-white slices of illumination scything through the night. Through it, Anna could see the rain slashing against the shore, the cold waves reaching up from the ocean.

The lifeboat.

As they stumbled on, figures ran towards them. All was confusion and the Crovie survivors were swept along.

David let her go and someone else grabbed hold of her. She couldn't see who it was until she got to the harbour and gloved hands touched her face, raising it to meet eyes she recognized looking at her anxiously beneath his drenched wool hat.

'Liam!'

'Are you all right?' she read on his lips.

'What are you doing here?' she tried to ask, but her words were torn away by the wind.

He pushed her towards the lifeboat. The others were already being helped aboard.

'Wait!' she shouted, 'Wait!'

She turned back towards the village, but it was impossible to see anything at all beyond the halo of light. Liam kept tugging her towards the boat. She dragged him close enough to bring her lips to his ear.

'Robert!' she bellowed. 'He went for Douglas McKean!'

Liam looked into the darkness, but there was nothing to see but storm. He pushed Anna towards the lifeboat again. Other hands took hold of her.

'No!' Anna shouted, as she realized what Liam was about to do. She'd only meant they should wait. 'You can't—'

There was no point. A second later he was lost to the darkness, forcing his way along the sea wall beneath the rain and waves. Anna found herself aboard the pitching, bucking deck. Someone wound a survival blanket around her, the silver glinting a vivid blue beneath the boat's shocking lights. She wrapped her arms around her stomach, as if she could keep the baby inside her safe from the world as it destroyed itself around them.

They won't cast off, she thought to herself, staring wildly into the darkness. *Not with three men left out there. Not with Robert and Liam and Douglas still—*

She became aware of a closer commotion happening behind her. Anna turned to see Frank on his knees, Pat holding his shoulders. Two of the lifeboat crew were with the couple, doing something that Anna couldn't make out. Had Frank fallen? The scene took on the strange effect of a stage tableau, the harsh white lights making everything unreal and staccato as they strobed into the storm. Anna couldn't understand what was going on. She could see only slices of action, movements frozen into frames. Everything was happening in stutters, disconnected, underscored by sounds too huge to mean anything at all.

Anna moved towards her friends. Time slowed. If felt as if she were fighting her way through mud. Then a louder roar took up behind her. It sounded like an ancient creature, bellowing into the falling sky. The rain took on a new smell, incongruous in the storm. Wet earth.

The cliff was coming down.

Anna turned, gripping the lifeboat's handrail with one hand, the other against the baby hidden away inside her. She could see nothing beyond the harbour but knew, clear as day, that there were tons of earth and rock raining down from the cliffs. On Douglas McKean's house. On the entire village. On Liam Harper. On Robert MacKenzie.

'*Please*,' she felt herself screaming impotently into the wind. '*Please—*'

Then there they were. Three figures stumbled out of the collapsing darkness. Two trying to run through a streaming torrent, either side of a smaller figure they were holding up between them.

Thirty

Frank hadn't fallen. It was a heart attack. Pat looked on in agony as the lifeboat crew did what they could, but they couldn't save the man who had been by her side for thirty-five years. Frank died on the way to Macduff, but it was Pat who looked like a ghost. She sat in the lifeboat station wrapped in a blanket, gripped by a grief that speared all who saw it.

'He'd been having trouble for while,' Pat sobbed, as Anna held her hand and let the tears slide down her own face. 'I tried to get him to slow down. But he wouldn't listen. Not to me, not to the doctors. Not to his own heart! Still kept on as he always had. "Can't teach an old dog new tricks, love," that's what he'd say. Oh, *Frank*—'

The storm was relentless. It had settled over the coast and was hurling itself at the land with everything it had. It wouldn't be long until the lifeboat would be needed again. Anna looked up from Pat's side and saw Robert MacKenzie talking to Liam, and the thought of him going back out into those waves scared her bone-deep. She got up, leaving Susan to take her place beside Pat. Robert saw her coming. His gaze looked past her to the sad gathering beyond.

'How's Pat?' he asked quietly.

Anna's eyes filled with tears again. 'In shock, I think. I can't believe it, either. Frank—'

Robert made as if to reach for her, but it was Liam who pulled her against him. He held her for a few minutes, then pulled back. 'I still think you need to go to hospital yourself, get checked out.'

'The paramedics say we're fine. I feel fine. And right now I need to be with Pat. Really,' she said, off Liam's look. 'I'm okay — thanks to you two and the rest of the crew. Liam, what were you even doing on the lifeboat?'

Robert cleared his throat. 'It was thanks to Liam that we knew the road was out. He called us.'

'When I couldn't get you on the phone I wanted to check you were okay,' Liam explained. 'Drove over and saw what had happened. Didn't know what else to do.'

'We'd all been called in,' Robert added, 'or I would have come over myself and seen the landslide earlier.' He nodded at Liam. 'This guy wouldn't let us leave without him.'

'It's not as if I can't handle myself in rough seas,' Liam pointed out.

'Well,' said Robert, 'if you were to stick around, we could use you, that's for sure.'

Liam glanced at Anna. 'I would if I could, believe me.'

Robert nodded and then pulled his keys from his pocket, passing them to Anna. 'Liam can take you and Pat to my place,' he said. 'Rhona's coming to get Terry and Susan. I've already called someone for Dougie and David's got a friend here in Macduff.'

Anna took the keys with a sense of relief.

'You stay as long as you like,' he added. 'The doctor's emergency number is on the fridge if either of you need it. The wee boy's with Barbara and I'll leave him there until the morning so you two can get settled. There's only one guest room, but—'

'I'll be fine on the sofa,' she said.

A siren began to sound throughout the building. 'I've got to go.'

'Robert—' Anna said as he turned to go, but then found she didn't know what it was she wanted to say. 'Thank you. For coming for us.'

'Any time,' he said. For a second it looked as if he might want to say something else, but instead he nodded to them both, glanced over at Pat, and went.

Liam drove Pat and Anna to Gardenstown and made them both cocoa in Robert MacKenzie's kitchen while the two women sat together. Anna wasn't sure that the events of the past hours had really sunk in for Pat. They hadn't for Anna, either. Despite her grief, Pat was exhausted, and at length Anna managed to persuade her into bed. She sat on the thick quilt in the MacKenzies' cosy attic room and held the older woman's hand as she drifted into sleep.

'I can stay, if you like,' Liam said as Anna crept back down the stairs with blankets for herself.

'I'll be fine,' Anna told him. 'All I want is to sleep.'

Liam nodded and then pulled her into his arms, resting his cheek against her hair.

'When I think about what could have happened—' he said.

'But it didn't,' Anna pointed out softly. 'Thanks to you.'

After he left, Anna lay down on the sofa beneath her nest of blankets and listened to the storm raging outside. She imagined Robert MacKenzie on the lifeboat. The thought of him out there, in the very midst of the storm, terrified her. She drifted into a fitful sleep, filled with dreams of darkness and ruin. In the middle of it all stood the Fishergirl's Luck. She woke with tears on her face, disoriented. There was a weak morning light pushing in around the curtains, but still the wind blew.

'Hey,' said a soft voice.

Robert was sitting in the armchair opposite the sofa where she lay. He'd changed into his usual clothes. His face was lined with exhaustion, dark smudges beneath his eyes. Anna said nothing, but reached out her hand. He took it, his thumb smoothing over her skin as they looked at each other. They sat like that for a long time, until Anna fell back into another unsettled sleep.

It took two more days before the storm had exhausted itself, and even then the rain still fell. When it had died down enough for a person to be able to stand upright, the tattered remains of the Usual Suspects assembled in Gamrie harbour and looked across the grey waters of the bay to Crovie. Even from this distance it was possible to see the huge scar of the landslide, a wide slash in the cliff behind the village. It was hard to see how any of the houses would have avoided the onslaught. The row was clearly still standing, but it was impossible to tell what damage the individual houses had sustained to their rear walls and foundations.

The Fishergirl's Luck still stood with her back to the sea. Anna was surprised how emotional seeing it there made her. There had been a part of her, she realized, that had expected it to have been swept over the sea wall and into the bay.

It was Anna who helped Pat with Frank's funeral arrangements. Doing so seemed surreal. She kept expecting the door to Robert MacKenzie's house to open and to see Frank walk through it, that smile on his face, the sound of laughter underlying his words.

'I don't know what I'm going to do now I'm on my own,' Pat said, more than once. Her grief was monumental, as if her bones were carved from it. They cried together, Pat and Anna, and in her darker moments Anna wondered how this grief was affecting the baby in her womb. More than that, she wondered why humans did it – why they fell in love at all when the loss of it caused such immense pain. Anna felt as if she'd lost her father all over again.

'I know it's not enough,' Anna said, on one of these occasions. 'But I'm here. You're not on your own.'

Pat squeezed her hand. 'I'm not your responsibility, love,' she said. 'You've got more than enough already. You can't stay in a village that's gone to rack and ruin, not when you've got more important things to think about.'

'There's no point talking like that until we know the

extent of the damage,' Anna said. 'It might not be as bad as we all fear. We know the Weaver's Nook and the Fishergirl's Luck are still standing, after all.'

Pat squeezed her hand again, but she was distracted, and Anna had distractions of her own. An email from Melissa about the cookbook had reminded her that life elsewhere was still going on. It was only in reading it that Anna realized that all her recipes were in the notebook that was with the other two she'd left inside the overnight bag she hadn't had time to pick up during the escape. Really, the cookbook was the least of her worries and she hoped that her editor would be able to understand that, as she said in her emailed reply. A few hours later Anna's mobile rang.

'Anna,' Melissa said, as soon as she answered. 'I'm so sorry.'

Anna rubbed a hand over her eyes. 'Look, this cookbook – I'm not sure it's going to work. Not anymore.'

'Don't even think about that now,' her editor said. 'I'm calling because I wanted to check on you as a friend. But also to put you in touch with someone. You know that we also publish Taymar Zetelli?'

'Oh, yes. I've got a couple of her books.'

'Well, since I've worked with her she's become a friend. We've talked about you – she's fascinated by what you've done in Crovie, and loves the sound of your food. After I got your email I called her and asked if I could pass on her number, in case she could offer a bit of moral support. She'd love it if you'd give her a call. Actually she said she's been thinking about getting in touch for a while.'

Anna frowned. 'She has? Why?'

'Probably to tell you how brilliant she thinks you're being. She's like that. I think a contact like Taymar might be exactly what you need right now.'

'Okay,' Anna said. 'Thank you. I'll give her a call.'

'Do,' Melissa urged her. 'And I'm always here, too.'

Once they'd hung up Anna looked at the number she'd scribbled down, thinking that perhaps Melissa was right, she could do with some moral support from someone who'd 'been there'. Taymar Zetelli was a colourful, larger-than-life character who had remained the chef-patron of her tiny eatery on the South coast through all three of her pregnancies. As her popularity grew, she'd opened more restaurants and every one of them had been led by women. Her cookery books had put her into a different sphere, as had the television series that had followed. Geoff hated her, 'on principle', although Anna had never understood quite what principle this was.

A couple of days later, Anna called the number she'd been given. The conversation that ensued went on for more than an hour, and in it Anna laughed for the first time since the terrible night that Frank had died.

Young Robbie was a great comfort to them all, but especially to Pat. He'd come in from school and immediately make her a cup of tea. He'd sit down with her and explain his day in detail, apparently understanding how much she enjoyed simply listening to his voice. He persuaded her to help him bake shortbread, and suggested that he

organize a bake sale at school to raise money for the villagers of Crovie.

'That's a lovely idea,' Anna told him, not having the heart
to point out that it was going to take a magnitude more than
any bake sale could raise to save the village.

Part of her wondered whether this would finish Crovie off
for good, the way the storm of 1953 had finally ended the
fishing industry there.

'That place has survived such a lot,' Robert told her a
few nights later, as they sat at the kitchen table together.
Pat and Robbie had gone to bed, and the two of them were
alone. 'I have to believe there'll be a way to get it back on
its feet again.'

'I can't help thinking it'll be too much work for people
who are beyond such things,' Anna said. 'Pat was already
slowing down, and losing Frank has knocked her for six.
Terry and Susan are going to struggle themselves. The
others – Phil and Marie, David and Glynn – they don't
live there permanently. I can't help thinking that they'll
all cut their losses and go somewhere else. Here maybe, in
Gardenstown. That'd be so much easier, wouldn't it?'

He nodded. 'If ever there were a time to move on, this
would be it.'

Silence sank into the room, and along with it a truth that
neither of them voiced. Anna reached for his hand. Robert
took it with both of his, frowning at the tangle of their fingers. Something had changed between them in the days that
she and Pat had been staying at the MacKenzie house. No,

Anna thought then, not changed – deepened. It remained unsaid, though, sketched only in moments like this, when one or both of them could have said something, but somehow never did.

'You have to do what's right for you,' Robert said. 'What's right for the baby. I understand that.'

Anna took a shallow breath. 'Living in a ruined village that has no access apart from by sea . . . Even if the Fishergirl's Luck is completely untouched, even if—'

'I know,' he said. 'I know.'

She shook her head, dumbly, unable to speak. In that moment she wanted him to lean over the table and kiss her, but he didn't. She could have done the same and kissed him, but Anna didn't do that, either. Where was the wisdom in starting something when she may have to leave this place, and soon? How ironic that she had spent her first days in the village desperate to leave, and these last ones desperate to stay.

'I'll take you there once the weather's set fair,' Robert MacKenzie said, in a voice that was barely loud enough for her to hear. 'Anyone who wants to go. We'll take the *Cassie's Joy*. When the weather's calm enough.'

The moment was broken, and Anna gently drew back her hand from between his. He let her go and stood up to take her empty mug from the table, keeping his back to her as he put it into the sink. Anna's eye was drawn to the photograph of Cassie, still in place on the fridge, and with a sudden flash of clarity knew that there was a future, somewhere, where another photograph could join it, a photograph which would contain her and the baby inside her that was growing larger with every passing day. She stood up and said goodnight while he still had his back turned, escaping while she still had the strength to leave.

'Don't close yourself off from it,' Cathy said, later still, as Anna lay beneath his blankets on the sofa in the darkness with her phone to her ear.

'I have to.'

'Why?'

Anna gave a short burst of laughter that had nothing to do with mirth. Cathy was the only one to whom she had confessed her new secret – that Taymar Zetelli had offered her a job as head chef at her next restaurant, which would be opening in Newcastle the following year. Taymar hadn't been fazed at all by Anna's pregnancy. The same couldn't be said for the owner of the only restaurant within driving distance of Crovie that had been looking for a chef. He had directed a pointed look at her stomach before telling her that the position had miraculously been filled overnight.

'How can I stay?' Anna said. 'It was impractical before. Now it would be plain crazy, wouldn't it?'

There was a pause. 'I want you to have the career you deserve. I really do,' Cathy said. 'You're so talented and you love the kitchen. But I also want you to have a life. A family. Love. If you take Zetelli's offer you'll have to leave Robert MacKenzie behind, and I don't think—'

Anna cut her off. 'He hasn't – this isn't – there hasn't been time for any of that. There *isn't* time for any of that.'

'But you know. Don't you?'

'I don't know anything,' Anna said, 'except that the only home I can call my own is in the village where nothing else may have been left standing, and I've been thrown a lifeline to start again elsewhere.'

Selkie lass,

I can't lose something that never was, and yet . . .

I lie awake at night and wonder how you would explain it, if you were the one telling, and Robbie was the one listening. I think you'd tell him that life is like the sea, with its own tides. I think you'd say that the tide takes things out, as well as bringing things in, and that life is like that too.

I tell myself that if she leaves — and how can she not, now? — that it's only the tide turning again. I tell myself that I'm not losing a thing, because a person can't be so lucky twice in a lifetime.

There cannot possibly be enough love in the world for that.

Thirty-One

Liam flew home the day before the villagers returned to Crovie for the first time. Anna took him to the airport in Inverness, where they both cried. He offered to stay for Frank's funeral the following week, but what would have been the point? Two or three days – two or three *weeks* – would have made no difference, except to give him an added expense he would not be able to easily afford. They had parted with the promise that he would call as soon as he reached home, and that was that. Anna was sanguine about it, really. Part of her thought she was probably numb.

The sea and the sky were still a uniform grey as the *Cassie's Joy* carried the Usual Suspects across the bay towards the stricken village. Robert MacKenzie had left a protesting Young Robbie behind in the care of his grandmother, and Douglas McKean had also remained in Gardenstown. Terry and Susan were with them, though, and David and Phil, too. Phil had been in close contact since the storm and had decided to make a trip specifically to assess the damage. Marie would join him in a couple of days, for Frank's funeral. Anna hadn't wanted Pat to come, had said they could report back to her, could even film it if she really wanted to see, but Pat had been adamant.

'It can't be avoided, love,' she said, in a voice that was a dull echo of how it had sounded before they'd lost Frank. 'It's something I have to deal with, that's all.'

Everyone was silent as the boat rounded the cliff. There was something eerie about the village before they'd even cleared the promontory, a stillness that made Anna shiver. It took her a few moments to realize that the absence was the sea birds. There were no gulls wheeling over the cliffs, screaming into the wind. The whole village felt like an empty house. There was no sign of life.

Robert brought the boat into the harbour and they helped one another out. There was debris strewn everywhere, littering the cars at the foot of the cliff and the concrete on which they stood. Anna's Fiat had shifted sideways on its wheels and was caked with mud and clods of earth. There were smuts of peaty soil everywhere, dark and wet, as well as splinters of wood that Anna belatedly realized were the remains of one of the wooden shacks that had stood at the rear of the car parking space. Most of the barrows had been dashed to pieces, lifted and dropped, lifted and dropped. The storm had smashed them to kindling. The air was heavy with the smell of earth. Anna took Pat's hand and held it.

To get to the Inn they had to step over ridges of soil and stones washed down from the collapse of the road. It was the first time anyone had seen what it looked like. They stood like the stunned survivors of an apocalypse, staring up at the ruin of cracked tarmac concertinaed beneath a muddy glacier of displaced earth and rock.

'God,' David muttered. 'How are they ever going to clear that?'

No one answered him and in the shocked silence, there came the whirr of helicopter blades. They looked up to see the aircraft coming over the bay towards the village.

'That'll be the news reporters,' Phil said darkly. 'There'll be more of them soon enough.'

They tried to ignore their overhead spectators and continued. The Inn seemed untouched apart from spatters of debris that had been thrown against the walls.

No one spoke as they picked their way along the sea wall. Robert kept one arm around Pat. The helicopter still hovered overhead and Anna was suddenly and ferociously angry at those inside. It must have been obvious who they were and surely anyone could understand how traumatic it was to be here, now, to be discovering for the first time how much of one's life and livelihood was lost. It felt intrusive to have it watched by outsiders, especially when she knew it would be broadcast around the world. She stopped, staring up, wondering who was flying the helicopter, if that person had any connection to this coast at all. But a low light was breaking through the incessant cloud, and the glare was enough to hide those inside from view. Anna felt someone brush her free hand with theirs. It was Robert, reaching back for her.

'Forget them,' he told her. 'There's nothing we can do and

after all, the footage they'll shoot will tell us more than we can see for ourselves right now.'

The debris worsened as they moved further towards the most affected end of the village. Any plant pots that had been outside the houses had either vanished or had been lifted by the wind and smashed into the ground or through windows. There were shards of glass everywhere. Something flapped past Anna and she realized it was a curtain from one of the rentals. Broken tiles were strewn across the concrete.

They reached the culvert in the centre of the village where the burn joined the sea beside the pier without too much trouble. Beyond, though, it was as if the cliff were a sack that had split its seams, spilling everything inside down on the houses furthest from the road. Anna had already known that the Fishergirl's Luck was still standing because she'd been able to see it from the harbour at Gardenstown. That had planted the vague notion that it might have some-how remained untouched. But as she walked closer her foot scuffed at something underfoot. It was a large splinter of wood, painted blue. For a second she couldn't place it, although it seemed familiar. Then she realized, with a sick jolt to her stomach, that it was part of one of the shutters that had covered her window. She'd known they'd been torn off, but seeing it there amid the soil underfoot stabbed a blade of misgiving into her gut. The feeling wasn't diminished as they got closer and she saw Liam's bench. It had been picked up from her garden and blown clear across the sea path to lean, upended, against the Weaver's Nook. One of the planks that made up its surface had been torn in half, the rest of it was ragged splinters.

Her fences had vanished, swallowed whole by the sea. Of the four chimneys she had planted with flowers, three were gone completely and the other was shattered almost beyond recognition. There were tiles and shards of glass everywhere, a sea of slate grey and reflected sky. Anna looked up from the garden to see that the window to her bedroom had been smashed clear out of its frame. Through the gaping hole, she could see the sky. For a moment her mind couldn't understand what she was seeing. Then she realized her roof had gone. It wasn't only the slate that had been lifted, either. The storm had ripped out half the supporting struts and the internal gabled ceiling. As she stared up in shock, it began to rain again. The Fishergirl's Luck was open to the elements.

With a cry Anna went for the front door. Robert held on to her.

'It won't be safe,' he said.

'I have to go in,' she said. 'There's something I have to— I didn't have time to pick it up when we left.'

He let her go. Inside the cottage the living room was eerily untouched, despite the cold damp blasting down through the open roof upstairs. Anna barely noticed. She saw the go-bag she had packed and then left on the floor when Robert had turned up with the lifeboat. She snatched it up and unzipped it, dropping it again once she'd pulled out what she was looking for. The photograph of her family, together on the beach all those years ago. She stared down at the picture, her emotions in turmoil.

'Now that we're here,' Robert said, at her shoulder, 'You should bring whatever you need.' He paused to glance at the staircase in the corner, bathed in a weird light from the ruined roof overhead. 'If you can get to it without going upstairs.'

Anna picked up the bag. 'I've got everything,' she said. It wasn't what was in the Fishergirl's Luck that was important to her but the place itself, and she couldn't take that with her. Bren's bothy would stay put, the rain seeping in, in a way it never had when its original owner had been alive.

When they stepped back outside, they found that Terry and Susan had gone with Pat into the Weaver's Nook.

'You wait here,' Robert said. 'I'm going down to look at Dougie's place and Pat and Frank's rental. Don't let her follow until I've checked it out, all right?'

Anna nodded. 'Be careful.'

He smiled at her, though his eyes were sombre. Anna watched him pick his way past the wreck of Liam's bench, over ridges of silt and what looked like crumbled stone.

As for the Weaver's Nook, all the windows had been blown out, the rooms water-damaged and scattered with debris, ruined.

Anna found Pat in the private sitting room above the kitchen, the one that Pat and Frank had kept for themselves for whenever they had guests staying. The window had blown in, but the rocking chair Pat had used each evening still waited beside the fireplace and the old oak armchair that had been Frank's remained on the other side. The two chairs faced each other as they had done ever since they were installed. Pat was staring at Frank's chair, tears streaming down her face.

'What am I going to do?' Pat said. 'What am I going to do without him?'

'Oh, Pat,' Anna said.

'He hadn't even started the crib,' Pat sobbed, as Anna held her. 'He was so determined to make it perfect for the baby, Anna. Look – there are his designs, still on the chair where he left them that last night.'

Anna picked up the notebook and saw page after page of sketches and notes detailing types of wood and measurements. It would have been a beautiful piece of furniture, Anna saw, made with such love that looking at the designs made her cry again.

'We shouldn't stay too long,' Anna said, through her tears. 'Pat, we'll come back again as soon as we can, but right now – what do you want to take with you?'

Pat gathered up a few things – photographs of Frank mainly, a few pieces of jewellery and some clothes.

'You keep that,' she said to Anna, of the notebook full of Frank's designs. 'He would have wanted you to have it. He would have wanted you and the baby to have such a lot of things.'

As they came back downstairs they saw Robert talking quietly with Terry and Susan.

'I want to see the rental next,' Pat said, holding one of the photographs of Frank that had been on the sideboard tight to her chest. 'I need to check out the damage.'

Robert smiled at her gently. 'Best not, Pat. Not right now.'

Pat's face crumbled. 'It's gone, then?'

'I think so, yeah,' Robert MacKenzie said softly, and Pat sunk her head against his shoulder with a sob that cracked Anna's heart wide open. Robert wrapped his arms around his friend and rocked her where they stood.

'Come on,' he said, after a few minutes. 'Let's head back for now, shall we?'

The helicopter followed them as they left, a weary band of survivors carrying what possessions they could. The sound of the whirring blades blurred with the noise of the waves and the increasing wind as the *Cassie's Joy* pulled out into the bay. No one spoke. They simply clung to each other. Anna studied Pat's face, but Pat had become silent, staring steadily out to sea, and Anna wondered whether she was seeing anything at all.

'I saw you on the news,' Cathy told her later. 'Oh Anna, I'm so sorry.'

Anna rubbed a weary hand across her face. The emotional strain of the past few days was taking its toll. She longed to hide away in a dark room, but she had arranged to meet up with Rhona to oversee the catering for Frank's funeral. It was the least she could do. Pat herself had asked Phil to take her into Elgin – something to do with a meeting with her bank. Anna had begged Pat to leave it for a while, but she had been insistent. Anna had the sense that she needed to feel in control of something again, and could see why that would be important.

'You'll know more about what the village looks like than me then,' she told Cathy. 'I haven't been able to bring myself to watch it yet.'

'It doesn't look good,' Cathy admitted. 'Two of the houses look as if they've been completely demolished. And that landslide that took out the road . . .'

Anna shut her eyes. 'I know,' she said. 'I know.'

The phone rang again almost as soon as she'd finished the call with Cathy. Anna answered it without paying attention to the number and regretted it immediately as she heard Geoff's self-satisfied voice on the line.

'Saw you snatching another five minutes of fame on the news,' he said. 'Getting to be quite the celebrity, aren't you?'

'What do you want?'

'How about a bit of gratitude?'

'For what?'

'For calling to give you another chance to say yes to my offer after seeing what a mess your life is in.'

'What?'

'That's right, I'm going to save your career,' he said, voice unctuously smug. 'You'll still come aboard in the new kitchen, although I've decided that I'm going to take on the executive chef role myself, at least to begin with. We can take it from there once I know for sure you can handle the pressure. So you'll be under me. But you always worked best like that, didn't you?'

Anna let a beat of silence hold the line as she contemplated what he'd said.

'Geoff,' she said then, with slow deliberation. 'Please believe that this is said with all due respect. You are *such* a dick.'

She cut the call and blocked his number.

Thirty-Two

Frank's funeral took place at the church in Gardenstown. The place was full – he'd had a lot of friends. The vicar spoke movingly about Frank's life, both before he moved to Crovie and since. Anna learned so much about him that she hadn't known, and it was the thought that she could no longer find out these things from him that made her weep. She hadn't realized how very important a figure Frank had become in her life, a fixed point by which she had begun to navigate. He could never replace the hole her own father had left, but she'd been thinking of Frank and Pat as her family for months now. It was only with the diminishment of their trio that she realized the true depth of that connection.

The wake was held in the Garden Arms in Gamrie. The pub was crowded, mostly with people Anna didn't know, or knew only vaguely. She stayed with the Usual Suspects, watching out for Pat. Anna was amazed by the woman's strength, by her grace, despite the deep well of her grief. Anna hated to think of her trying to deal with the aftermath of the storm alone, trying to sort out the mess that was the Weaver's Nook, let alone the devastated rental house.

'You'll help her, won't you?' she said quietly to her gathered friends. 'I mean, obviously I know you will, it's only that I hate the thought of not being here to do it myself . . .'

Rhona glanced at the others. 'Sounds as if you've made up your mind to leave, hen,' she said.

Anna stared into her glass of lime and soda. 'Realistically, I don't know what else I can do.'

There was a pause. Rhona raised an eyebrow at Phil. Susan nudged him. Terry nodded. Marie shrugged.

'What?' Anna asked. 'What's going on?'

Phil looked over his shoulder to where Pat was talking to another knot of people, then back at Anna. 'Excuse me for a moment.' He extricated himself from their circle and went over to Pat, apologizing for the interruption and then speaking a few words in Pat's ear. Pat looked over at Anna and nodded. As they came towards her, Anna felt a terrible feeling of misgiving.

'Can I talk to you for a moment, love?' she asked. 'Outside. I could do with a bit of air, to tell you the truth.'

Anna looked at the others, who offered smiles and nods as she followed Pat outside. Together the two women walked down the Strait Path that led from the pub to Gamrie's shore. The tide was out again, the sun was warm, and there were families with small children playing among the rockpools. Across the bay they could see Crovie's battered shoreline. The weather was lifting, no more storms forecast for the immediate future, and a low light was breaking up the cloud, pale sunbeams casting God-light over the damaged houses.

From this distance it looked like a toy town, carelessly dropped from the pocket of a passing toddler.

Pat settled herself on the old stone wall. Anna perched next to Pat and felt, not for the first time, that her belly was beginning to swell into a proper pregnancy bump. She laid a hand there, and Pat smiled.

'You're really beginning to show.'

'I know,' Anna laughed. 'At least I have more than one excuse to buy a whole new wardrobe.'

Pat smiled again and looked out to sea. 'Poor Frank. He was so excited about the baby, you know. Could hardly talk about anything else.'

'Oh, Pat—'

Pat reached over to take Anna's hand. 'Don't fret, love,' she said softly. 'You'll start me off, and that's not what I wanted to talk to you about. Now, before I begin, it's important to know that there's no reason for you to feel pressured. It's likely that we would have thought of doing something of the sort whether or not you'd been here, given what the storm's done to the village.'

Anna shifted on the stone, uncomfortable and anxious. 'What are you talking about, Pat? Do what?'

Pat looked out to sea again. 'We've decided that we're going to buy the Crovie Inn. All of us, I mean.'

Anna blinked. 'What?'

'We had some savings put by, Frank and me, and he would have thought it a fine idea. Obviously the offer's low-ball, taking into account the current state of the village, and it's dependent on a structural survey.' Pat turned to Anna, her grey eyes tired but lit by a brightness that hadn't been there since Frank's death. 'I've invited the rest of the Usual Suspects to be part owners in it, too, and they've all agreed. Phil and Marie, mainly – they're the ones with the most to invest, besides me. But Terry and Susan, Rhona, David and Glynn, Old Robbie – when I suggested the idea, they all wanted to be part of it. And together, we can afford it.'

Anna was utterly stunned. 'But ... Pat, the rest of the village – the rental house – won't you need any savings you have to deal with all of that?'

Pat shook her head. 'I've seen the news footage, love. The rental house is done with. The most I can hope to get out of it is some insurance to pay off the last of what we owed on the place, and that some other party will want to take it on for a rebuild. Terry and Susan will need somewhere to live while they assess how to deal with their place, and possibly permanently if it can't be saved. So will I, for the time being – I can't live in the Weaver's Nook right now, and I can't impose on Old Robbie forever. If it turns out we can all go back home eventually – which is what we're all hoping – we'll run the Inn as a B&B. We can do it up ourselves while we live there, bit by bit. Together.'

Anna was silent, processing this information. She looked out at the bay, at the gentle blue-grey-green waves rolling into shore. When it was like this it was hard to imagine it being any other way – hard to conceive of the violence of the storm that had shattered their lives and yet also bound them all together even more closely than before.

'There'll be room for you and the baby,' Pat said quietly. 'If you decided you wanted to stay. And there's the downstairs, of course.'

'The downstairs?'

Pat smiled, but she was looking out to sea again. 'The kitchen, love. The dining room. There's a whole restaurant sitting there, waiting for someone to make use of it, just as Phil's been saying since the night he first met you.'

Anna couldn't speak.

'I know it's a lot to put on you, and today of all days,' said her friend, grasping Anna's hand again. 'We – *I* – am not trying to trap you into anything. I want to be very clear about that. I don't want you to feel obligated to stay. It's another option, that's all, and God knows none of us will hold it against you if you don't take it.'

Pat went back to the wake a short while later, but Anna felt that she needed some space.

She walked slowly down to the harbour. The water was still calm, the waves barely enough to break white against the sea wall. As she looked across at Crovie, a single shaft of sunlight broke through the cloud and glanced against the roof of the Fishergirl's Luck. From here it didn't seem damaged at all. It seemed whole, as self-contained as it had been when Bren had first converted it into a home.

Anna made her way towards the village. The snook that ran around the base of the cliff was clogged with debris thrown up by the storm – rotting seaweed, bits of old net, sand, rocks and mud. It took her some time to pick her way along the route. When she reached the village, it was as silent as it had been two days before. Anna wiped the worst of the detritus from her shoes and stood looking up at the Inn. It seemed as untouched as it had during her last visit.

She passed it, walking carefully along the sea wall to the Fishergirl's Luck. Inside, sound was muted, overlaid by the intermittent flap and ripple of the tarpaulin that had been fixed over the broken roof. For a moment Anna stood listening to the sound of the gentle sea filtering in from outside, such a contrast to the event that had brought her here, to this point. A bright shaft of sunlight gleamed through the cloud – she could see it gilding the tiny window over the sink, naked of its shutters – and blue light suffused the room, refracted through the tarp. Anna lifted her face, for a moment feeling as if she and the Fishergirl's Luck had been caught in the tank of some huge aquarium.

Anna wandered about. She wanted to go upstairs but dared not risk it. From beneath the tarp came the pervasive smell of damp. Everything in her bedroom would be ruined, she knew, as would the wardrobe and probably all her clothes. Maybe even the floor.

Downstairs, though, much had been protected. The kitchen, certainly, was virtually untouched, though still cluttered with everything they had dragged across from the Weaver's Nook. Even the bench table beneath the stairs had been spared the brunt of the rain thanks to the staircase – which Anna thought would probably need replacing. Anna looked up at her cookery books, still snug in their narrow bookshelves overhead. She reached up for one of Taymar Zetelli's, wondering whether it would be damp. She couldn't reach, but before she could find something to stand on, a voice spoke from behind her.

'Let me help.'

It was Robert MacKenzie, strangely smart in a suit and jacket, although he'd taken off the tie he'd worn for the funeral. He came to stand next to her and reached up to pull down the book she'd been reaching for, handing it to her without a word.

'I wanted to see if they were wet,' she explained. 'I wondered whether the damp had got into the floor upstairs.'

Robert looked around. 'It's not safe to be here.'

'I needed to see it again,' she said. 'To be sure.'

He turned back to look at her, his eyes in shadow. 'To be sure? Of what?'

'Of what to do with the Fishergirl's Luck. It needs *so* much work.'

There was a silence. In it he turned away. 'What will you do? Sell it?'

'I don't want to. Really, I don't. But it needs so much repair. I can't let it go to ruin. There's so much history here. I can feel it, can't you? It's in the walls. It'd be wrong to let it rot because I can't afford to fix her myself.'

Robbie didn't answer, and for a few minutes there was nothing apart from the faint snicking of the tarp, the flickering of the strange blue light.

'Pat said you've put money into the Inn,' Anna said.

Robert nodded, still not looking at her. 'Dougie's going to need somewhere to live.'

Anna looked at him in astonishment. '*Douglas McKean's* going to live there? Do the others know that? Does *he* know that?'

He laughed at that. 'Yes. There's nowhere else for him to go, Anna. He's never lived anywhere but Crovie. I can't make him go into a home, at least not for a while yet. I couldn't do that to him, not now.'

There was another brief silence. 'Maybe he should live here.'

Robert froze for a second, then turned towards her. 'Sorry?'

'Once the roof and whatever else needs repairing is fixed, Douglas McKean could live here, at the Fishergirl's Luck. Do you think he would?'

Robert MacKenzie didn't say anything. He turned his head away, towards the light visible through her kitchen window. Anna watched him.

'You—' he said, and then stopped before trying again with a slight shake of his head. He slid his hands into his pockets. 'You've already decided, then. To leave Crovie. The Fishergirl's Luck.'

It was a statement, not a question. His tone made her heart thump.

'Look at the place, Robert. Even before the storm hit, raising a child here would have been tough.' She glanced down at the book in her hands, at Taymar Zetelli's face smiling at her brilliantly from the cover. 'I haven't told any of you this yet, but . . .' she held up the book. 'This chef has offered me a job.'

Anna could feel Robert's gaze fixed on her face, though she couldn't bring herself to meet his eye.

'She wants you to work for her?'

'Yes. She's opening a new place. She needs a head chef. She's a good person to work for, she's got a good reputation for being supportive of women with children. It's a great opportunity for me. I mean, it would have been whatever the situation, but now . . .' Anna trailed off.

'Where?' he asked. 'Where's the restaurant?'

Anna swallowed. 'Newcastle.' She tried for a slight laugh. 'It's not as far as London.'

He nodded, turning away again.

'Pat says—' Anna started, then had to stop and take a breath before trying again. 'Pat says there'll be room for us both at the Inn. Me and the baby, I mean. There's no way I could live with Douglas McKean, not even temporarily, but if he could stay where he is until this place is renovated, and then move here – that would work.'

She watched him go very still. Slowly he turned towards her again. 'What?'

Anna put the cookbook down on the table, light-headed, every nerve-ending jangling. The moment was coming crashing towards her, as powerful as a storm, and as inescapable. *What are we? What am I to you, what are you to me?*

'I'll live with Pat at the Inn. Even if Terry and Susan have to stay there for a while, there'll still be more room. It'll be easier with the baby – I can have a monitor with me in the kitchen, I'll always be able to hear if I'm needed, and there'll be other people around. It's always better to live on-site, especially right at the beginning of a start-up, it makes everything far less complicated, cuts down on costs, and—'

Anna realized that her nerves had set her rambling. Robert had moved closer, his face no longer cloaked in shadows.

'You're going to stay?'

She let out a laugh, a tiny explosion, a release of pressure. 'Of course I am. Of *course* I am! Did any of you really think I wouldn't if there was any chance – just a *chance* – I could work out a way to stay?'

'We ... *I* thought you might not,' he confessed. 'I wasn't sure there was enough here for you, not when it would be so much easier to go elsewhere.'

Anna looked around. 'You're right,' she admitted. 'Taking Taymar's offer would be easier.'

He took another step closer. 'Then why stay?'

Anna was aware she was looking anywhere but his face. She took a deep breath, and then looked up at him.

'This is home,' she said simply. 'And I don't want to be anywhere else. And there are things here ... *people* ... I can't imagine ever being able to leave without leaving a part of myself behind, too.'

He smiled, and Anna thought, not for the first time, that she could spend a lot of time watching him do that.

Robert moved closer still, until they were almost toe-to-toe. He hesitated for a moment and then reached out to take her hand. He rubbed his thumb across her palm, his eyes downcast to her fingers. Anna's heart was out of control. She wondered what he was waiting for, whether he needed her to be the one to make the first move, and then worried that he wasn't on the same page at all, that this was nothing more than another show of friendship, of the kind Auld Robbie MacKenzie had been offering her so steadfastly since before she had even moved into the Fishergirl's Luck.

'I—' she said, desperate to break the tension. 'Oh!'

The sensation took her utterly by surprise. Something fluttering in her belly.

'What?' Robbie asked. 'What is it?'

'I think—' There it was again. The faintest tickle, a curl of bubbles unfurling. 'I think I felt the baby!'

Anna moved his hand to her stomach, pressing it to her. They stood silent, for another moment, and then—

'There! You feel it?'

'Yes!'

'God, that's weird,' Anna laughed, her hand still over his. 'Poor thing must be protesting at my heart rate.'

His laugh resolved into a smile and a raised eyebrow. His hand was still on her belly. He moved it, sliding it around Anna's waist and pulling her closer, until she was pressed against him. 'Your heart rate?' he said. 'Why, what's wrong with it?'

She couldn't breathe. He was warm and so very close. 'Oh,' she managed. 'A bit fast, maybe.'

He grinned. 'Really? Why?'

Anna shook her head. 'No idea.'

He dipped his head. 'None?'

'None at a—'

The rest of the word was lost against his lips. They moved over hers, gentle and soft, and to Anna it felt both like home and like nothing she'd ever felt before.

Later, they left the Fishergirl's Luck and walked hand in hand to stand outside the Inn.

'Do you think we can do it?' Anna asked, looking up at the peeling paint, the faded sign.

Robert lifted her fingers to his lips and kissed them. 'I know we can. I know *you* can.'

'It won't be easy.'

'Nope.'

Anna nodded, then turned to look out over the sea. The sun was beginning to set, edging the ragged clouds with vivid bursts of orange and pink. Out in the bay, Anna spotted movement. They moved closer, a series of sleek curves leaping out of the waves. Up, and up, and up again.

'Well, would ye ken that, Anna Campbell?' said Old Robbie, slipping his arm around her shoulders and pressing his lips to her hair. 'The dolphins have come to wish us luck.'

Epilogue

Anna put down the phone and stared at the colourful proof pages spread across the desk. The cookbook was almost complete, and she had three more days to check everything one last time before letting Melissa know of any changes she wanted to make. Anna picked up the pencil she'd been using to make notes and drummed it briefly on the image of the gooseberries she had harvested and photographed in the kitchen on the day that the new worktops downstairs had been fitted. The sun had been out, pools of bright light pouring through the windows, shining on the space in which Anna now spent a lot of her time. There were still three months until she'd open her first service at the Crovie Inn, but Anna already knew the kitchen like the back of her hand.

She stilled her pencil, tried to read another sentence, failed, sighed, drummed the pencil again.

From behind her came a gurgle, and then a tiny but distinct giggle. Anna smiled and went to pick up her daughter from her nap. The baby was lying on her back in the crib that Robert had built from the designs Frank had left behind. Months he had spent on it, wanting it to be perfect, wanting to make sure it would hold the memory of the man that the baby who would sleep within it would never know.

'Well now,' Anna said, showering kisses on her daughter's chubby, delicious neck as she scooped her up. 'Look who's awake already. Did you have a good sleep?'

Her answer was a headbump, aimed softly at Anna's shoulder, as the happy baby pumped her arms and legs, excited by the sheer prospect of being awake and loved.

Anna left her proofs where they were – she couldn't concentrate on them anyway, not now – and went out into the hallway. The faint sound of music from a radio filtered in from somewhere, along with the murmur of voices coming from one of the Inn's almost-finished bedrooms.

'Pat, Susan!' Anna called. 'I need a break – we're popping along to the Fishergirl's Luck. We won't be long.'

'All right, love!' Pat called back.

Downstairs, the baby murbled as Anna slipped her into the carry sling on her chest before pulling a tiny hat over her daughter's downy hair. 'I know, you don't like it,' she said, kissing the little forehead under her chin, 'but if the wind's up, you'll need it.'

She opened the Inn's back door and stepped out onto the path. The wind was brisk, but the day was warm with it, the sun bathing the coastline in gold and turning the grasses to a russet blush. She turned and waved to the digger driver up on the landslide and saw him wave back from his cab, the noise of the vehicle joining the sound of the waves and the screech of the gulls overhead. It had only been a matter of days since the work had progressed enough to be seen from the village. Speculation was rife about how much longer it would be until the road was clear, and then how long after that it would be useable for the villagers. It had taken months to get to this point as it was.

'Anna!' a voice shouted as she turned away. It was Young Robbie, making his way along the path from Gamrie with his ubiquitous binoculars strung around his neck.

'What are you doing here?' Anna asked as the boy ran towards her, tugging her down so he could kiss the baby soundly on the cheek. 'You didn't come over on your own?'

'Nah, Rhona's behind me,' Robbie said. 'She's got something to show you. Dad said he couldn't go out with me today because he's so close to finishing the Fishergirl's Luck but I needed to do dolphin patrol, so I said I'd come. From the path is better than nothing.'

Anna rubbed a hand through his hair – so like his father's – and looked up again to see Rhona appear along the snook path.

'Ach, hen,' her friend said, when she got close enough. 'Where are you off to on this fine day?'

'I've been struggling with the cookbook proofs all morning. Thought I'd take a break and see how Robert's doing at the bothy.'

Rhona cooed at the baby. 'Aye, fair enough. I've got a couple of new glazes for you to look at though, in case you want to add them to the comparison test next week. And I want a cuddle of the bairn, so not too much canoodling, eh?'

'Yuk!' Young Robbie screwed up his face. 'I don't need to know about that!'

Rhona flicked the boy's cheek gently. 'Come on, then. Let's you and me go and make Pat and Susan a brew.'

'They're upstairs, sorting the curtains out,' Anna said, as Rhona steered Robbie towards the Inn. 'They could probably use a break. And help yourself to lunch – the bread's still warm.'

Anna made her way along the path, murmuring to the baby as she went. The water lapped against the sea wall, white foam peeking over the edge before dropping away again with a whisper. Around her, the sounds of industry echoed from the houses as she passed. Faces smiled at her from replaced windows, along with the occasional shouted 'hello' and wave. She waved back at the neighbours who, since the storm, had become an even closer-knit community. No one wanted that night to cap the village's long history with tragedy and desertion. Even the cottage owners who visited once a year had made a pact to ensure that Crovie was restored. It was happening, though progress was slow. Heavy work had been made even more difficult than usual with no road access and money was short without the income from the rental properties that needed repair.

At the Fishergirl's Luck there was no sound at all, no hammering or banging, no echoing rasp of a saw. Anna saw why when she spied the two figures sitting at Liam's bench. Robert MacKenzie had repaired the broken seat himself, though it would have been easier to simply buy a new one.

It was important to the place's history now, had been his reasoning. It deserved to be repaired alongside the tiny home of which it was part. Anna was glad. The place had seemed incomplete without it.

One of the figures glanced up at Anna and lifted his old chin in a kind of silent greeting as she approached. The other turned to see her coming and smiled as he got up. Robert came towards her, hair lifted by a sudden breeze.

'Hello, you two,' he said as he reached them, wrapping his arms around Anna and leaning down for a kiss, before planting one on the baby's head, too. 'How's the cookbook going?'

'Ugh,' Anna said, making a face. 'I can't tell if it's good or terrible. I go from thinking it's one or the other minute to minute.'

Robert kissed her again. 'It's brilliant.'

'How do you know?' Anna laughed. 'I haven't let you read it yet!'

'Stands to reason. Everything you do is brilliant.'

'Flatterer.'

'Saying it how I see it, that's all.'

'I don't—'

There came the sound of a throat being cleared by the old man sitting behind them. Anna peered around Robert.

'Afternoon, Dougie.'

He raised his chin again, but said nothing.

Robert grasped Anna's hand and she let him pull her towards the bench, though Anna wasn't sure she really wanted to sit down. She and Douglas McKean had silently agreed an uneasy kind of truce, but they weren't really on chatting terms.

'Let me take the bairn for a wee while,' Robert said, and Anna undid the sling, smiling as she watched him hold her daughter against his chest. He sat down beside Douglas, and Anna slid in opposite. The sun was warm, the sea was calm, one of those days when it seemed impossible that the weather here was ever anything but gloriously beautiful. Behind the line of houses, the scar in the cliff was already being filled with grasses and wildflowers growing into the rivulets of soil left overlying the red rock. At this rate the slip would be invisible in a year, though the story of that night would remain part of the village's history forever, and two of the houses below would never recover.

Anna brought her attention back to the table to find Douglas McKean looking at her through shrewd eyes. She tried for a smile.

'Did you come to check out progress on the Fishergirl's Luck, Dougie?' she asked.

He nodded slowly. 'Aye. Auld Robbie brought me o'er in t' *Cassie's Joy.*'

'And . . . what do you think? Hasn't he done a great job?'

McKean's gaze drifted out to the ocean. 'Ne'er seen inside t' place afore. Nae got a thing to compare it tae.'

Anna glanced at Robert, who smiled and gave a tiny shrug. The baby laughed.

'Heard ye called the bairn Bren,' said Douglas McKean. He surprised Anna by reaching out one gnarled hand, waving a finger in front of her daughter until the baby caught hold of his calloused fingertip.

'Yes,' Anna said. 'It . . . seemed kind of fitting.'

'Aye, well, what wi' her being made in the Fishergirl's Luck,' McKean agreed.

'Dougie, that's really not—' Robert MacKenzie began.

'She's a strong one, a'right,' the old man went on, as he and Little Bren battled for control of his finger. 'Just like that auld harpy herself. Aye, tis a fit name for a bold wee lassie. Ye'll have ye work cut oot w' her. An' mayhap she'll end up in the bothy when I'm deid and buried. That'd be fit, too.'

Anna was taken aback by the old man's comment. There was something she'd never even thought about. That in a few years' time, Little Bren Campbell – or maybe, just maybe, by then she might be Little Bren MacKenzie – might end up living in the Fishergirl's Luck. There was something about that idea that made Anna smile. What would the village look like then? Some of the faces might have changed, but she thought that Crovie itself would probably stay very similar to how it must have been back in Douglas McKean's younger days.

'Yes,' she said. 'You're not wrong, Dougie. That would be very fitting.'

Anna looked at the way her baby's fingers were still wrapped around his, the eldest and youngest residents of Crovie connected by a sliver of time that might perhaps prove too narrow for Little Bren to remember in years to come. The thought cast Anna's mind back to the phone call she'd had with Melissa.

'Something's happened,' she said.

Robert looked up with a frown. 'What do you mean?'

'Nothing bad. A bit surprising, that's all. Melissa phoned.' Anna took a breath. 'They've had an approach from a production company. They want to make a series to follow the cookbook.'

Robert's eyes widened. 'Wow. That's amazing!'

Anna smiled. 'Is it? I'm not sure. I've never been interested in being on camera. It's not my kind of thing. Writing a cookbook, yeah, but—'

Robert reached out one hand to cover Anna's. 'Hey. You don't have to do it if you don't want to.'

She squeezed his hand. 'No, I don't. And my first reaction was to say no. Melissa told me to think about it, and the thing is . . .' Anna looked around at the village, slowly coming back to life around them. 'It doesn't have to be about me, does it? It could be about Crovie. My food would be a part of it, but there could be so much more to it than that. Local history, stories. I could talk about Bren's notebook, cook recipes from it, go foraging the way she did. Her notes are tales in themselves.'

Little Bren murbled and Robert kissed her forehead. 'That sounds like a great idea.'

'I should talk to everyone else about it. See what they think.' Anna looked at Douglas McKean. 'What about you, Dougie? How would you feel about being on camera? I bet you've got a ton of stories you could tell, given the chance.'

Douglas McKean grinned, a surprisingly warm expression given his pronounced lack of teeth.

There came a shout from along the sea wall. They all looked up to see Young Robbie running towards them, helter-skelter, his cheeks red, his sandy hair flying in the wind. He was shouting.

'They've done it!' he yelled. 'They've got through! They've cleared the road!'

Well now, my selkie lass,

   Robbie and Anna have filled the house with daffodils.
They bought jars of pickled beetroot, too. The house is a riot
of purple and yellow, just for you.

   Happy Mother's Day, Cassie.

   We love you.

Author's note

The first time my husband and I visited Crovie was in 2017, during a spring tide so high and a wind so brisk that we dodged the waves all the way down the short line of houses, and failed to dodge them coming back. By the time we had returned to the point at which we had started, we were both soaked, and I was captivated. I have always been drawn to the idea of living somewhere that others would consider impractical, and in Crovie I seemed to have found that to a perfect degree.

By that point I had already encountered the meticulously converted mill pony shed that would become the Fishergirl's Luck. The wonderful owner, Marie West, had invited me to tea and told me her stories of living in such a tiny place. The building is in another small fishing village on the same coast, but once I had visited Crovie, with beautiful Gardenstown visible across the bay from her narrow shore, I realized that putting the two together would give me the basis for the story that had taken root in my head.

Thus the Crovie in these pages is a version of the real place, but it is not an absolutely faithful rendering. The real Crovie is often busier than the one in my story. Homes are owned by people from all over Europe, and in summer families celebrate friendships renewed every time they and their children meet. They are all passionate about the village, fully aware that they are preserving a place that supported a way of life no longer in existence but still important to remember.

In September 2017, the threat of a landslide closed the single road into the village. It took a year for it to be shored up, during which time the only way in was on foot or by boat. This could have turned the village into a ghost town, but it didn't, just as the huge destructive force of the Great Storm in 1953 didn't stop families from thriving here. Choosing to own a home in Crovie requires tenacity, a willingness to take the weather as it comes, and to live amid the echoes left by centuries of people who did the same.

As I write this I am sitting in the kitchen of number 33, where I have spent the past few days polishing the manuscript of *The House Beneath the Cliffs*. It is 7 a.m., and through the window I can hear the engine of a fishing trawler crossing the bay beneath a sky that is lead grey after days of sun. I love it here, whatever the weather. I hope you did, too.

22 July 2020, Crovie.

Acknowledgements

Thank you to Polly MacGregor, Angela Ritchie, Jess Woo and Amanda Lindsay for their continued encouragement, support and varying expertise, and for Marie West for showing me around her beautiful tiny home.

Thank you to my amazing agent Ella Kahn – without you I would never have believed I could write adult fiction.

Thank you to Charlie Haynes and Amie McCracken of the Six Month Novel: their online bootcamp forced me to get back to my keyboard and produce the first draft of this in the wake of surgery. During the writing of the first draft I also stayed just outside Pennan at the Mill of Nethermill, where Lynn Pitt's beautiful Millshore Pottery became the inspiration for Rhona's talents.

At Simon & Schuster, a huge thank you to my wonderful editors Clare Hey and Alice Rodgers for your expertise, kindness and diligence; to Pip Watkins for the beautiful cover, Genevieve Barratt for marketing, Sara-Jade Virtue for brand direction, Anne O'Brien for the copyedit, Maddie Allan and Kat Scott in sales and production controller Francesca Sironi, who kept the whole shebang on time.

The tiny inkling for the idea that would eventually become *The House Beneath the Cliffs* was planted during a holiday on the Aberdeenshire coast with my then boyfriend more than ten years ago. He is now my husband, and the publication of this book coincides with our ten-year wedding anniversary. Adam, it's been a wonderful decade, and none of it would have happened without you. Thank you.